AN I
TO DIE FOR

Mike Phillips was born in Guyana, came to Britain as a
child and grew up in London. He has been a broadcaster
for the BBC, a journalist, a university lecturer, Curator
of Cross-Cultural Programmes at Tate and a trustee of the
National Heritage Memorial Fund. He co-wrote *Windrush*:
The Irresistible Rise of Multi-Racial Britain with his brother,
Trevor Phillips. Mike is best known for his series of crime
novels, beginning with *Blood Rights* which was adapted
for television by the BBC. He was awarded the Crime
Writers' Association Silver Dagger Award for *The Late
Candidate*, the second book in the series. In 2007 he was
awarded an OBE for services to broadcasting.

Praise for Mike Phillips

'This is Mike Phillips' best novel, brutal and caring,
totally authentic'
The Times

'Could have come from the pen of the master,
Raymond Chandler'
Today

'There's much here to suggest that Phillips could be one
of our bravest, most incisive social commentators'
Mail on Sunday

By Mike Phillips

The Dancing Face
Windrush
The Name You Once Gave Me
A Shadow of Myself

Sam Dean Novels
Blood Rights
The Late Candidate
Point of Darkness
An Image to Die For

MIKE PHILLIPS

AN IMAGE TO DIE FOR

HarperCollins*Publishers*

HarperCollins*Publishers*
1 London Bridge Street,
London SE1 9GF

www.harpercollins.co.uk

HarperCollins*Publishers*
1st Floor, Watermarque Building, Ringsend Road
Dublin 4, Ireland

This paperback edition 2022

1

First published by HarperCollins*Publishers* Ltd 1995

ISBN: 9780008542948 (PB)

Typeset in Meridien by Palimpsest Book Production Limited,
Falkirk, Stirlingshire

Printed and bound in the UK using 100% renewable electricity
at CPI Group (UK) Ltd

MIX
Paper | Supporting
responsible forestry
FSC™ C007454

This book is for Ivan, Kwesi, and Jenny.

*All is true, but in time
we'll come to the end
of the small hours.*

1

When I walked past the girl in the white sweater she had less than half an hour to live, but judging by the way she smiled at me, the last thing on her mind was the thought of sudden death. It was a bright morning in May, one of those days when the brilliance of the sun seemed abrupt and unreasonable, because the previous fortnight had been dank and grey. The girl was standing by the entrance which led into the courtyard of the building behind her, and, framed against the dark mouth of the passage, she seemed to be glowing with reflected light. For a moment the illusion of a halo was so strong that she didn't seem quite real, but as I came closer she pointed a finger at me and spoke my name.

'Sam Dean?'

I gave her my best smile, assuming that she was part of Davis's production team. That much was obvious when I came to think about it. Her sweater and jeans were nothing out of the ordinary, but she wasn't wearing make-up, and her face, framed in a smooth sweep of glossy fair hair, had a cheerful open confidence which seemed like a declaration that she didn't belong here on the estate. It wasn't the worst council estate in this part of London. Unlike the high-rise disasters of the decade before, it was built in red brick, and its outer fringes consisted of jagged lines of low terraced houses which effectively disguised its mammoth size and complexity. It was when you got to the central blocks of flats through the zigzag mosaic of alleyways and internal courts, that the increasing murkiness of the walls, the vandalised shrubs, and the overturned dustbins began to tell the story of the place. Even without those clues I already knew that this estate had the usual problems: drugs, adolescent delinquents, and a general air of municipal depression. I had come in through a passage which ran along the back of the flats and I hadn't seen many of the residents, but I knew instinctively that the girl in front of me didn't live on the estate. No one who lived here had this air of sunny well-being.

'Jill Dunn.'

She put her hand out and we shook hands. This was strange too. Her accent and her appearance made her middle class, south counties, but the spontaneity of the gesture suggested that she must have lived abroad.

'He was waiting for you,' she said, 'but they've had to start the interview. Go on up anyway. It won't take long.'

I nodded as if I understood what she was talking about, and went on up the stairs. After the sunshine I'd just passed through, entering the grimy block was like going into a dark tunnel, an impression reinforced by the gloomy lighting along the corridor. Up ahead I could see a bluish white glare flooding out from the open door of the last flat in the row, and I guessed that this was where Davis would be. My footsteps echoed loudly in the empty passage, and someone must have heard me coming, because, as I got within a few yards of the open door, a young woman, who, apart from the fact that she had black hair, seemed like a clone of the one I'd just met, peered round the edge of the door and put her finger to her lips.

I knew this meant that my approach was registering on the sound equipment they were using, but there was something about the signal which made me feel patronised, so instead of freezing on the spot I gave her a puzzled look and walked on breezily. As I did so, the dark-haired woman came all the way out from behind the door and gave me a look of cold interrogation. From inside I could hear a buzz of voices and people moving about, and I guessed that they had stopped filming till someone had dealt with the interruption.

'Sam Dean,' I told the girl at the door, but this one didn't smile or offer her hand. Her expression grew marginally less frosty, but that was all.

'Oh. Yes,' she said. 'Wyndham's expecting you, but we had to start on time. You'd better go in.'

I gave her a nice smile and squeezed past, following the long black cable which snaked through the hallway. Halfway down, as I went past what I took to be the door of a bedroom, I heard a low rumbling growl, startling in its menace, immediately followed by a furious scrabbling. I leapt a few inches in the air, and heard the woman behind me smothering a giggle.

'Don't worry,' she called. 'He's locked in.'

A few feet further on the cable curved round to the left, and I emerged into an L-shaped room. The lights were set up on tripods in the elbow of the room, pointing away from me. The cameraman was bent over, fiddling with the monitor by the side of his camera. Squatting behind him on the floor a man wearing headphones was playing with the knobs on his machine. In front of the camera Joan Foster was sitting in an upright chair facing someone I couldn't see. The last time we met she'd been a bouncy young researcher. Now she looked older, thinner and more fashionable, the tangle of mousy hair I remembered shortened into a lustrous mass which swung heavily when she moved her head. On the other side of her was Wyndham Davis, towering above everyone else. Nowadays he wasn't bearded, but the mop of blond curls made him look as eccentric as ever. As I came through the doorway he glanced round and glared at me.

'Sammy,' he said loudly. 'I was waiting for you.'

'But you had to get started,' I finished the sentence for him.

'I was expecting you earlier.'

'You're lucky I'm here now,' I told him. It was now half past ten, and it was only twelve hours since he'd rung me.

As if recognising that he was being unreasonable, Davis grimaced, grinned at me, and flipped his hand in a noncommittal gesture.

'You know Joss and Lou, don't you?' he said.

The cameraman winked at me and his mate Lou waved without looking up from his equipment. I knew them both too, the way you know people with whom you've spent a fortnight working intensively on something difficult.

''Course I know the bastards,' I said.

'Oi. Oi,' Lou muttered, 'he's started. We'll have to train him all over again.'

'Right,' Davis cut in before I could reply, his tone making it clear that he didn't want to waste any more time. 'Let's get on. You ready, Joss?'

Joss grunted and Davis looked over at me again.

'Why don't you hang on a bit, Sammy? We'll be finished soon.'

I looked round. There was a sofa against the wall behind

4

me and I sat on it, the imitation leather squeaking loudly as I relaxed. Davis waited until I was settled, then he bent over and peered into the monitor on the camera.

'All right, Joss,' he said quietly. 'Go on then.'

'Rolling,' Joss announced.

Joan sat up a little straighter. In front of her I could see the lower half of the interviewee's legs, stretched out and crossed at the ankles. He was wearing jeans and an expensive pair of trainers, but that was all I could make out.

'Let's pick up where we left off. You were talking about where you saw him,' Joan said encouragingly. From her tone I guessed that she was smiling sweetly, and from what I knew of Joan, that would mean she was acting her head off.

'I was in the van going up Beulah Hill,' a voice said. The accent was London, and the timbre of the voice told me that it belonged to a white man.

'How far is that from here?' Joan asked.

'Dunno. Ten miles. Something like that.'

'Hold it, Dave,' Davis said suddenly. 'Never mind the miles. Can you say when you left the estate and how long it took you to get to Beulah Hill. Then say you saw him. OK?'

The man must have signalled his assent.

'All right, ask the question again,' Davis muttered.

'I left here about ten o'clock,' Dave's voice said, 'and I was going up Beulah Hill about half ten. That was when I saw Leon Ross. He was leaning over the bonnet of his car. It was definitely him, so he was miles away at the time. Right?'

'That was fine,' Davis announced, 'but let's just do it again. I don't want to put words in your mouth, but you told us that when you looked back there was a car coming the other way and the lights shone on his face, otherwise you wouldn't have recognised him.'

'Well, I knew the car. Didn't I?' Dave replied triumphantly.

'Right,' Davis explained patiently, 'but even so, it's helpful that you saw his face. So it's useful if you say that, and it would help as well if you go on a little bit about the dog being in the van and recognising the car because you'd seen him around here with his head stuck under the bonnet. That kind of stuff. Everything you told us before. Remember, it's not about truth. We know what you're saying is true. But it's about credibility. The image. That's what counts. OK?'

'Gotcha.'

'All right, Joan,' Davis muttered.

That's how it went for the next twenty minutes or so while they stopped and started, trying to get the man to deliver the story that Davis wanted, in the precise style and shape he was after. I was losing track of time, but I'd got the gist of it in the first few minutes. Davis wasn't nitpicking. He wanted the story to sound like the sort of evidence that would be credible in a court of law. He'd given a brief summary of the project on the phone, and I could see why he was anxious. His company was a small independent, and he'd landed a commission to make a series of six programmes on current miscarriages of justice. They were all based on recent murders, the bloodier and more bizarre the better, and this was the first, the pilot on which the network bosses would decide whether or not to go ahead with the series. So Davis had chosen the juiciest murder with which to kick off. This was the slaughter of a young woman and her child, which had taken place in a flat on one of the upper floors, about a hundred yards away from where we were. The story was stark and simple. Around midnight a neighbour had noticed the open door and gone in to be greeted by a scene of carnage, blood everywhere, blood sticky underfoot, blood smearing the walls, and blood soaking into the toddler's little mattress. Next day the police arrested the husband, Leon Ross, and he was subsequently tried and convicted. Davis was claiming to have turned up overwhelming new evidence that Leon couldn't have killed his wife, Helen.

On the phone he'd been cagey, but I guessed that this interview was only a small part of what he had, a piece of testimony he'd be using to buttress something else. In that case, I thought, I wished that he'd get on with it, so he could let me know what he wanted. The tension of sitting still on the squidgy plastic sofa was beginning to make my muscles seize up, and I had just determined to get up, go out and wait outside the building when the dog in the next room began making a series of terrifying noises.

I suppose the word barking describes what he was doing, but it didn't get near the monstrous intensity of menace and rage communicated by the sound. It started with a low rumble, so low that I had the illusion I could feel it through the soles of my feet. Then it rose rapidly into a coughing roar, which ended in an ear-splitting crack. A nanosecond of silence and it started again, faster, louder and more devastating than before.

Everyone in the room froze for an instant. Lou was the first to react. He ripped the headphones away from his ears, switched his machine off, and began adjusting the knobs.

'Bloody hell,' Dave said loudly. 'What the fuck's going on?'

He stood up and I saw him for the first time. Fair hair

cut short. A gold earring glinting in one ear. Acne scars on both cheeks. The right side of his neck was tattooed with the open beak and staring eyes of an angry dragon whose tail and clawing feet climbed out of his T-shirt to curl round his bulging biceps.

'Hang on,' Lou called out. 'Microphone.'

Dave looked down at the microphone pinned halfway down his T-shirt and began fiddling with it impatiently. Joan stood up and started helping him to unclasp it. As she did this we heard the thud of a heavy body against the door, and I realised that the dog's barking had changed to a continuous sobbing snarl, which didn't stop or alter its pitch even when he threw himself against the door.

In the same moment we heard the woman shrieking Wyndham's name. She might have called out before, but it would have been impossible to hear above the noise the dog was making. In any case, judging by the sound, she was already in the flat, her footsteps clattering through the hallway.

Wyndham was the first to move, driving his way out of the corner by the window and squeezing past me on the sofa. As he did so I sat back, pulling my legs aside to let him pass, so I missed seeing the woman stumble into the room.

'Oh. Shit,' Wyndham said suddenly, the word echoing the shock I felt as they appeared.

The screams had been coming from the dark-haired woman who'd been stationed at the door of the flat, but now I barely recognised her because her face was smeared with blood. She had her arm round Jill Dunn, half carrying, half supporting her, and the blood with which both of them were drenched seemed to be coming from Jill. There was still a small white patch on Jill's sweater, but the rest of it was painted a wet squelching red.

Somehow the red stuff had spurted on to her hair and it hung down lank and straggling, some of it plastered against her face, framing her rolling desperate eyes. Her nose and mouth were running with it too, and as she lurched against the other woman she seemed to be trying to say something which came out as a pathetic moan, the blood gushing as she opened her mouth. Wyndham held her as the other woman let go, and, kneeling, lowered her gently to the floor.

'Ambulance!' he shouted. 'Ambulance!'

Before any of us could move, there was an explosive, splintering crash and almost before the sound of it registered, the dog leapt, snarling, into the room. He was only a dog, black and tan, writhing muscles, scrabbling feet, slavering jaws, and a long continuous growling. It was as if a violent blizzard had blown into the room. He hit Wyndham head on, knocking him back against me, and turning, fastened his teeth in Jill's shoulder, his head working back and forth as he tore and worried at her flesh.

The one thought in my mind was to get the dog off her, but Dave got there first. As the dog came into the room he'd started towards it, his mouth wide open, shouting something I couldn't catch. He hadn't yet managed to free himself from the microphone and as he moved he pulled the wire behind him, dragging the camera and its tripod, which Joss caught in his arms, falling back on top of me. Behind him the spotlight fell against the windowsill and exploded with a loud bang. For a moment I was trapped, caught in a tangle of arms, legs, black plastic and rods of sharp steel. By the time I'd fought my way out of the sofa, Dave had the dog by the collar, whacking him violently in the ribs and hauling him back out of the room, still snarling and snapping his bloody jaws. Jill was now motionless on the floor, and when I dropped to my knees beside her I didn't need to touch her to see that she was now dead. Next to me, Wyndham sat back on his heels and hung his head. Then he looked up at the woman who'd brought Jill in and was now standing pressed against the wall. Somehow I hadn't noticed it until that moment, but her mouth was open and every few seconds she was making a thin, high noise, like a door creaking as it opened and shut.

'Why don't you shut up?' Wyndham shouted.

She reacted immediately, jumping back against the wall as if she'd been struck. At the same time she put the side of her hand between her teeth and bit down on it, as if by reflex. I put my hand on the side of Jill's neck, feeling for the pulse, but there was nothing. Beneath the mask of blood, there was already a pallid, drained look to her skin. I thought for a moment about giving her the kiss of life, but, looking at her I knew it would be pointless. Under my knees the carpet was sopping with her blood. I reached out to feel her neck again.

'It's no bloody good,' Wyndham said angrily. 'Leave her alone. Can't you see she's dead?'

I turned to look at him. His eyes were fixed and staring, his skin suddenly transformed into a fragile paper-white. Behind us I could hear Joan's voice, talking in a cool, level tone to the emergency service. In that moment I felt an anger so intense that I could have smashed my fist into Wyndham's face. Instead, I got to my feet and held my hand out to help him up.

'There's an ambulance on the way,' Joan said. She didn't look any more agitated than usual, but I noticed that she was staying on the other side of the room, as far away as she could get from the corpse.

'You need the police as well,' I told her. 'Call them now.'

2

I woke early the next morning. I'd only had a couple of hours of distressed sleep, the dark pit in my head roaring with the fragments of murky nightmares. I kept seeing the girl's face. Her blue eyes had been open, staring with that iron fixity of purpose that only the dead seemed able to achieve.

The policeman who interviewed us had eyes of the same colour, but his had a busy darting look to them, restless and nervously alive. At the station they'd kept us waiting around for the better part of the day, and by the time we'd made our statements, the horror of the scene in which we'd taken part was being swamped by boredom. The worst of it was the fact that we had very little to tell, apart from what we'd seen. Katrina, the woman who'd brought Jill in, had found her stumbling along the corridor. That was all. During the afternoon the police had been making door-to-door enquiries, but no one had seen or heard anything to suggest how Jill had come by the knife wound which killed her. When I left, the police were still interviewing Wyndham, and I guessed he was being pumped about the possibility that the stabbing had something to do with the film he was making.

In the taxi we shared coming back through west London, I tried to get Joan talking about what was going on and whether it was connected with Jill's murder, but she couldn't or wouldn't tell me much. In any case, I had the suspicion that she didn't know as much as she would have liked about where the project was headed.

'Wyndham wanted you for a job,' she said. 'But he'll ring you later and tell you about it himself.' She looked away from me. The sun was still shining, and as we went past the new block of luxury flats which had replaced the hospital annex in Harrow Road, bright points of light winked at us from the glossy surfaces of fresh paint.

'What was the job?' I asked, but she didn't look round and I guessed she wasn't going to tell me. I felt a sudden stab of anger when I realised this, and as if she could tell what I was feeling, she shifted uneasily, moving a little further into the corner of the seat. Her posture hadn't changed, but I kept my eyes on her, casting about in my head for a tactful way of expressing my irritation. She seemed smaller than I remembered. Other things had changed too. Half a dozen years ago, she'd had a clumping, sporty look about her, a lady cricketer just out of the shower. Now she was wearing high heels, a tight dark suit, and under it, one of those bras which thrust her breasts forward like a pair of perfect twins.

'He'd better tell you himself,' she said. 'I'll make sure he rings you today.'

I was dubious about that because I suspected that she didn't like me very much. If the way she was reacting to me was anything to go by she hadn't forgotten the last time we'd worked together, and it had all ended, literally, in tears. The job had been for an independent company and we'd been preparing an educational series which never got on the screen. But the development stage, during which we'd done dozens of interviews and a lot of research, took three months.

At the time, Joan had just left college and most of what she said about the project had a grinding sloganising tone about it, as if she was still trying to prove herself the brightest young thing in the seminar group. Within the first few weeks her tight, irritable manner had got on everyone's nerves, and at the end of the month she had a spectacular row with one of the other researchers, a recently divorced woman who was working her way back. It became one of those office feuds where everyone took sides. In this case Teresa had the majority vote, especially after she invented the Great Joan Foster Sweepstake. To enter the GJFS you had to guess how many times Joan would use a particular combination of words before lunch-time. It was a sneaky tactic which isolated Joan and ensured that nothing she said would be taken seriously. She didn't know exactly what was happening, but she could feel the vibes, and her paranoia grew more and more intense. On the morning I lost patience with her I'd spent most of the previous night reading a series of school inspectors' reports, my head ached, and I was beginning to suspect that the project we were working on was a dead duck. That was also the morning I guessed, correctly, that Joan would use the phrase 'strong women' at least twenty times before lunch. During all the covert merriment that my triumph provoked, Joan must have heard or sensed something untoward, because she came back from the sandwich bar where she went to munch salads and confronted me head on. What was all the sniggering about? By then I'd had enough, and I was beginning to feel guilty about my contribution to Teresa's campaign. So, without beating around the bush, I told Joan what had been going on. She listened, staring at me without expression. Then, without a word, she turned away and sat at the word processor. I was hovering, uncertain about whether or not to apologise, when I realised that there were tears splashing down in front of her on to the desk, but before I could take in what was happening she leapt up again, ran the length of the room and slammed into the ladies' loo. Half an hour later she emerged and went home without a word to anyone. She was back the next morning, but from that time she'd stopped speaking to me, except for essential matters of business. Fortunately, the project was wrapped up during the next fortnight when both our contracts came to an end, and I went back to scuffling for part-time shifts and occasional articles on any paper that would have me. Joan went, as I'd half expected, to a job in the BBC. Now she was Wyndham's partner, and a player in what passed, among us, for the big time.

In the circumstances I had the feeling that Wyndham must have had a very strong motive for wanting me. He rang a few hours later. By then the gloom was staining the bit of the sky that I could see from the window of my loft, and the rumbling surf of traffic running down to Paddington had started to fade. My flat, which consisted of a couple of rooms and a kitchen, was at the top of three tall storeys. The house was a sort of anachronism. It belonged to the Church of England, and it couldn't be changed or torn down because it was part of a listed Georgian terrace. The street was full of rich people, and the house was probably worth a millionaire's ransom, but the tenancy had been passed on to me by a friend who'd got it from another friend who'd lived there since the postwar years when the district was full of cheap rented housing. Nowadays the neighbouring streets were choked with newly built apartment blocks which seemed to be occupied by throngs of wealthy Arabs. But these were luxurious places in comparison to my house, where the roof leaked and where I was usually out of breath by the time I'd climbed the four flights of stairs. On the other hand, the rent was still extremely low because it was tiny and inconvenient. I loved living in the centre of the city, and I loved the feeling of being on top of a tower, isolated and inaccessible. Lying awake at night, I would listen for hours to the rumble of the traffic round Marble Arch, mingling with the cooing of the pigeons on the roof.

'Sorry we couldn't talk this morning,' Wyndham said. 'I want you to do a bit of a job, nothing too fancy, you know.'

'What is it?' I asked.

'Well,' he said, 'I want you to find a bloke. Jill was sorting it out.' He paused, while we both thought about the implications of that fact. 'Well, I don't quite know how far she'd got, actually. I don't think it was anything much to do with her being killed.'

'Much or little, mate,' I said, 'I don't really fancy that kind of job.'

'You haven't heard what it's all about.'

'Tell me.'

The story was simple enough. Wyndham's new slant on the case was to do with a former lover of the murdered woman who he believed was either the real murderer or knew, somehow, who the real murderer was.

'What makes you think it's not the husband? They convicted him.'

'I don't believe it,' Wyndham said. 'For a start, he's got an alibi. We've been finding witnesses who confirm it. You saw one of them this morning. And I'll show you

15

the transcripts of the statements and the case. They make interesting reading.'

I didn't hesitate. I'd made up my mind already, the night before.

'Got to say no, man,' I told him. 'Even if I was interested I would be completely pissed off that you didn't dream of giving me a job in the first place when it was just an ordinary reporting job. Now you've run into a problem which needs a black ferret to crawl down whatever hole you've got in mind and you call me. Your suspect is black. Right?'

I'd guessed that from the moment he said he wanted to see me. In fact, the husband who'd been convicted was black too. I wasn't sure whether or not that made the point stronger, but it seemed to get home to Wyndham.

'Sammy. Sammy,' he said, halfway between soothing and apology.

'Don't Sammy me,' I told him. 'I never liked being brought in to do the black stuff, and I don't want to do that any more if I can help it. What bugs me is the fact that it's you. I don't care if it didn't cross your mind a couple of months ago when you started your project that I could have done with the work. But you've known me for years and you know this is exactly the kind of crap I've had forced on me the whole of my working life. I don't feel like it any more.'

I put the phone down feeling easier and lighter. Getting that off my chest had been a pleasure. Not that it would do me any good, I thought. Ticking off Wyndham had given me a short-term lift, but turning down the prospect of paid work had been a rash move. In any case, I had an uneasy feeling that I hadn't heard the last of the whole affair, so that when the doorbell rang next morning I guessed immediately who the caller was.

As it happened I was wrong. I'd expected to see Wyndham standing on the doorstep, but instead of his hulking form, the person I saw looking back at me through the spyhole in the door was a woman. Tall, blonde, wire-rimmed dark glasses, which gave her features a haughty, enigmatic look.

I opened the door slowly. I knew who she was, but I couldn't guess what she wanted, and, in any case, I wasn't sure that I wanted to speak to her.

'Can I come in?' she said. An ironic lift of the eyebrow, her favourite affectation and the only one I could remember. I stood aside and she walked past me and up the stairs without hesitation. At the top, she paused, looked round quickly and went on into the sitting room. I followed her, still puzzled by the fact that she'd come to see me. We hadn't been alone or had an informal conversation for more than ten years, and I'd have been happy to keep it that way.

'Not much change, I see,' she said.

I guessed she was referring to the shabby look of the place, but I couldn't tell whether she was needling me or sympathising, so I merely shrugged. She must have taken that as an invitation, and without waiting for a reply she took her glasses off and sat down. I sat opposite and looked at her. At that moment her composure had me confused, and I couldn't think of anything to say. Our relationship had come to an end after a long, slow build-up of indifference and irritability. At the back of my mind was a question about whether she'd ever told Wyndham what happened between us during the times he'd been away researching or filming somewhere. I doubted it, but the possibility added a touch of insecurity to my feelings.

'I saw Wyndham yesterday,' I said.

'I know.' There was an undertone there but I couldn't read it. 'That's why I came to see you.'

She was wearing a dress which came down to her ankles, and was cut to fit her body. Close up it was a riot of tiny flowers in maroon and beige, with big round buttons running all the way down the front. Under it, a see-through white tunic, about the same length, flirted out of the opening at the bottom of the dress.

'I want to ask you a favour.'

She unfastened three buttons and leaned back in the sofa. The dress fell apart around her in graceful folds. Through the transparent material I caught the gleam of her flesh, its colour a pale and dusty gold. She must be close to forty now, I thought, but the look of her body was richer and more sensuous than I remembered. My mind struggled with the comparison. When we first met she'd been very different. In the winter she'd worn tweedy slacks and dull blouses. In the summer she'd worn shape-less flowery dresses, and her fair hair and pale skin had given her a sandy, washed-out look. If I had to guess I'd have said she was the English teacher in a suburban grammar school, and probably married to the head of the history department. But the passage of time, augmented by considerable sums of money, had done her a favour by transforming a persona which used to be only moder-ately attractive into something confident and sexy.

'Come on, Sarah,' I said. 'This is overkill. Tell me what you want and get out of here.'

She gave me a small knowing smile. Her eyebrows curved.

'You like the dress.'

'I love it. So what's up?'

'Wyndham,' she said. 'Getting you on the project was my idea. Wyndham needs you.'

'It's a pity neither of you thought of me in the first place.'

'We did,' she said. Her tone was impatient. 'But what he needed was a couple of kids who could run their little tails off for the minimum wage. You're past all that. Anyway, you know I've always thought you were good; so does Wyndham. If it had been right for you he'd have got you.'

I'd known that all the time, but it was hard to make distinctions after living on the receiving end for so long, and it was more convincing hearing it from her, partly because we'd first met when she hired me to work on an arts programme she was producing: and after that she'd always made a point of hiring me when she could. We'd been friends and occasional lovers long before I met Wyndham, and she hardly ever talked about him or their life together. So when he got in touch with me one day and asked if I'd work on a programme he was producing, I was intrigued and curious. Sarah, on the other hand, turned out to be angry and upset because I took the job without consulting her. Nothing was the same after that, and our relationship cooled in direct proportion to the warmth of my relations with Wyndham. By the time it was finished, our meetings had become dull and difficult and spiky with resentment. Ten years later, I could hardly remember exactly how we'd brought it to an end, apart from the fact that we both stopped wanting to meet.

'All right,' I said. 'That's fair enough. But I don't understand what it's got to do with you.'

When Wyndham decided to strike out on his own the idea had been that he and Sarah would be partners, but a couple of months after they'd secured the commission for their first independent TV series, she'd told him that she wanted to work by herself, as a freelance writer. Since then she'd made a career writing for various glossy magazines. She was almost famous, well known enough to command a couple of grand for a thousand words, and as far as I knew she didn't have much to do with the company.

'I still own part of the company,' she said. 'But that's not it. The point is that there's something going on that I'm uneasy about. Wyndham can't handle it. Besides, he's got other things to do.'

'You don't need me,' I told her. 'Wyndham can get anyone to find this guy he's after. Get a private detective or something. He'll probably be more efficient.'

'It's more complicated than that.' She twisted round and picked up her handbag. As she did so, the last button popped open on the dress. She didn't make any effort to do it up again. Instead, she opened the bag and took out an envelope. 'Look at this.'

It was an ordinary white envelope. On the front was a label with Wyndham's name and address printed on it. I opened it cautiously. Inside there was a plain sheet of paper on which there was a sentence made up of words cut from newspaper headlines and pasted together. The sentence said: **STOP THE FILM OR YOU DEAD**. When I looked up, Sarah was watching me, her expression unreadable.

'What's this about then?'

'I don't know,' she said. 'He's had about three of these.'

'What do the police say?'

She hesitated. Her right hand made a fist which she tapped repeatedly on the arm of the sofa.

'He hasn't shown them to the police.'

'What? After what happened yesterday he's crazy not to.'

She frowned.

'Wyndham doesn't think these are anything to do with

yesterday. The police think that Jill was attacked by one of the gangs on the estate.'

'So why are you so worried?'

I could just about see Wyndham's point. Anyone in his position would have had at least one death threat from a crank at some stage in his career. But Sarah's tension seemed to be signalling that there was something more she hadn't told me.

'He doesn't really think this is from some harmless lunatic.' She took the envelope out of my hand, put it in the bag and snapped it shut. Then she looked straight at me. 'He thinks this might be something to do with the man he wants you to look for. He disappeared at the exact moment that Wyndham started digging.'

'Yeah, but that doesn't make him a murderer.'

She sighed, and sat up straighter.

'Wyndham got a phone call. There were some threats. It might have been the same man.'

'That sounds dangerous. Why doesn't he go to the police? I mean, that's concrete. Guy rings up and threatens you on the phone.'

'Well.' She fiddled with her glasses, uncertain for the first time. 'That's just the problem. Wyndham hasn't got any evidence to connect this man with the crime. He needs to build a case. Having the police snooping around might destroy any chance he's got to stand up a miscarriage of justice. They're not going to help him make them look stupid. Anyway, you know Wyndham. He's got it into his head that he's going to do it his way.' She shrugged. 'It's a risk whatever he does.'

'So you want me to take the risk.'

'It's not like that. He simply wants you to do a job.'

'Come off it, Sarah. I don't even know what it's all about.'

She leaned towards me, her eyes looking deep into mine. Right then I knew that I was going to do what she asked. The strange thing was that the last time I'd been with her I was bored and impatient to get away. Now I was so excited I could hardly breathe. It was all coming back, a stream of images shooting through my head. During our last months the sex had become furious and intense. She'd been provocative and passive in turns. Each time had felt like the last time, and, pinned together by an agonising spike of anger and guilt, we'd wriggled ourselves into exhaustion. Looking at her now, my memory of the frustration was like something I'd read once in a book or been told about. Unreal. Reality was the hot damp feel of her body.

'He'll tell you the details,' she said. 'I don't know much about it anyway. It's just that he needs someone he can trust.'

'What makes you think he can trust me?'

She gave me that knowing smile again.

'Oh, I'll keep you in order.'

'What exactly is it you want me to do?'

'Go and talk to Wyndham. Ring him at the house. He's there now trying to sort things out. I'll be out all day. You can go and talk to him. Please, Sammy.'

'All right,' I told her. 'I'll talk to him, but I won't promise. OK?'

'OK.'

She got up, as if satisfied that our business was concluded, and buttoned the front of her dress carefully. When she was finished, she took a quick pace towards me, bent over and kissed me quickly on the cheek.

'Thanks,' she said.

'I haven't said I'll do it.'

She shrugged, straightened up, turned round and walked to the door. Halfway through she looked back.

'No need to tell Wyndham I came to see you. I don't want him to think I'm interfering.'

'But you are.'

'Just don't tell him. OK?'

I nodded. 'OK.'

She smiled, fluttered her fingers at me, and then she was gone. I sat where I was, trying to think through what she'd been telling me, and listening to her clattering down the stairs. Halfway down, just before the second landing, the sound stopped. She's coming back, I thought, and I began getting up to open the door for her, but after a brief pause the footsteps started again, and in a moment I heard the street door slamming shut.

3

'He's got something to hide,' Wyndham said. 'Whatever it is I need to know about it.'

I wasn't sure what he meant because I still wasn't certain about the details of the case. I was about to say so when his eyes flicked sideways and he flashed a smile and a wave of the hand at someone who'd just come in. I looked round, and saw two women walking across the restaurant. The older one was a plump blonde dressed in black from top to toe, her clothes billowing around her as she advanced. Behind her was a younger woman, tall, thin and black, with a supercilious expression. As a pair they made an oddly ludicrous impression, contrasts fitting together, like a couple of comedians. Wyndham didn't seem to notice. Instead he got up and gave both of them an ostentatious peck on the cheek. He didn't appear to be making any moves to introduce me so I stayed where I was.

'I've been meaning to get in touch, but I'm up to my neck,' the blonde woman said. 'I've read it, but we need to talk.'

'I thought I'd leave it till I heard from you,' Wyndham told her.

She nodded seriously. 'Give my secretary a ring.'

She smiled vaguely at me before turning away.

'Bloody cow,' Wyndham muttered. Suddenly I realised that he was angry. His face had gone red with the effort of holding it in. 'I've been waiting three months for an answer from that bitch. I sent her half a dozen pages three months ago and she still hasn't made a decision. She hasn't bloody read it.'

To an outsider his rage might have seemed excessive, but I understood his bitterness.

When Wyndham set up his own company he'd become a freelance, like me. Unlike me, he was cushioned by generous redundancy payments and two easy commissions, and for a couple of years he made more money than he'd ever done as a staff member. Then the overheads began to mount up, wages, VAT, insurance, all the usual catastrophes associated with running a small business. Wyndham still made a living with commercial videos and short films for backwaters like schools television, but he'd had to get rid of his office and the staff he'd hired. In the circumstances the time he spent waiting for a decision about a commission represented money down the drain. Thinking about it, I began to have a sense of how desperate he'd be to make a success of the film he was working on.

'Who is she?'

He looked over to where the women had settled themselves at a table in the corner, then he moved in a little closer and told me that she edited one of the big documentary series.

'You should have kissed her ass.'

This produced a sudden mood change, typical of Wyndham. His scowl disappeared, then he sat back and barked with laughter. 'I did. I did. But it didn't do any good.'

'Who's her friend?'

'She presents one of those children's programmes. She's one of those nice black lady graduates they're grooming to represent the multicultural face of the organisation. And very nice too. Don't you recognise her?'

I clicked my fingers. Recognition had been slow because I'd only ever seen her on TV, striding about a studio stroking a furry bundle, and all I could remember about the occasion was her ingratiating grin. But when she'd paused at our table the grin had been absent. When her eyes rested on me they'd been deliberately blank, and when I smiled she hadn't responded. Wyndham must have guessed what I was thinking because he gave me a grin which had a sarcastic edge to it.

'You're not important. They're probably talking about a contract. An ambitious young tiger like her wouldn't want anyone to think she hung out with a clapped-out old freelance like you. Besides, they're sisters. Middle-aged men are the enemy. Middle-aged black men are like from Mars.'

I guessed he was right, and I also guessed that he was telling me this in order to dump some of the humiliation he'd felt. For a moment I cast about for a snappy comeback, but it suddenly seemed a childish game to play, so I changed the subject instead.

'I'm not sure I get the reason why you want to go to so much trouble to find this guy. Even if you do, you won't necessarily be able to pin anything on him.'

He gave me an impatient look. As usual, he'd stated his conclusions without telling me how he'd arrived at them, but the fact that I couldn't keep up with his thought processes still irritated him.

'I've arrived in the middle of this,' I told him. 'I need to know more.'

Calming down visibly, he put on a businesslike face.

'I picked this as the pilot for the series for two reasons. One is that the conviction is shaky. Leon Ross, that's the husband, was out on the night the family was murdered. He came back to the estate sometime after midnight, where he found his wife stabbed to death in the sitting room of the flat. He found the child in the bedroom with its throat cut.'

'I know all this,' I interrupted.

He shrugged. 'You said you didn't.'

I took a deep breath. He was being awkward, but in this mood there was no shifting him without a row, so I let him go on.

'He had an alibi. He said he'd been with a woman in south London all evening. At first she backed him up, then she said that he'd actually left earlier than he claimed. So he changed his story. He said he'd lied because he was scared that no one would believe what really happened. His car had broken down on the way back. He'd fixed it, then it had broken down again. Each time he had to wait for the engine to cool down, then he'd run out of petrol. Altogether it took him over three hours to get back. The cops couldn't find anyone who'd seen him or who could confirm his story. I don't know how hard they tried, but no one came forward anyway. That was bad enough, but it turned out that he was covered in the victims' blood. He said he'd got the bloodstains when he was checking on them, before he rang the police, but there were no signs of a break-in and no indication that anyone else had been in the flat.'

I interrupted again, before he could embark on the details of the trial.

'Where's this other geezer come in then?'

He leaned forward eagerly.

'Well, that's the interesting bit. That's the other reason I chose it. It's like this. True-crime reconstructions are two a penny now. We're long past the days when Edgar Lustgarten could stand up there and shock and amaze you with boring crap about the forensic genius of the Yard. Your average punter wants blood and guts smeared over the walls. So we'll get a lot of mileage from a beautiful young woman and her innocent darling strangling in a pool of gore, but even that isn't quite enough any more. The real hook is the detection angle. Blood, brutality and an unsolved mystery. The police screwed up and put an innocent man behind bars, while a bestial killer is still roaming the streets, and we can point the finger straight at him.'

'Suppose he's innocent?'

I knew the answer to that one, but his enthusiasm was making me nervous.

'Doesn't matter. Our job is to broadcast the doubts about the verdict in the interest of justice. If there's a valid suspect who's never been looked at, it makes the case stronger.'

'What do the police think about your theory?'

He grinned. 'What do you think?'

I thought they'd be pissed off.

'So how'd you get on to this?'

'More luck than judgement. You need to know the background.'

The waitress arrived with lamb and strips of polenta for Wyndham, trout for me. He waited till she left.

'These estates are a bit like the old working-class districts in some ways.'

I nearly interrupted to ask how he knew. Wyndham's father was a senior civil servant, commuting from a village in Buckinghamshire. Wyndham himself had attended a public school nearby. He was probably in his mid twenties before he went anywhere near what he was calling a working-class district.

'Old working-class districts.' I laughed. 'You're a typical history graduate, believing all that stuff.'

'Oh, bollocks. You wanna hear this or not?'

I waved him on.

'All right. The point is that quite a lot of people around the estate seemed to have known that Helen Ross had a boyfriend. Amaryll Johnson.'

'Amaryll?'

'One of your beautifully archaic Caribbean names. The husband's named Leon, the boyfriend's name Amaryll. You know what you're dealing with right away.'

I ignored the jibe.

'How come so many people knew about Amaryll if the husband didn't?'

'Oh, they were discreet. Leon was a bouncer and he worked at night a lot of the time. When he was out, Amaryll was in.'

I shrugged. 'Gossip.'

'Yes and no. The thing is that they were the only mixed-race couple on the landing. She was young, in her twenties, good-looking. You know how that is. Causes excitement. The place was full of old biddies of every sort watching her. The word is that Amaryll used to be watching for Leon to leave before he slipped in, and just before Leon came back he'd come rushing out, and we've got that from too many reliable sources for it to be just gossip.'

He gave me a triumphant look, but just as I was about to ask my next question his attention switched to a couple who were on the way out. A portly grey-haired man in an expensive suit, trailed by a thin young woman, boots, tight black jeans, and tight black sweater and short black hair. Next to her companion she looked like a teenager out for a treat. We'd missed seeing them before because their table was in a secluded corner partly concealed by a large potted palm. Wyndham smiled and waved. The grey-haired man nodded briefly and continued on his way, while the woman averted her eyes and went past with her chin in the air.

'Hello,' Wyndham said. 'Did you see that?'

'What?'

'Very, very big. Head of department.' He named the man. 'She's a trainee. A few months out of Oxford. Taking the new girl out to lunch proves he's a new man.' He made a comical face. 'Pity people in his department are soooo cynical.'

I shrugged the whole thing off. This was the raw material of the gossip which would be flying around for the next couple of weeks, and the question of whether or not this girl was screwing the boss, or merely stringing him along, would become the subject of earnest discussion among various groups of serious men and women. The problem was that their careers could sometimes depend on knowing who actually had the boss's ear.

'Did someone see him that night?'

Wyndham looked blank.

'Amaryll,' I repeated patiently. 'Did anyone see him nipping into the flat that night?'

'Well, no. But they were seen together that day. The point is that he could have been in the flat later on, and if Leon's alibi holds up Amaryll is the obvious suspect.'

'How come that didn't occur to the police?'

He shrugged again.

'It might have done. They questioned him, but I imagine that Leon looked like such a good bet they didn't push it too far.'

'Why not?'

He frowned. The question was making him uncomfortable, and as if in response I began remembering details.

'Wasn't he supposed to be a wife-beater?'

Wyndham slapped his open palms on the table. The look on his face suggested that I was being deliberately obstructive.

'All right. Leon had a record of domestic violence.' He hesitated. 'And he had a stretch in Broadmoor.'

'Broadmoor? What for?'

Wyndham shrugged.

'Aggravated assault. He sent another guy to hospital. It was just an ordinary street fight, but the papers made a big thing out of it. I think that's why they convicted him. What got the police excited was the fact they'd had a fight that morning and there were scratches on his face. But none of that means he killed her. He's got an alibi, and we've found a witness to support it. That was the lucky bit. You'll like this. The way we got on to it was that I took on a schoolkid for this work experience thing they do. We use him as a messenger mainly. But he happened to live on the estate, and he came up one morning and told me this story, complete with a local suspect, and a friend of his elder brother who claimed to have seen Leon at the time when his wife was being murdered. He wants to break into TV and he thought I'd be grateful, which of course I am, because when I checked, the whole thing stood up. Bingo!'

The grin on his face reflected the joy he must have felt at that point, but then he must have sensed that my mood was unsympathetic, because he put his hand over his mouth and smoothed his features into sobriety.

'All I want to know,' I told him, 'is what's the point of going to a lot of trouble to find Amaryll when you don't have any evidence against him and all the circumstances are against the guy they've already convicted?'

Now he looked angry, his patience finally exhausted.

'Come off it, Sam. You know what I'm doing. The issue isn't Leon's innocence or guilt. That's about truth, and about truth I don't bloody know. The issue is the story, the narrative. Leon's alibi gives me enough to cast doubt on the verdict, but there's no punchline. I need the suspect to round it all off and make it gripping. When that goes on the screen the logic of the story will hold a couple of million idiots and stop them from touching the remote control till they find out what happens at the end. Have you got it now?'

'What about the threatening letters?'

He looked surprised.

'What threatening letters?'

'I heard you got some letters and telephone calls.'

A pause.

'Oh, those. There're a lot of nutcases about. We're working in what amounts to a village. There's bound to be some nonsense going on. I don't think there's any connection.'

'And Jill?'

A longer pause. I could sense that we were both seeing the same image of Jill's blood-smeared features. He pushed his plate away.

'A coincidence,' he said. 'It's horrible, but it happens.'

Our eyes met.

'Why me?' I asked him. 'It doesn't follow that because the guy is black I can find him. I'd need to know who he is and where he comes from. It's a lot of work with no guarantees. There's a lot of people with more expertise in finding lost people.'

'Like who?'

'Police, detectives, debt collectors, social workers. I don't know.'

Wyndham sighed.

'That's just it. Those categories are specific, you see. If some dodgy businessman runs off, he's going to use his credit card in the Isle of Wight, they track him through computer records, that sort of thing. Someone on income support registers for the dole in Brighton, they get him sooner or later. Some kid runs off from Peebles and ends up in the West End, the police pick him up and find out who he is. If you check out and you're reasonably intelligent and you don't get yourself into any official lists, and you don't go around telling people who you are you could disappear forever. It's a needle in a haystack job.'

'So what makes you think I can do it?'

He gestured vaguely.

'I don't know what I think. Except that you're different. You won't look in the voters' register or sit in front of a computer. You're interested in people, where they come from, where they go. I've heard you rabbiting on and on about populations shifting across Europe. All that kind of stuff.' He struck an attitude and stuck his finger in the air. 'The inexorable movement of peoples across the landscape.' He grinned at me, his eyebrows raised, and after a while I smiled back at him.

'People talk to you,' he went on, 'and you'll make guesses. Creative imagination is what we need here, and you've got that.' He paused, and leaned closer. 'The other thing is that I don't want him to think I've sent the cops or some other agency after him. If he's really got something to hide he'll just run off or shut up. You're different. He might well have heard of you. You're less likely to frighten him off than most people, and I want you to persuade him to be interviewed on camera. If you can get to him and start talking you can do it.'

'Suppose he knows that he's being stitched up.'

'Don't talk like that, Sammy. It's bollocks. We're just giving him the chance to answer a few questions about his involvement. Clear his name.'

I gave him a sceptical look.

'I know what you're saying,' he said. 'But have you considered the possibility that Leon is innocent and this guy might have the information that will save him. I truly believe that, and who made you judge and jury?'

In that moment I was thrown by his sincerity.

'It's not a game,' I said. 'Not with a bunch of people dead and a guy serving several years in prison.'

Wyndham shrugged, impatient.

'Don't you think I know that?'

'Let me think about it,' I told him.

Later on I realised that I'd already made the decision, and I spent the early part of the evening going through the transcripts of Ross's interrogation by the police, which was among the bunch of papers Wyndham had stuck in my hand before we left the restaurant. Along with these there were a number of interviews with witnesses to a series of violent incidents between Leon and Helen. The police seemed to have gone overboard on these. Or maybe there were so many of them because most of the neighbours seemed to have seen or heard something of the kind. Someone in Wyndham's office had provided an index and there were four statements from women who'd seen Helen running out of the flat, pursued by Leon, on the morning of her death. I worked through the rest of the interviews looking for statements about Leon's whereabouts at the time of the murders, but the closest they

34

came was the testimony from a neighbour who claimed to have seen Leon's car parked in the slip road for most of the evening. Under questioning he had admitted to being uncertain that it actually was Leon's car. It was, however, the same make and colour, and the police had found another witness who backed up his story. This was probably the detail which had convicted Leon Ross, largely because the second witness had been a patrolling police driver who hadn't taken the number but could certainly remember that a white Ford Escort had been parked there at the time that Leon claimed to have been poking about under the bonnet of his car in south London.

Leon himself, under questioning, sounded shifty and uncertain. He hadn't actually confessed, but his story was so thin that I found myself wondering why he hadn't made up a better one. There was no mention of Amaryll. Not specifically. Several of the witnesses testified to the fact that Helen had received gentleman callers at odd hours while Leon was away from the flat. I half expected the transcripts to show the police going after Helen's rumoured infidelity as a motive, but as I read on I realised that they'd been contented to focus on the frequent quarrels between the couple, and Leon's pattern of violent behaviour.

By the time I'd worked my way through the bulk of the statements it was nearly midnight, and I was no closer to forming an opinion about Leon's guilt or innocence, but I was beginning to see why Wyndham needed another suspect to firm up his claim that this had been a glaring judicial error. Something else was beginning to worry me. My arrangement with him was that I'd look at the papers then telephone him. I'd been hoping that before I spoke to him again something about the evidence would give me a feel for what had happened, perhaps help me begin sketching out a theory which would contradict the police case, but after all I'd read I still couldn't make up my mind.

I picked up the phone and dialled Wyndham's number. He answered right away.

'None of these people in the transcripts mention Amaryll by name. How come you know who he is and how often he visited the flat?'

A pause. I guessed he was working out what to tell me.

'Before we go any further,' he said, 'I need to know whether you're in or out. Otherwise it just gets too difficult.'

When I dialled his number I'd almost decided to tell him that I wasn't interested, but there was something about the situation, a puzzle waiting to be unravelled, that made me want to know more: and apart from my curiosity about the case, I had promised Sarah.

'All right,' I told him. 'I'm in.'

4

The boy was tall, with the strung-out look of a professional cyclist. I guessed he was about sixteen. He might have been older but I had the feeling that the way he was wearing his hat, with the peak pointing backwards, was something to do with still being a kid. Beneath the hat what I could see of his head was shaven, the dark roots speckling the sides of his skull, as if it had been dusted with black pepper.

'You're Jamie,' I said.

He made a sound halfway between a grunt and a sniff, which I took to mean yes. We were sitting in the offices of Wyndham's production company. They consisted of a large room which seemed to be sprouting with computer terminals. Actually, there were only six of them, but their presence seemed to dominate the room. Joan Foster and Katrina were sitting at one end working at separate desks. They'd both looked up and said hello when Wyndham brought me in, but after that they'd ignored me. Wyndham had gone off to his own room, which was up another flight of stairs on the floor above, and I'd sat in the corner waiting for the boy Jamie to turn up.

'What I really want to know,' I told him, 'is about this guy Amaryll. Do you know him? What makes you think that he had anything to do with the murder?'

His face flushed red. I could see the stain climbing all the way up to his hairline. He shifted his chair a little so that he was a couple of inches further away from me.

'Dunno.'

I waited.

'Everybody said that. You know what I mean?'

'Everybody like who?'

'I dunno.' He hesitated. 'My mum. Dave.'

Dave was the man in whose flat Jill had died.

'How come no one told the cops about this?'

He grimaced.

'Dunno.'

I choked down my impatience. Wyndham had said that the boy wanted to work in TV, but if he made it he wouldn't be reading the news. That much was certain.

'Thanks,' I told him. He ducked his head and grunted in reply. Then he got up and hurried out of the office without looking back. Katrina saw him going and jumped up hastily from her desk waving a big beige envelope.

'Jamie,' she called out. 'I want you.'

She hurried out of the door after him and I heard them talking in the passage. Feeling Joan's eyes on me I looked round. I half expected some show of curiosity, if not sympathy, but she merely gave me a sarcastic smile and turned away to focus on her terminal. Wyndham had told me to ask her for any information I wanted, but her manner irritated me too much to bother, so I got out of my chair and headed up the stairs.

He was sitting in a swivel chair, staring out of the window at Camden High Street. It was the middle of the morning and the traffic had eased up a bit, but even so, on the street the cars and lorries were crawling, the air blue with the hot smoke of their fumes. Wyndham made a gesture of greeting without turning round.

'I moved in here not long after the IRA bombing, and the rents were fairly low. They've gone up since then. People don't remember anything further back than a few months. It's the death of history.'

'No, it's not,' I told him. 'I remember the bomb. My son was at a record shop down there. He missed the explosion by a few seconds.'

'How is he?'

'Not bad. He's doing his exams this year. University in the autumn.'

He took this in without comment. There was a lot more I could have said about my son and about how I thought he was, but I'd learnt long ago that the subject bored people who didn't have any children, and many parents who had a stroppy teenager on their hands reacted in the same way. Looking at the back of Wyndham's head I wondered what he was thinking. He and Sarah hadn't had any children and I'd always wondered why, but it didn't seem the right time to ask.

'How'd it go with Jamie?'

'He didn't know anything more than you'd already told me.'

Wyndham swung his chair around.

'I never said he did. You're the one that insisted on talking to him.'

'All right. Have you got an address for Amaryll? Any place I could start?'

'Joan will have all that.'

'I'd prefer you to tell me.'

He stared at me, then shook his head and gave an

impatient grunt. Then he leaned forward and began tapping at the keyboard in front of him.

'I'll print you out a list of addresses.'

Half an hour later I was on my way down to west London. Wyndham had said that Jill had been working on drawing up the list of addresses he'd given me, but they didn't amount to much. The first one was Dave's flat, and the other two were places where Amaryll had lived. I had the feeling that they'd be useless, but at least they were a place to start.

Turning off the Harrow Road into the little maze of streets which ran down into Harlesden, I found myself wondering whether I was doing the right thing. Everything about this job made me uneasy, including the fact that I wasn't at all sure that it could be done. As usual I needed the money, but I'd have felt happier if that had been the only reason I'd said yes to Wyndham. In any case, I couldn't share his confidence about the eventual outcome, and somewhere at the back of my mind there was an uncomfortable feeling that however I played it someone was going to get hurt.

I was so busy turning over the prospect in my head that I almost drove past the first address on Wyndham's printout without noticing, but, just in time, I caught a glimpse of the number – 29 – painted in faded white on the crumbling gatepost. I slammed the brakes on, pulled over, and parked. On the pavement I looked around, gearing myself up to confront whatever I'd find. Ahead of me the row of terraced cottages ran straight down to Queen's Park, and suddenly the monotony of the street arrangement and the similarity of the buildings reminded me that this too was a low-income estate, built more than a century ago. These were houses built to an identical model, two storey, sash windows, a tiny strip of front garden, now overlaid with concrete. But there was also something about the patterns which sketched out the outlines of communities which had long since vanished. On the way in, I'd gone past a couple of chapels and a meeting hall, all constructed in the same sub-Gothic style, and I guessed that they came from the era when the district was home to a reservoir of artisans and skilled workers. In recent years the last vestiges of the industrial landscape they'd built disappeared, and nowadays middle-class professionals were spilling over from Maida Vale and Notting Hill, drawn by the relatively cheap housing of the area and its proximity to the centre of the city.

As if my thoughts had magicked up an illustration of what was happening to the place, I'd parked right in front of a house which shone with whitewash and new brick-work. Its sash windows had been replaced by a huge sheet of smoked glass, and a row of potted plants trembled against the basement wall. In the context there was something oddly foreign about the conversion, and, as if to confirm that idea, a short, thickset woman with a cloud of wavy black hair opened the front door and came out, followed by two blond toddlers. When she saw me standing on the pavement she hesitated, as if uncertain about whether or not to come down the steps. I smiled at her and got a frightened look in return, so I gave up and moved on to 29.

When I rang the bell there was no answering sound, so I rapped with my knuckles. As I did so something moved in the smelly dustbin beside me, and a cat jumped out and streaked away. Nothing else happened for a while, so I abandoned discretion and banged on the door with my fist. I'd got in one or two good blows before I heard

41

a rattling noise and the door opened to a width of about six inches or so. In the gap a tall thin man appeared, his face wrinkled and scowling.

'What do you want?' he said.

I hadn't prepared a story, but looking at him, I knew I needed one. His greasy brown hair was tied back in a ponytail and a straggly tuft of hair dripped off his chin. Grungy and suspicious, his little brown eyes were glaring at me with what seemed like an habitual rage. Definitely not the friendly type.

'I'm looking for Amaryll.'

'There's no Amaryll here.'

His expression hadn't changed, but he'd hesitated for a second. If I had to bet on it I would have guessed that he knew who I was talking about. I gave him my most harmless smile.

'He's my brother,' I said.

A look of puzzlement crossed his face, closely followed by scorn.

'You're never his brother,' he said. 'He's half-caste.'

I kept my face straight, although the revelation had given me a buzz of irritation at the fact that, up to now, no one had bothered to mention it. I could understand it not cropping up in the witness statements. The statements about Helen's visitors had come from whites, and white people were notoriously unobservant about physical differences between black people. Hypnotised by skin colour, the average English person often failed to pick out the most dramatic differences of height, weight and shape. Not surprising in the normal run of things, but Wyndham wasn't average. He should have said something instead of leaving me out on a limb like this.

'We've got different mothers,' I said.

His eyes narrowed and he stared at me intently, but I

42

met his gaze with a vague smile which I hoped made me look innocent.

'Who's that?'

This was a woman's voice, coming from somewhere behind the ponytail, and he turned his head to answer without unblocking the doorway.

'Some geezer says he's Amaryll's brother.'

I'd been angling for a more positive reaction and now I got it. There was a shriek, a scrambling noise, and the door flew wide open. The woman who elbowed Ponytail out of the way and confronted me was about the same height, and her hair was also scraped back into an oily ponytail, but the resemblance ended there. Where he was skinny, she was broad, and she seemed to fill the doorway.

'What you want? Who are you?'

Scottish, I guessed. I also had the feeling that she'd heard everything I'd said to the man, but this was her way of imposing herself on the situation, so I went through my explanation again, adding the details which occurred to me as I went along.

'He's my young brother. We haven't heard from him since Christmas. We got a card with this address on it. I'm just looking him up, see if he's OK. If he's not here can you tell me his new address?'

Pretty good, I thought, but what I was saying seemed to drive the Scotswoman into a fury. Her face swelled red with rage, her bosom heaved and she leaned towards me, her arm thrusting her partner backwards as if clearing the decks for action.

'You see that dirty bastard, you tell him I see him round here again I'll smash his face in.'

'What's he done?' I asked.

'Rip off,' the man's voice echoed from the depth of the hallway. 'He's a fucking rip-off artist.'

43

Immediately the Scotswoman turned her head to snarl at him.

'Shut your fucking mouth.' She turned again to face me, frowning, as if surprised to see me still standing there. 'And you. Piss off.'

She slammed the door shut before I could speak. I stayed where I was for a couple of seconds, wondering whether I should try again. But in the end I did the sensible thing and walked away.

Back in the car I considered my options. I hadn't got much from Amaryll's friends, that is if they'd ever been friends. But at least I'd learnt that there'd been some kind of trouble. Perhaps that was the reason he'd vanished. Not that it mattered. It was clear that knowing what the trouble was wouldn't help me find him, and finding him was the point. I knew that Dave would have to be my next visit, but I'd been putting it off, hoping against hope that something would turn up. Now there was no alternative.

I got there in a few minutes. The estate didn't look much different from the way it looked the day before, except that, at this time in the afternoon, there were several young women walking about pushing prams or hauling kids along the walkways. In front of Dave's block there was a little group of three women complete with baby buggies and a couple of crying toddlers. They were looking at the building and talking animatedly, but when they saw me coming they fell silent and watched my movements intently as I went past and into the entry.

Dave's door was half open, and in the hallway I could see a battered suitcase and a couple of sports bags. I couldn't see the dog, but I guessed that he was locked in the bedroom. Before I could knock, Dave opened a door off the hallway. He hesitated for a moment, frowned in recognition, then walked towards me, skirting the bags on the floor without lowering his gaze. He didn't speak. Instead he put one hand on the edge of the door and posed in front of me, his pale blue eyes cold and fixed. I could sense that he was trying to intimidate me, but he didn't quite cut the figure he intended. Seeing him briefly the day before, his tattoo, his hairstyle and the aggression of his movements had left me with the impression of a muscular neo-Nazi. Facing him now in the doorway I realised that his close shave disguised the fact that he was going bald, and where his vest rode up around his middle there was the beginning of a substantial potbelly.

I didn't bother with any preliminaries.

'I want to talk to you about Amaryll. You know him, don't you?'

'I told your lot all I know,' he growled back. 'And I ain't got no time to piss about.'

'You moving?'

'Upstairs. Temporary. Till they get this lot cleared up.'

He indicated the room where Jill had bled to death with a wave of his hand.

'I just want to ask you a couple of questions.'

'Dunno. What's it worth?'

It struck me that Wyndham must have doled him out some money for the interview. That would have gone down as expenses, but now he was convinced that anyone connected with the telly must have pocketfuls of notes to hand out.

'This isn't an interview or anything like that,' I told him. 'I just want to ask you a couple of questions.' His eyes didn't flicker. 'All right,' I said, giving in, 'I can do a tenner. That's all.'

He thought it over, then he nodded, let the door go

and moved back into the hallway. I followed him in, but he stopped after a few paces and leaned against the wall. That was fine as far as I was concerned, I thought. I didn't want to go back into that room.

'So what do you know about Amaryll?' I asked him.

He shrugged. When he did that the dragon curled round his biceps danced, and for a couple of seconds we both watched it in silence. Then he began talking. He didn't know much about Amaryll, he told me. He'd seen him around quite a bit, in the local bookie shop, in the nearby pubs and sometimes around the estate. He came from somewhere up north, to judge by his accent. He never heard about him working. He wasn't a dealer either. What it was, Amaryll fancied himself as a bit of a gambler. But the way Dave heard it, he was a loser who pawned his stuff and borrowed from the local moneylenders when he ran out of dosh. The story was that someone had threatened to do him unless he paid up.

'Who's that he owed money to?'

'I dunno, mate,' he said. 'None of my business. Y'know what I mean?'

'Leave off,' I told him. 'If you know what's going on you know who's doing it. It's not like this is a teeming metropolis.'

He frowned, then he leered, then he leaned back against the wall and gave me a blank look.

'I can do you another tenner,' I said. 'Give me a name.'

He thought it over for a moment, then his eyes shifted.

'It didn't come from me.'

'On my life,' I said.

'Give us the money.'

I felt around in my pocket and gave him my petrol money. He pocketed it with a grin of contempt.

'Flanagan.'

'Where do I find him?'

His face rearranged itself into a scowl.

'That's your problem, mate.'

He straightened up as if to indicate the interview was over.

'Does he live locally?'

He scowled at me and put his hand on the doorknob nearest to him.

'That's it. I gotta let the dog out now.'

Behind the door I could hear the long sobbing gasps of the dog's breathing. Dave stooped, picked up a length of chain and leather which was draped over one of the bags and looked at me with a nasty smile on his face.

'All right, Dave,' I said, 'I'm going.'

5

I rang Wyndham from the telephone box down the street.
There was a large turd in one corner and the remains of
a chicken tandoori in the other; the smell was overpow-
ering, so I propped the door open and made my call half
in and half out of the box.

Wyndham listened to what Dave had told me without
comment.

'Shit,' he said eventually. 'The creep didn't tell us that.'

'You didn't pay him enough.'

A moment of silence, then he cheered up.

'Maybe, but this is great.' There was no mistaking the
enthusiasm in his voice. 'It links up with the estate and
all the other stuff going on there. Adds another dimen-
sion.'

'What are you talking about?'

'Never mind. It doesn't matter now. Let's just try and
nail this guy down. I think the thing to do is chase this
one up. Even if we don't find him in the end we could
have a good story there.'

'You think so?'

I was being mean. He was probably right about it being

a good story. It was just that I didn't really want to be the one to do it.

'Yeah. It's going to be all right. Call me as soon as you've made some progress. OK?'

'OK.'

I put the phone down and got back in the car. It was obvious that Wyndham wanted action sooner rather than later, but I could only think of one source which might be useful, and it was still too early in the day to find him. For the better part of a minute I thought about how to occupy myself for the rest of the afternoon, then I gave it up. Instead, I started the car and drove back towards Marylebone Road. I had the vague intention of going back to the flat and reading the transcripts of the police interviews again, but when I got to Edgware Road I turned left, drove round the back of Lords and entered Regent's Park by the gate next to the mosque.

I found Sophie in the rose garden. She was sitting on the grass with a group of young Arab women. At first I had a little difficulty in picking her out, because she was wearing a three-quarter-length black dress and her hair was covered by a scarf, but then she moved, speaking to one of the women and gesturing with her hands.

Seeing her like this, completely unaware of my presence, gave me an odd sense of being a voyeur, spying on something private. In a way I was, because she was now working on one of the projects she'd been planning for a long time. This was a book of photographs of Muslim women. She'd already been working on it for more than a year, and she was spending more and more of her spare time with the women she was about to photograph. That was how she went about what she described as her serious work, and in the moment I saw her it struck me that she wouldn't want to be interrupted.

I walked past at an angle which would bring me into her line of sight, then I waved. She looked up, saw me, grinned and waved, but she didn't get up or make any other sign, so I kept on going down to the pond where a couple of big ducks were waddling around hopefully, on the lookout for the next instalment of the free food laid on by the daily stream of tourists. After a few minutes I heard her footsteps coming up behind me. She put her hand round my arm and squeezed.

'I came on the off chance you had a minute,' I said.

'It's OK.'

She leaned against me and when I looked round she grinned.

'They were going anyway.'

The early summer sun had turned her skin darker again, and it would have been easy to mistake her for someone from the Middle East. In fact, she had been born in Argentina, but the combination of her half-African mother and her Scottish father had given her the sort of appearance which was unremarkable in many parts of the world. With her pale beige skin and dark curly hair, she could have been from anywhere, an attribute which, in the last few years, she had begun to use to her advantage.

'How's it been?' I asked her.

She'd been away for a week, doing a freelance job for a newspaper.

'Boring.'

I waited but she didn't elaborate. Beyond her the group of women she'd been with came off the grass and moved along the path towards us. From a distance they'd looked like a drab and uniform collective. But as they came closer I realised that the black robes were made of a silky material which shimmered in the sunlight, and through the

50

slits at the sides I could see more silk, in gorgeous patterns of bright colour. In the same instant five pairs of hot black eyes fixed themselves on mine, and the tallest woman in the group gave me a smile that was half amusement, half flirtation. Then they were gone, leaving behind the impression that a flock of exotic birds had just swept past. Beside me, Sophie sniggered.

'Not what you expected?'

She was teasing me. I shook my head.

'Nope.'

'They're all aristocrats. Very rich, very powerful. They spend their time in London shopping, walking in the park, gossiping, and flirting very discreetly.'

The women receded into the distance, in a long stately glide, like black swans floating through the bushes.

'Let's walk,' Sophie said.

We walked through the rose garden and along the wide avenue.

'So what's happened?' she asked.

I told her about Wyndham's programme, about the murders and about the job he'd hired me to do. I mentioned Sarah but I left out the fact that she'd come to see me. Halfway through the recital we sat on a bench opposite two elderly Arabs. One of them was fat, with that look of being stuffed into his trousers, and he was carrying a walking stick with which he kept on drawing lines in the dust at his feet. From time to time, the fat one would address a remark to his companion, and when he did so, he would tap emphatically on the ground with his stick.

'I can't think about it right now,' Sophie said, 'but it sounds to me as if they're using you somehow.'

I didn't answer. This was a signpost to an old argument about how I earned my living. She'd begin by telling me

I was too good for what I did, and that I always let myself be exploited. I would reply by telling her that I'd always lived in circumstances where I had to do what I could.

'So what are you going to do?'

'I'll do the job and see what happens,' I told her.

I dropped her off at her flat a couple of hours later and drove back up the Harrow Road towards Neasden. Just before the Kensal Rise junction I turned off into the yard of the old sports centre. The shadows of the evening were growing thicker, and next to the building, the darkness seemed to be closing in. Through the gloom I made my way to the entrance, guided by the sound of the basketball bouncing, like some huge and drunken insect dancing on a drum. There were still no bulbs in the corridor which ran between the toilets and the changing rooms, but in the reflected light from the big hall I could see Georgie standing at the door, waiting to collect the boys' fees as they came in.

'Sammy!' he called out as I approached. 'You're not a member. Two pounds for you.'

Georgie was a tall spindly black man in a blue tracksuit. He was in his mid thirties, but he affected the style and language of someone ten years younger. He'd been running the centre for more than half a dozen years, and his fanatical love of basketball had turned the team into one of the best in London. On the other hand, no one had ever seen him play and by all accounts he was a terrible coach, but everyone could see how much he cared about what he was doing.

'Do I look as if I'm going to play, Georgie? I've come to see my son, if he's in there.'

Georgie made a sound of patient exasperation.

'He's in there. But cha man. You have to pay. This club costs money to run y'know.'

No point in arguing. I paid him and went in.

The hall was painted in a fading institutional green. A game was in progress and seated on the benches around the court there were more than thirty young men, watching what was happening in the middle, or merely lolling around talking to each other. At first I had the impression that everyone in the room was black, then I saw a white boy sitting on the end of one bench, his head turned to talk to the boy behind him.

I sat on one of the benches at the back, near the wall. I couldn't see my son anywhere, and I guessed that he'd gone to the loo or to fetch a drink, then all of a sudden I looked at the court and realised that he was one of the players. In the same instant, he caught the ball, feinted with it right and left, then set off down the court in a blur of motion. Halfway down he passed, ran a few steps, caught a return pass and soared into the air. A flick of his arms and the ball thudded against the backboard and through the ring.

In my excitement I nearly stood up and cheered.

'Yeah. Yeah,' I muttered involuntarily, and louder than I intended.

For the moment no one else seemed to be reacting to my son's glorious shot. Then, two benches ahead of me, a boy turned his head, and gave me a smile.

'Yeah,' he said lazily. 'All right.'

I sat back, laughing at myself a little, because my instinct had been to get up and cheer and say to the person next to me – 'that's my boy'. But the enthusiasm of a spectator would have been out of place here. None of the boys came to watch. They came to play and all of them were waiting to get a game. I settled down, trying for the combination of relaxation and alertness which would signal that I was a connoisseur of the finer points, but the sight of my son springing about the court filled my eyes. Watching the aggression with which he moved I remembered that he had just taken his last school exams and was now waiting to hear whether he'd go to university. This would be a bad time for him, but somehow I could only focus on the memories of my own youth which kept flooding back. At his age I'd been an athlete too, a runner, and stepping on to the old cinder track at Finsbury Park used to be a sort of adventure, like setting off on a trip where you knew the destination would be pleasurable. Sometimes, as I trained, I'd race along, marvelling at how little effort it took to fly over the track, my feet bouncing back off the surface as if it had been paved with springs. One time, walking home after a training session, the nervous tension in my legs gave me a push and I was off, belting along the High Street, laughing with the delight of being young and strong and full of speed. I'd run about a hundred yards when I heard the police siren, but before I could react the car cut in front of me, and two policemen jumped out and grabbed me. Fortunately, I was too astonished to struggle, because the first question the cops asked after they'd pinned me over the bonnet was why I'd started running when I saw them. It took me a while to convince them that I hadn't been running away from them, but the shock of that evening cured me of running in the street, even in the days when jogging was all the rage.

Remembering that incident made me think of Aubrey. I had told him once about the anger I'd felt all those years ago, and he'd been genuinely amused, because, growing up in this area, he was accustomed to being stopped and questioned by policemen, and he took it as an inevitable and natural part of a young black man's life. It was Aubrey who'd first brought me to this gym. My son had discovered it years later and on his own initiative, but whenever

I came here Aubrey was never too far from my thoughts. He was the youngest son of a woman I knew who lived nearby. As a youth I'd hung out in her house and so I'd known Aubrey from the time he was a toddler. The sport he went in for was actually karate and although being the baby of the family had made him a sweet-tempered and good-natured person, he had a fearsome capacity for physical violence which had got me out of trouble more than once. I used to think of him as invulnerable, a ton of rippling muscles topped by a big grin – *no problem, Sammy*. But Aubrey's size and shape and reputation made him a notable figure on the street, and one night he'd been stabbed several times and left to bleed his life away on a dark pavement in south London. A year later I still found it hard to believe that Aubrey was gone, but thinking back, it struck me that I had begun to avoid this district where I could hear his voice and imagine him swinging through the streets.

'Hello, Dad,' my son said in my ear. His voice gave me a start of surprise, because swamped by my memories I hadn't noticed the end of the game. 'You OK, Dad?'

I nodded vigorously.

'Yeah. Good game.'

He gave me a polite smile which told me that he knew I didn't know the difference.

'How's your mum?'

'Fine.' He sat down. 'You never rang.'

In the normal way of things we spoke to each other on the phone most days, and if I was going to turn up I'd have told him.

'Spur of the moment,' I said. 'I need your help with something.'

His smile widened. He loved it when I told him there was a way he could help me.

'What's up then, Dad?' He leaned forward. All business.
I told him what I wanted.

'Right. You're in luck today, Dad. There's this friend of
mine lives on the estate. He'll be here in a minute. He'll
know. Just wait a few minutes.'

We leaned back against the wall, watching the game.

'Funny thing,' I told him. 'Some of these kids look
American.'

The fact was that the long shorts, socks and trainers
they were all wearing gave them the authentic loping air
of American players, but several of the boys were also
wearing vests which carried the logo of various high
schools, and from time to time, one of them would call
out in what sounded like a genuine American accent.

'You're nearly right,' my son said. 'About a dozen of
these guys went to the States to play. Trying to get into
the NBA or get a scholarship. One or two of them did,
but the rest came back. They played in high school, but
that's all.'

'You're kidding me,' I said. 'They went that far?'

He shrugged. 'They're crazy about the game, and it's
crap in this country. No money in it. You can't even get
a regular game with good players. If you're really into
basketball you have to go to the States. All the black kids
who love the game, that's what they want to do.'

For a moment I thought about the level of passion and
frustration this represented.

'What about you?' I asked him.

He laughed.

'I used to think about it. If I'd had the chance a couple
of years ago I'd probably have gone. But I think differently
now.'

He leaned closer and lowered his voice.

'When I don't come here for a while I get back and I

see the same guys been coming here for ten years. Now they're old. Twenty-five. Twenty-six.' He made it sound geriatric. 'They're still doing the same things. They've spent most of their lives playing, they've been to the States and come back. They have some crap job or they're unemployed, and they're still coming here every night they can, hoping for a break. I want to do more with my life.'

The seriousness of his tone was unexpected. All of a sudden I was looking at an adult I didn't know.

'What is it you want to do?'

He hesitated, his expression speculative, as if he was wondering whether I would understand.

'Something to do with identity, being mixed race, what it means.' He paused again, looked round, then back at me. 'I don't know what it will be, but that's where I want to go.'

His eyes were fixed on mine and I had the feeling that this was a test of some kind. But before I could speak he looked round, stood up, and waved. A tall black boy with a carefully shaven head was coming towards us. He grinned, vaulted a couple of benches and slapped hands with my son. His name was Steve. He was a business studies student, my son said, and when he heard what I wanted, he frowned with concern.

'Yeah,' he said, 'I know who they are. They live up the next close, y'know. But you don't want to have anything to do with them people, Mr Dean. They're like' – he gestured – 'Rangers supporters. They go round doing people up and that.' He lowered his voice. 'You can get guns from them.'

'Rangers supporters?' I was genuinely puzzled by that.

'What he means, Dad,' my son broke in, 'is that they're like the worst sort of people round here. They're

57

dangerous. You can't have nothing to do with people like that. You don't know these people, Dad. They're bad.'

'No problem,' I told him. 'It's just work. I only want to talk to them.'

A quick look passed between the boys.

'All right, Dad. Me and Steve will come with you if you're going up there.'

It was a mindset which went with his age, I thought. Sometimes he couldn't help implying that I was a simple-minded old fool.

'Look here,' I said, 'I've been living in this country for longer than the two of you put together have been alive, and I've been dealing with people like this all that time.'

I was playing the irascible old man and the boys grinned at me, enjoying the act.

'All right, Dad,' my son said, mimicking alarm, 'we know you're real bad, but be careful. That's all I'm saying.'

He pulled a face, and Steve broke up into shouts of laughter. I made a furious face back, then broke out laughing myself, to keep them company and for the pleasure of the thing.

'All right,' I said when they eventually calmed down, 'don't worry. I'll be careful.'

6

The gloom of the evening deepened into a dark stain which arranged itself in ragged borders around the patches of illumination punctuating the crescents and alleyways of the housing estate. It was early, still an hour and a half to go before the pubs closed, and the only residents I saw on my way in were groups of teenagers lounging along the paths. The Flanagans lived in a house at the end of a cul-de-sac near the heart of the complex. According to Steve, they'd managed, by some weird alchemy, to manipulate the local housing authority so that the last three houses on the row were occupied by members of the same family.

I recognised the spot from his description of the vehicles lined up in the cul-de-sac. A big Ford transit, a rusting Rover, a new BMW, and a customised Vauxhall with a scarlet devil creeping across the bonnet, his pitchfork pointing relentlessly into the middle distance. I squeezed in between two of the cars, walked up the pathway to the house and rang the bell. Behind the door I heard chimes, but there was no response. I tried again, then, when there was no answer, I put my finger on the button and let the chimes repeat themselves a few times. After a while I heard the rattle of a chain and the door snapped open a few inches.

'I ain't bleeding deaf,' a woman's voice said.

There was a dim light in there, and I could just see part of a woman's face. It was a big moonface, topped off by a scrub of coarse, greying black hair. That much I could make out. Somewhere in the house a baby was crying.

'Mr Flanagan?' I asked.

'What you want?'

'I got some money for him,' I told her.

The woman didn't move or speak for a moment, and I realised that I'd pushed the wrong button. Perhaps she knew I was lying.

'Come back tomorrow,' she said eventually. The door slammed shut before I could respond. I thought about ringing again then gave it up as a bad job.

Back in the car I looked at the shadows and wondered about Flanagan. Postponing our encounter until the next morning seemed a reasonable proposition on the face of it, but even if I did I could find myself up against the same brick wall. I'd have lost the advantage of surprise, if it was an advantage. In any case, I had psyched myself up to do this tonight, and I wanted it over and done with.

I drove back towards Kensal Rise, but when I got to the gym the building was dark and the gates were locked. For a little while I tried to guess where my son and his friends might be, but in a couple of seconds I gave that up as a hopeless task. Instead, I eased round the round-about before the cemetery, drove up Harrow Road again, and stopped at the pub nearest to the estate.

I spotted Ricky Costello immediately I was through the door. It would have been hard not to. He had coarse

60

reddish hair, textured like the fibre you find inside the shell of a coconut, a pale, tan-coloured skin dotted with big dark freckles, and bright-green eyes. He was sitting by himself at a small table in a corner near the door, and it struck me that this was the first sign that my luck was improving, because I'd been nerving myself up to check all the pubs within walking distance. As I approached he gave me a blank stare, which was an indication of his mood, rather than a sign that he didn't recognise me.

'Mr Costello,' I said, 'let me buy you a drink.'

His scowl said that he didn't want company, and he wasn't fooled by the offer of a drink. I took it as a greeting and went over to the bar. When I got back he was sitting in the same position, but his glass was empty. I put the pint in front of him, sat down and asked him how he was doing.

'What you want?'

Ricky had never been particularly sociable, but a few years ago he'd been different. That was before he went back to the Caribbean. This was the first time I'd seen him since then, but I'd heard through the grapevine that the experience had left him bitter and angry. But it was an understandable reaction, everyone said, if you considered that when Ricky sold up and left Britain he'd been a respectable businessman with an attractive wife, two pretty toddlers, and money in the bank. Two years later he'd stepped off a plane at Heathrow, divorced, broke and without the energy or will to start again. Rumour and counter-rumour had obscured and distorted the details but there was one fact that no one disputed. Ricky's downfall had been an Act of God. Things hadn't been going badly at the time. He'd built his own house on the island and started up a version of the car repair firm he'd established in Ladbroke Grove. He couldn't match the local cowboys' prices, but Ricky was reliable, honest and qualified, a fact which he demonstrated by displaying a blown-up copy of his Higher National Diploma on the wall of his garage. After a few months he was getting a fair amount of business, and he was beginning to feel a certain amount of confidence that he'd make a go of his new life. The hurricane changed all that. Ricky had lived in Britain for most of his fifty years and he'd forgotten about hurricanes. When the big wind hit, he'd been wandering around his property, stacking loose timber and picking up tools he'd left behind. Even so, it wasn't the amazing force and vicious strength of the storm which terrified Ricky, it was the sudden explosiveness of its arrival. One minute he was bending over to lift a shovel, the next minute he was stretched full length, clinging to the ground and sobbing with the shock of it. There were sheets of zinc, planks of wood and old car tyres flying through the air straight at his head, and the wind seemed to be aiming with deliberate and malevolent intent to snatch him up and obliterate him from the earth. He wasn't very far from the house, and when the first fierce blow slackened a little, he got on all fours and began crawling through the murk, but in the same moment, a six-foot sliver of metal dropped out of the air and buried itself in the ground right in front of his nose. He lost his nerve then, and summoning up every last reserve of strength, he jumped for the nearest solid structure which just happened to be the concrete septic tank he'd put in six months earlier.

This was how Ricky had spent the night, up to his waist in shit, shivering, crying and shouting curses into the insane howling of the wind as it swept by above his head.

It could have happened to anyone, but when the story

got out, he was a laughing stock all over the island. The local radio station broadcast the story, and the press picked it up and spread it all over the region. Before Ricky had recovered from the terror of the night the entire world was laughing at him. His wife, fed up with being linked to the man who had spent the night covered in shit, packed up and went home to her mother, and a couple of months later went off with a man who owned a small hotel in Grenada, taking the children with her. Ricky started drinking, neglected his business and within a year had lost everything.

'I'm trying to locate a guy,' I told him, 'and I figured you're the man round here. Maybe you know.'

'I don't know shit,' he muttered. His morose expression hadn't altered, but I wasn't discouraged. Before his trouble Ricky had been working as a mechanic in the area for more than twenty years. The vehicles in front of the Flanagan house looked as if they'd had a lot of work done on them, and it was likely that he'd come across them at some point.

'Try a short,' I urged him. He grunted. I took that as a yes and went to the bar again. By the time I got back, the pint had gone the way of all booze.

'Flanagan,' I said. 'A Vauxhall with a big red devil on the bonnet.'

Ricky's hand moved across the table. His expression didn't change, and the rest of him didn't move. Only his eyes flickered at it, and we watched the hand reaching out and curling round the glass, as if it was an independent agent.

'Come on, Rick.'

The hand lifted the glass up to his mouth, and he took a big swallow.

'Live on the estate,' he said reluctantly.

'I been there. He's not home. Where would you look for him?'

Ricky took another swallow, and the hand put his empty glass back on the table.

'Which Flanagan you talking 'bout?'

'They have more than one?'

Ricky sniggered.

'They're tinkers. Nowadays they'd call them travellers, only now they don't travel no more. They settled down. There's the old lady and about half a dozen sons. All live same place.'

'So where they hang out?'

'Try Kilburn. Paddy Flynn's.' He'd been fidgeting with the glass as he spoke, but I had ignored the hint, and he gave me a smile that was full of malice. 'I wouldn't advise you to go down Flynn's asking questions 'bout no Irishman. You know what I mean?'

I knew what he meant, but I still had another question for him.

'Which one is the moneylender?'

'The moneylender? Oh. That's the mother.'

7

I approached Camden Town by way of Regent's Park. Coasting through the park at twenty something miles an hour made the trip a lot slower than it needed to be, but I guessed that my day was going to turn rotten soon enough, and meandering through the sun-dappled greenery was like storing up compensation for whatever crap was coming later.

As it happened, the morning had started surprisingly well. I'd woken up from a sleep in which my dreams had been too innocuous to remember, and within a few seconds of opening my eyes, I'd solved the problem of how to deal with the Flanagans. When I rang Wyndham and told him I wanted some money and why I wanted it, he hemmed and hawed, but in the end he agreed, and said I could swing by the office and pick up some cash.

It was all so easy that even the prospect of having to encounter the cold hatred of Joan's aura didn't spoil my mood. In the event I needn't have worried. Katrina was the only person in the office, and although she was firm about making me sign a receipt for the money, she stood close to me and smiled, and I suddenly noticed how good she smelled, and how smooth and supple her shoulders were as they flowed out of the sleeveless sweater, and I got out of there feeling a nice warm glow.

The mood hadn't evaporated by the time I got to the Flanagans' front door. Everything looked much the same, except that it was now light enough for me to see, stuck next to the doorframe, a notice which I'd missed the previous night. It showed the picture of a snarling Rottweiler. Under it, a caption said: HE CAN GET TO THE GATE IN ONE SECOND. HOW FAST ARE YOU?

I ignored it, and pressed on the bell with the lunatic confidence of euphoria. Nothing happened for a little while, but I had the sense that someone was watching me, and when I listened I could hear movement behind the door. I pressed the bell again and the door sprang open.

There were two of them, and although the door wasn't quite wide enough for them to stand shoulder to shoulder, they gave the impression that it would take a battering ram to get past. It wasn't that they were big. Both of them were shorter than I was. But they looked almost identical. Auburn hair, sharp, foxy faces decorated with a bright-red stubble, and a shambling, bulky look.

'Mrs Flanagan?' I enquired. I was trying for a business-like tone, but as soon as the words were out of my mouth it struck me that the question sounded ridiculous. The two men in front of me grinned at exactly the same time. Their teeth were stained dark grey and brown, but the one on the left had lost half of the bottom row.

'Does either one of us look like a missis?' the man on the right said.

'No, you don't. But I want to see Mrs Flanagan.'

The men's faces were still creased in mocking smiles, but their eyes were giving me a fixed angry stare. They were a pale blue colour, with a damp milky shine which I associated with alcohol and unpredictability. In the dark hallway behind them someone called out. I couldn't make out the words, but I recognised the voice from the previous night.

'What d'you fucken want?'

This was the one with the full set of teeth. He was losing patience, and in any case, the grins had vanished as suddenly as they'd appeared.

'Tell her it's money,' I said. 'She's owed some money, and I've got it.'

Not strictly true, but if I was right it would come to the same thing in the end.

The man propping up the left-hand side of the doorway spoke for the first time, turning his head and shouting back down the hallway.

'Fucken money, he sez.'

The reply was an indistinct mutter which, once again, I couldn't make out, but she must have told them to let me in, because they stepped back from the door and pressed up against the wall so that I had room to pass.

'Walk right in, Paddy,' the one who'd done all the talking said.

I glanced at him to try and work out whether I should be smiling at the irony, but there wasn't a trace of humour on his features, so I walked right in without comment. I was facing a steep flight of stairs. A fat woman was sitting on the bottom rung. She wore a shapeless olive-coloured dress with an ancient grey cardigan pulled over it. On her feet she wore red socks and a pair of fluffy bedroom slippers. Topping off all this was a huge round face which seemed to bulge with blubber, the cheeks stained with the angry mauve of broken blood vessels. Behind her, perched on the stairs, were four small children of various ages. By the side of the stairs, in the passage leading back to what I took to be the kitchen, stood two replicas of the men who'd greeted me at the door. That made four of them, and I guessed their ages at something between twenty and forty. I was the centre of their combined gazes, the same weird blue eyes reflecting back at me everywhere I looked, and I had the peculiar sense that I was being granted an audience at some sort of twisted regal court.

The woman made a sudden movement, put one hand to her face, and clamped her jaws round a set of teeth. The blubber heaved, then reassembled itself into identifiable features.

'I don't know nothing about no money,' she said abruptly.

I'd expected this, and I was ready to handle her initial denials.

'I'm not from the council,' I said, 'and I'm not looking for any trouble. What it is, I've got some money that belongs to one of your customers and I can't find him. I reckon if you can help me locate him I can make it worth your while.'

Her little eyes glinted at me out of the slits in her face.

'I dunno what you're on about.'

She had a deep voice with a staccato intonation, but the words were muffled and blurred, as if they had to travel a long way through a tunnel lined with fur. I drew a deep breath. She knew exactly what I was talking about, but I'd have to go along with the game.

'Amaryll Johnson,' I said. A sort of ripple ran through the crowd round me, and the fat lady made a sound that was halfway between a wheeze and a sob. The teeth clicked, a sound that was tiny yet distinct. 'I want Amaryll for a job, but I can't find him. I heard that he owed you a few bob, so I reckoned you might have some idea. You

68

help me and I'll pay off some of what he owes you. Take it out of his wages later.'

'What kinda job?'

I couldn't read the expression on her face, but I guessed that the little light I could see gleaming under her eyebrows was greed.

'You don't want to know.' I held her gaze and smiled. 'You really don't.'

That convinced her, as I thought it would. She wheezed some more, and I was about to suggest that someone patted her on the back when I realised that she was chuckling. After a few seconds, the sound stopped.

'Brian,' she gasped, 'me book.'

One of the boys in the passage turned and walked through the nearest door. No one spoke, and apart from the sound of the boy opening and closing doors, all I could hear was the fat woman's breath wheezing in and out. In a moment Brian was back with a big green ledger. He handed it to his mother, and she opened it, then riffled through a couple of pages.

'Eleven hundred and eighty-three quid,' she said.

She was looking at me.

'How much of that is interest?' I asked her.

'Fuck off,' she growled immediately. All around me her sons stirred like a pack of dogs hearing a familiar signal.

'Wait a minute,' I said hurriedly. 'What it is, I thought it was like five hundred. I was reckoning on giving you about ten per cent.'

'That's no good,' she came back at me. 'Hundred and eighteen. That's ten per cent. Innit?'

This was a woman who knew about bargaining. I'd halved her offer and she'd doubled mine, so we were back where we started.

'Eighty,' I told her.

'Give us it then.'

She stretched out her open hand. At the end of the wobbling pink column which was her arm it seemed amazingly small and delicate.

'Hold on a bit,' I said. 'Where is he?'

'I got his address here.'

'I've been to two addresses already,' I said. I told her where they were. 'I'm not paying for those.'

She looked uncertain for the first time.

'That's what I got.'

I should have known. With this bunch at her beck and call she wouldn't have been likely to let Amaryll escape owing her more than a grand if she could have laid her hands on him.

'Sorry,' I said, 'we can't do business.'

Her face twitched with fury. Suddenly I was conscious of the sound of the brothers breathing behind me, and I shifted slightly to bring them into my line of sight. Somewhere at the back of my mind I began wondering how I was going to get out of this hallway.

'The girlfriend,' the talkative brother grunted. I switched my attention and looked round to find him giving me an oddly ingratiating smile. 'Do you want to know where the fucken girlfriend lives?'

'Will Amaryll be there?'

'I don't fucken know,' he snarled. 'Fucken find out for yourself.'

In the end it was a bargain in which both sides got both less and more than they wanted. I hadn't discovered Amaryll's whereabouts, but I'd found another trail I could pursue, and I'd managed to beat the Flanagans down from eighty to forty pounds for telling me about it. I had the suspicion that their willingness to sell me the name and address of Amaryll's girlfriend was motivated by the fact that they'd already spoken to her, met with a blank wall and now believed the information to be worthless. I wasn't so sure, because somewhere inside me there was still a little warm spark which kept on telling me that today was a day when everything would go right.

I experienced my first setback about fifteen minutes later. Amaryll's girlfriend was named Linette Holder, and she lived on the top floor of a house off Queen's Park. It was a crowded little street but after I'd cruised up and down a couple of times I found a space next to the pavement and walked up the road to Linette's house. Three bells. I pressed the top button and waited. Nothing. I pressed it again, then, when no one answered, I tried the other two. Still nothing. I looked at my watch. It was the middle of the day and the occupants of the house were probably all out at work.

I felt a chill of frustration. I'd have to come back later, and that would be another day wasted on a hunt which might well turn out to be fruitless.

Back at my flat the answering machine was blinking lazily. Two calls. The first one was from Wyndham. On the second one I heard Sophie's voice. I reset the machine and rang Wyndham. He answered immediately, as if he'd been sitting waiting to hear from me, but after the preliminaries he said that all he wanted was to know how I was making out. I told him what I'd done that morning, and about going to see Linette later.

'Fine. Fine,' he said. His tone was absent, almost distracted and it stirred distant memories. This was how he sounded when he had something delicate to say. He'd beat around the bush till he was asked.

'What's going on?' I said.

71

'Couple of things,' he answered readily. 'There's a do at the channel tomorrow, and I thought if we went a bit early we could see the editor of this series. We need to talk anyway and it would be nice to have you along. He likes you.'

I took that with a pinch of salt. I'd first met the man when we were both starting out, freelancing for a rock music magazine. Now he was an important TV executive, and I could well believe that when my name came up he'd be friendly and nostalgic. How much good that would do was another matter.

'What's the other thing?'

He hesitated.

'Why don't you come over? Let's have a late lunch. Sandwiches or something. Let's talk. Yesterday was all business and I didn't really have a chance to get anything else. How about it? It's a long time since we met to talk.'

I agreed, choking down the astonishment I felt. I would have called Wyndham a friend, but it had been so long since we'd met on any kind of intimate terms that, apart from talking about the job in hand, I couldn't imagine what we'd say to each other. The thought that Sarah had finally confessed flashed through my mind, but I pushed it away. All that was so long ago.

I was still wondering what Wyndham might be about to spring on me when the phone rang. Sophie. Her voice sounded warm and relaxed.

'What's happening tonight? I want to see you.'

I told her about going to visit Linette.

'You want to come?'

'You sure?'

I told her I was sure and that I'd pick her up later.

Half an hour later I was at Wyndham's office. This time we decided to forget about lunch and, instead, took a walk along the canal towards Regent's Park. A little family of ducks kept pace with us for a while, and the sun sparkled invitingly off the tops of the ripples, but the smell of sewage came off the surface of the water, and the margin of the stream, where it lapped sullenly against the brick walls, was strewn with a raft of pizza boxes, half-eaten tandoori-chicken bones, condoms, and filmy scraps of tissue paper. It was a fine day, but we had the towpath to ourselves. Typically, it was one of those places in the middle of crowded London which turns out to be deserted.

'When I was a kid,' I told Wyndham, 'people used to fish here. Twenty years ago there used to be a big canoe club right over there. Then they discovered that the rats peeing in the water was giving the kids some horrible disease. Now nobody uses it for anything.'

'Except estate agents. The canal keeps property values up.'

He bent down, picked up a big chunk of gravel and skipped it over the surface of the water. It was a typical gesture, but it drew my attention to how much he'd changed. When we first met he'd been slender and athletic, his movements fast and nervy, the long blond hair and the beard giving him an air of fashionable eccentricity that I came to understand he cherished. Now he was growing into stolid middle age, going soft around the waistline and dressed in the sort of tweed jacket and grey flannel trousers his civil-servant father would have worn.

'I keep waking up in a rage,' he said.

'You were always a bad-tempered sod.'

He waved the comment away impatiently.

'That was just work. This is different. The thing is, I'm bored. I don't know whether that's the word for it, but it will do.'

We'd come to the end of the path, and I touched his

arm and suggested going up into the park. He grunted absently, still lost in his own thoughts, and followed me up the stairs, across a couple of roads, and into the park gates facing St Mark's.

'When I went independent,' he said, 'I thought it was the end of hassling with idiots. I thought I'd get to control my own work, be creative without some bureaucrat looking over my shoulder all the time. But that's not quite how it works. Nowadays I'm censoring myself before I put the idea to them. What's really humiliating is scrabbling around doing jobs I wouldn't have touched a few years ago just for the sake of making a living. And coming up with some lame crap to get it just because all they can cope with is lame crap. I know how stupid they are, you see.'

He paused, but I couldn't think what to say. In any case, I had the feeling he wasn't looking for a dialogue. My role was to listen. We were going past the zoo. I hadn't walked this way for a while, and I found myself noticing that it had begun to look rundown and mournful. Up ahead the giant cage Lord Snowdon had designed drooped like a sparrow caught in the rain.

'I'm a generalist, you see.' He gave an abrupt bark of laughter. 'Oxford did that for me. Then I learned to make the organisation work. Like a machine. You put in a certain amount of energy and the pistons move, the wheels spin, pretty girls gather round and flatter you. I miss all that shit. It didn't occur to me that it could happen, but leaving was like abandoning my whole identity. That wouldn't have mattered if I'd got to do the sort of work I wanted. Instead of which I'm up to my neck in the sort of boring crap I always hated. I invent the wheel every day, only it doesn't feel like invention. Wouldn't matter if I was an entrepreneur. Unfortunately, I'm more of an artist.'

Ten years ago, I thought, he'd have boasted about that.

'I used to get up and charge out to get things done,' he said. 'I don't feel like that now. Sometimes I wake up swearing, I'm so angry.'

'How does Sarah feel about that?'

He glanced sideways at me. Something sneaky about the gesture.

'I don't know. We went through a bad patch a little while ago. There wasn't any money coming in. Sarah was the breadwinner for a bit. I twiddled my thumbs. Sat by the phone waiting for people I used to chat to every day to return my calls. I didn't like that much. It didn't help.'

I made a noncommittal noise. I didn't want to hear the details of his problems with Sarah, but he was in flow and I couldn't think of a way to stop him.

'She's different. We can't talk any more. We don't even get mad at each other. Not much. I suppose we're both angry in different ways.'

He gave me that sneaky look again.

'You used to know her as well as anyone,' he said. I repeated the noncommittal sound I'd made before. It saved me the trouble of thinking about how to reply. 'Has she said *anything to you*?'

I screwed my face up to show I was thinking about it.

'No. I don't think so. We've talked on the phone a couple of times, but just the usual stuff. Hello. How are you? That kind of shit.'

I waited for him to start again, but the flow seemed to have come to an end, and we walked on in silence. A few seconds later he looked at his watch.

'I need to get back.'

We walked out into Prince Albert Road and caught a taxi back to his office. At the door we shook hands. Wyndham said it had been good to talk, and to phone him as soon as I'd seen Linette. Then he plunged into the doorway and sprang up the stairs.

I walked back to the car thinking about our conversation. On the surface he could hardly have been more open about his emotions, but I had the nagging sense that I was missing something. Everything Wyndham had said was perfectly straightforward, and I had no reason to suppose that there was anything more to it. At the same time, there was a warning bell jangling somewhere in my brain, and although I was trying hard, I couldn't quite shake off the feeling that the monologue had been swimming with meanings which I couldn't quite grasp.

8

We were on Linette's doorstep round about six o'clock. She was a young black woman with hair which had been straightened then bobbed. She was also short, plump, and carrying a year-old baby on her hip. When she opened the door she took us both in with a swift glance, but her face stayed impassive.

'I'm looking for Amaryll Johnson,' I told her.

Her eyes were on me, carefully ignoring Sophie, but I realised right away that bringing her had been a mistake. Linette probably took her for an English person, and seeing us together had raised her hackles before I had a chance to say a word.

'I don't know nothing about him,' she said. 'He doesn't live here.'

'Have you seen him lately?'

Her mouth tightened scornfully, and when she spoke her voice was loud and sharp.

'I told you I don't know and I don't want to know nothing about Amaryll or his dodgy friends, or his white women.'

She put her hand on the door and shifted the weight

of the baby on her hip as if she was about to slam it in my face. But the venom of her tone had decided me. No more Mr Nice Guy. I took a deep breath.

'I'll be honest with you, love,' I said. 'We're from a newspaper.'

That got a big reaction. She recoiled slightly, and the baby gave a subdued wail. I reached into my pocket, brought out my union card, held it up dramatically, then put it back with a flourish. As a document it had no status whatsoever, but it said 'PRESS' in big letters and she'd have caught sight of that.

'Don't worry,' I said, 'there's no trouble. Your name won't be mentioned. At all. On my life. It's nothing to do with you or his personal life. I swear. What it is, Amaryll got in touch with us to sell us a story. He's asking for big money and if it checks out he'll get it. I got some money for him right now.'

I patted my pocket.

'Everything's going all right except we can't get in touch with him. He's given this address and another two.' I named them. 'But he isn't there. The thing is, right now we have to check he is who he says he is before we go ahead. I've got fifty quid right here in my pocket for you if you can help us out. No trouble for you. Your name won't be mentioned, I swear. It's just what we call background. Like where he comes from. What kind of bloke he is. It's easy. Just a few questions.'

She wavered, and I put my hand in my pocket and hauled out a bundle of notes. I still had a hundred or so of Wyndham's petty cash.

'Fifty quid,' I said.

'What's it all about then?'

She'd lowered her voice, and now she sounded almost furtive. I hadn't overestimated her gullibility, I thought.

78

On the other hand, tabloid newspapers had established such an outrageous reputation that most people would believe almost anything about them.

'I can't tell you that, darling,' I said. 'Amaryll wants to tell you, he can. Till then it's confidential. We never reveal our sources. You know what I mean?'

By now I knew that I had her. She began moving away from the door, but then she squared up to me again.

'What paper did you say you were from?'

'Can't tell you that either, darling. Not till it's signed and sealed. We've got to be careful nowadays with the press council and that. I'm not allowed to invade your privacy. Know what I mean?'

She nodded understandingly. Behind me, Sophie made a stifled sound which turned into a choking cough. Linette looked past me at her.

'Who's she then?'

'Photographer.'

She drew back in alarm.

'No pictures.'

''Course not,' I said. 'She'll wait in the car.' I turned to Sophie. 'Go on then.'

She gave me a little wave and went off. When I turned back to Linette, she had stepped back from the door, and was climbing the stairs. I followed her up. At the top she showed me into a sitting room facing the street. It was cluttered with the baby's things. A walker, a playpen, a pram, a playmat, and an assortment of brightly coloured plastic toys strewn over the floor. At one end of the room there was a big TV set tuned to the news, and opposite it, a brown corduroy sofa splotched with shiny stains. She cleared a jumble of nappies and clothes off one end of the sofa and made room for me to sit.

'Just a few questions,' I said. I still had the money in

my hand, and she kept flicking her eyes at it. 'Tell me where you met him.'

Over the next half an hour, I found out all she knew about Amaryll, which, as it turned out, wasn't much. He was in his twenties. His father was from St Lucia and his mother was from Yorkshire. He'd been born up north and come to London as a teenager. They had met in McDonald's two months previously, when she'd been out with a couple of friends while her mother looked after Adrian, which was the baby's name. He'd told her that he managed a group of young rappers but she'd begun to doubt that when she noticed that he never had any money, and she'd packed him in after she'd turned up at a dance in Wembley where they were playing and discovered that the group had never heard of him. This wasn't too unusual in her experience, because Adrian's dad had made out to be working for an insurance group and when he vanished she went to their office, but they'd never heard of him either. On the other hand, Amaryll had been a bit weird. Unpredictable, and subject to sudden rages which frightened her. After the Wembley fiasco, her friend Shelley had seen him in a car with a white woman. She'd knocked on the window, but Amaryll had ignored her. She'd never seen him again.

'Do you know who this woman was?'

'No. Just a white woman. Some slapper.'

'Have you got a photo of him?'

She went to a corner of the room and dug out a pile of photos from which she sorted one out and handed it to me.

Amaryll had small regular features, wavy black hair and a moustache. He had posed for the photograph, but he wasn't smiling. Instead, at the moment the flash went off his mouth had begun to tighten into an expression of anger.

'He never liked this photo,' she said. 'He said to tear it up. I dunno why I bothered to keep it.'

That was about all there was. I'd been in the room for more than half an hour, and the baby, back in its playpen, was beginning to bash against the bars with a music box and make steady wailing noises. It was obvious now that she didn't know where Amaryll was, and I had no idea whether there was anything else that might be worth knowing. I dithered for a few seconds, then I gave her the money. She took the notes with an air of reluctance, but her mouth had arranged itself into a self-satisfied smile the instant that her fingers touched them. I asked her whether I could take the photo and I tucked it away into my jacket pocket.

'Hold on a minute,' she said, 'he left a book here.'

She went over to the same corner where she'd got the photos and came back with a book. It was a paperback manual about how to improve your management skills. I flipped it open and an envelope fell out. I picked it up.

'Is this his?'

'Yes. He took the letter out. Said it was from his auntie.'

I turned it over. There was an address on the back flap, and I stuck it in my pocket with the photo. Then I gave her my phone number, and told her to get in touch if she heard from Amaryll. She said she would. I said goodbye and left.

Sophie was sitting back in the reclining position listening to *The Archers*. When I got in and started the engine, she sat up and switched the radio off.

'What was all that stuff about?' she asked.

I looked over to check on her expression. She looked amused.

'I was impersonating a bloke I used to know,' I told her.

81

I hadn't known I was going to do it until I started, but once I'd got into the swing of things it felt as if I'd been taken over by a tabloid reporter who used to be notorious among the hacks I encountered. They called him Lucifer, a nickname he played up to by wearing black all the time. Black socks, black shoes, black hat, black shirt, all of it topped off by a swirling black cape.

'Up to the time I met this guy,' I told Sophie, 'I used to think that cleverness and subtlety went together like some natural law. But he was simple and obvious. His favourite thing was patting his pockets and going: "I've got a hundred quid right here for you." Always seemed to work.'

'Did it work for you?'

I gave her the photo and the envelope.

'She said the letter came from his auntie. So the address might be useful.'

She studied it, slanting the envelope up to the window to catch the light from the streetlamps.

'It's up above Sheffield. I've been there. It's like a road junction with houses.'

'That's good,' I told her. 'If he's there he shouldn't be hard to trace.'

By the time I rang Wyndham from Sophie's flat I had convinced myself that Amaryll was holed up in Yorkshire. Wyndham had no doubts about that either. He desperately wanted to believe in a swift conclusion and perhaps this was it. We agreed that I'd go up and take a look, but he wanted me to leave it for another day.

'I've made this appointment for us,' he said, 'and it would be a bit awkward breaking it.'

There was an undertone of anxiety to his voice which told me that, for some reason, the meeting with the editor of the series was a serious matter.

'He's trying to keep them sweet,' I told Sophie later. 'It's like they're always in danger from the competition. Until practically the moment they go on the screen no one can be certain that the powers that be won't decide to postpone or pull the series for one reason or another, because until that moment they can cut their losses by not showing it. So the producers have to keep selling the project until the countdown begins, and producers like to calm their nerves by staying close to the people with the power, or anyone they think can intercede for them if things get rough. He probably wants to show me off. Another precious resource he's throwing into the ceaseless struggle for higher ratings.'

'Poor guy,' Sophie said.

'Eating shit is part of the job,' I told her. 'It goes with the badge.'

I was shouting so she could hear as she moved about the kitchen. She was roasting lamb. I refused to eat beef, and she wouldn't eat pork, which left lamb. Sometimes I would argue that we ate too much meat anyway, but she'd always reply that her roots were in the pampas and savannahs, where people cut their teeth on beef, the way I'd cut mine on sugar cane, and she had no intention of becoming a herbivore.

After dinner we sat in the dark watching the sky. Her flat was a studio with a sloping roof, the last third of which was a couple of rows of glass panelling. During a storm the effect could be spectacular, with thick snakes of water rushing down the surface of the glass, and dazzling forks of lightning flowing majestically across our line of sight. On this night there was a moon. Behind it the sky was clear enough for stars, and from time to time a line of silver-edged clouds sailed slowly across the background of dark-blue steel.

'That girl we saw today,' Sophie said, 'suppose she wore a veil and lived according to a set of rules which governed every part of her life. How much worse off would she be?'

I guessed she was thinking about the Muslim women she was hanging out with.

'You getting religion?'

She stirred impatiently.

'I'm serious. Think about it. And the other one who was murdered.'

I thought about her, and the cold-blooded description of the murder scene I'd read in the police notes flashed across my mind. Amaryll was prone to sudden rages, I thought, and his photograph told the story of an angry and disturbed youth. Maybe he was the type.

'Hey,' Sophie said loudly. 'I'm talking to you.'

It struck me then that I must have been silent for longer than I realised, and I struggled to focus on what she'd been saying. We'd both lived in the margins. In her case, it was a stronger, more immediate experience, but I also knew how it felt to move in and out of groups whose background or whose instincts I didn't share. Sometimes the sheer mobility we owned struck me as a kind of freedom. Sometimes it felt like the restless and perpetual movement dictated by the curse they laid on the Flying Dutchman. Sometimes you could feel an almost irresistible tide washing you towards the nearest fixed point – religion, political crazes, prophets of doom – all these shone like beacons home. Every immigrant I knew of struggled in the eddies of this dilemma. How to harness the winds of fate. Where to belong.

'I don't know,' I told her, 'that you can always control what happens to you by the way you behave. The world's full of earthquakes, traffic accidents, hurricanes, airplanes fall out of the sky, people slip on a bar of soap and break their necks. Then there's a whole mob of evil bastards who like to hurt and kill people. Anything can happen. You know that.'

She made a soft sound, as if she was clearing her throat, but she didn't reply otherwise, and I clenched my fists, digging the nails into my palms, in a reflex of irritation at myself. The father figure Sophie adored as a child had later been exposed as a torturer and assassin, and I hoped that she wasn't thinking about him. At the same time, I was certain that she was. I looked at her out of the corner of my eye, but she was staring straight out of the window, her profile cold and immobile.

'People live as best they can,' I told her, 'and good luck to the ones who can find help. Living by one set of rules or the other might make you feel more secure, but the truth is that there's no guarantees. The way I see it, we're all in trouble.'

9

Wyndham met me in the lobby of the TV company. It was late afternoon, but the place was crowded with people coming and going. Behind the desk the two receptionists handed out visitors' passes as if they were pieces of the Host, and some of the visitors had the look of grateful awe you used to see on the faces of pale-skinned, white-robed Western hippies as they filed into the presence of their guru.

'Nick's waiting,' Wyndham said in a low but urgent tone. This was Nick James, the editor we were going to see. He lowered his voice. 'Vanessa is going to be there as well.'

I'd already heard the gossip about Vanessa. When Nick met her she'd been a freelance researcher. Within a year he was getting a divorce, they'd moved in together, and she was his assistant. The insiders said that nowadays he couldn't make any kind of decision without her approval.

'I thought that this meeting was only about saying hello to Nick.'

He lowered his voice another notch.

'Yes. That's what it is. But Vanessa's important.

Everything goes through her. If she doesn't like what you're doing you're dead. So far she's on our side. Let's keep it that way.'

I shrugged, trying to hide the flush of irritation I was feeling. I understood Wyndham's agitation, but this wasn't a drama in which I wanted to be involved.

'Let's go,' he said, then he grabbed my elbow, and steered me to the lift, where a young woman dressed in billowing mauve pantaloons and a tight black sweater was waiting. Wyndham told me she was Nick's secretary, Sandy, and she gave me a tight little smile. I'd been five minutes late, and I guessed she wasn't going to waste much charm on me.

When we got out of the lift, Sandy pointed us down the corridor and said that Vanessa was waiting. There was actually no one in sight, but as Sandy walked away, a door opened and a tall woman emerged. She was wearing a short, tight black skirt with a black shirt tucked into it. Above the ensemble was a long, narrow face framed by wings of shiny black hair which turned into a ponytail dancing on the nape of her neck. At first sight I'd assumed she was in her mid twenties, but close up I realised that she was at least ten years older. She greeted Wyndham with a warm smile but it cooled down several degrees when he introduced me.

'Nick's waiting,' she said, then whipped around and led the way, at a fast clip, to the door of the next office, where she knocked softly, opened it and ushered us into the presence of the man himself. He'd been sitting at his desk, and now he turned round, and stood up.

Nick was in his forties, and shorter than average height. He'd never been the athletic type, but now he was going wobbly round the waist and he had a bald patch in the centre of his greying brown hair. But age had improved his appearance. In his early twenties he'd been furtive and weedy. Now his manner had a new confidence and authority, which I guessed came with his professional status. The odd thing was that the image of the young Nick which my memory called up seemed to be wearing exactly the same clothes, a dark-grey suit, with a white shirt open at the neck. In a moment, though, I realised that the clothes I remembered had come from a cheap chain store, while the suit he was now wearing had the broad shoulders and the floppy look of a designer label.

'It's been a long time,' he said. He gave me a limp, moist handshake.

'And now you're a big boss.'

His laughter had more than a hint of self-satisfied complacency about it.

'That's an exaggeration.'

Vanessa was already seated. She had her legs crossed and her thighs seemed to stretch halfway across the room.

'We're running late,' she said abruptly. 'I won't be able to stay very long. I've got some things to do.'

Her tone was curt. If I hadn't known better I would have assumed that their roles were reversed and that she was the head of the department with Nick as her assistant.

'So how far have you got?'

'We're nearly there.'

Wyndham sounded confident and relaxed. In response both Nick and Vanessa gave him grave and understanding nods, as if they knew what he was talking about, which was more than I could manage.

'I've done most of the interviews,' he said. Then he gave them a quick summary of how he wanted to present the case, dwelling on the alibi he'd established for Leon, and the role he intended for Amaryll. 'That's the only incomplete line of enquiry,' he said at the end. Then he flicked a sidelong glance at me. 'Now we're waiting on Sammy to do his stuff.'

The moment the words were out of his mouth I knew exactly what I was doing there, and why he'd been so anxious to get me, and I was kicking myself for being a sucker. I was an old acquaintance and a former colleague of Nick's, and Wyndham had consulted him about hiring me for this job. So if I succeeded everything was fine and they'd all look good. If I failed, it would all be my fault, and Wyndham couldn't be blamed for hiring a loser who came with a recommendation from Nick. I'd been stitched up, and it was too late now to cut and run, because it would give me the appearance of cowardice or incompetence.

'What progress have you made?' Vanessa asked. Her tone was brusque, and I was about to say something rude in reply, when Wyndham cut in quickly.

'We've got a lead on the chief suspect. Up north. Sammy's going up tomorrow. I would think we'll know one way or another in a couple of days.'

'So we're still on track,' Nick said suddenly.

'Very much so,' Wyndham told him.

I opened my mouth, then shut it again. The man was desperate. In any case, even if the Amaryll angle fell apart, he still had a story. The point was to keep Nick and Vanessa happy.

'I've got to go soon,' Vanessa said. 'Just one more thing. We were discussing this earlier. It would make it stronger if you put more detail into the social background. It's significant that they're a mixed-race couple. I think you should do more to bring out the pressures she was under in dealing with the black patriarchal model, and link it with what we know about persistent battering and child abuse.'

I had determined to sit back and let Wyndham do the talking, but there was something about the assurance with which she spouted this jargon that made my blood boil, and I leapt right in before he could head me off.

'The basic difficulty there,' I said, 'is that if you're going to argue that the police case is up the creek, you can't really trot out all this black patriarchy stuff as a motive. I mean it's gratuitous. You can't say that the man didn't do it, but these are the motives he would have had if he did. Your argument calls for certainty about what happened, the whole drift of the project is to establish uncertainty.'

The room was silent. A horizontal line appeared in the middle of Vanessa's forehead. Her eyes were light green, flecked with brown, and, for the first time, they were resting steadily on me. I had the sense that she was surprised, not so much by what I'd said, but by the fact that I was contradicting her.

'The issue isn't the motivation of the murderer,' she said. 'The issue is that, as a woman, she was vulnerable, and like a lot of other women, she ended up as a victim.'

'The issue is whose victim she was,' I interrupted. 'Suppose she was killed by a stray racist. That would involve a totally different slant on the background.'

The line across her forehead deepened and her eyes narrowed to a squint. She looked at Wyndham.

'There's no indication of anything racist, is there?'

Her lips puckered on the word, as if she was tasting something nasty. Wyndham shook his head.

'No,' he replied hesitantly. 'Not on the face of it.'

'Well then,' Vanessa said, 'let's not get hung up on political correctness.'

'All this is hypothetical,' Wyndham declared firmly, forestalling whatever he thought I was going to say. 'Why don't we meet up in a couple of days, after things have shaken down, and go through the script. Then we can sort all this out.'

'That sounds good,' Nick said.

Shortly afterwards the meeting broke up. Vanessa went out with a brief smile at Wyndham and a cold stare at me. Nick shook hands and said it had been nice to see me, and then we hurried out of the building and into the nearest pub.

'What was all that about?' Wyndham asked. He looked a bit miffed, and I guessed that he was working himself up to have a go at me.

'Don't bullshit me, man,' I told him. I looked him in the eye and got my retaliation in first. 'I'm the scapegoat. I can accept that, but don't bullshit me.'

'Who's bullshitting you?' He sounded as truculent and aggrieved as I felt. 'I'm using you. All right. But I never told you any different. That's how the game is played.'

I'd known that from the beginning, I thought. Suddenly my mood changed and I smiled at him.

'So what are you so pissed off about?'

He gave me a wry grin.

'You should have ignored Vanessa. She's a notorious pain in the ass. I handle it by saying yes and then forgetting what she said. If the film looks OK, and Nick likes it, she'll persuade herself that I've obeyed her every word. Arguing with her at this stage simply causes trouble.'

'I couldn't help it,' I told him. 'It sounded like she was about to add wife murder to the list of crimes your average black man is programmed to commit.'

Wyndham smiled.

'Maybe. But can you see me making the film that way?'

'I don't know,' I said. 'Taking a swipe at nasty black macho men is one way a new man can establish his pro-femme credentials.'

I'm not sure what answer he expected, but this one didn't please him.

'Don't confuse me with that lot, Sammy.'

I shrugged. This had turned into a variant of an old argument which had no resolution or conclusion, and the only way out of it was to change the subject.

'How about Nick?'

He frowned.

'I'm not sure what's going on with him. She's his commissar. When he wants to he ignores her, and she winds up agreeing with him. I have the suspicion that he uses her as a mouthpiece. Good cop, bad cop. Keeps people on their toes.'

'I wouldn't put it past him,' I told him. 'He looks like the same cunning little nerd he always was.'

Wyndham looked pensive.

'He's doing pretty well for a nerd,' he said. 'His last series got terrific ratings.'

The party was intended to mark the launch of a new series about forgotten Victorian knife murders, entitled *Friends of the Ripper*, and the grapevine suggested it was going to pull in a massive audience. Wyndham wanted to be there so he could keep his finger on the pulse, but we'd agreed that this didn't mean actually watching the thing, and we loitered in the pub long enough to make sure that we'd arrive well after the formal showing of the first episode would have come to an end.

The venue was the same building where we'd seen Nick, and the lobby was still dotted with anxious petitioners. Beyond it, the atmosphere in the inner sanctum of the conference room was thick with laughter and congratulations. Towards the middle of the room, the crowd of guests seemed to swirl into a solid clump, and

I caught glimpses of the celebrity, who was presenting the show. A comedian with a surly manner, he was flanked by the chairman of the company, both of them puffing at cigars with the ineffable air of men who were masters of all they surveyed. The building had a no-smoking policy, but I suspected that no one had yet had the nerve to tell the chairman.

Beyond them I caught a glimpse of Joan, talking earnestly to another woman. Like most of the women in the room, she was dressed in black. Next to them were a couple of researchers I'd met recently. Looking past them, I realised that I knew several of the people I could see, and I had the disorientating sense that it would be hard to tell this gathering apart from any of the TV parties I'd attended in the last year. The established players, editors and producers, were fixed stars, each one with a cluster of courtiers, one or two talking fast and confidentially, the rest waiting their turn, smiling vaguely, trying not to look as if they were waiting their turn to kiss whatever part they could reach. Circling around these groups were the aspirants, hungry kids just out of a six-week course on video and film directing, a hurriedly typed up proposal for recycling some idea which was a cliché to start with burning a hole in their briefcases – Andy the Rent Boy, Battered Wives, Women Slaves, Blacks on Death Row, Aids: The True Story, Reggae and Gang Violence in Kingston JA, Gang Violence and Rapping in Downtown LA, Forgotten Women Artists, Forgotten Women Writers, Forgotten Women Musicians, Forgotten Women Poisoners, Forgotten Women, The New World Music, Sex Slaves of the East – the lists went on and on, the kids muttering their titles at speed into the ear of any editor they could get to hold still, keeping their voices low in case any of the others heard them and stole their creative efforts. From a distance they looked like scavengers, a pack of slavering dogs slinking nervously around, making a quick dash from time to time to snatch up a stray piece of meat.

Someone tapped me on the shoulder, and I turned, expecting to see Wyndham. Instead, I saw Nick at my elbow. He looked on edge, his eyes swivelling back and forth. I guessed that the reason for his nerves was the young woman who was hovering about a foot away, gazing intently at the side of his face. She was done up in party mode, a short black dress and a frizzed-up hairstyle which seemed to be dripping black corkscrews; but her stiff posture and her hot, anxious eyes contradicted the idea that she was there to celebrate anything. At that moment she seemed to be pursuing Nick. I couldn't be sure whether they'd been talking or whether she'd followed him over, but in any case he seemed to be studiously ignoring her.

'Sammy,' he said. 'Glad I saw you. Can we talk? Some things I wanted to ask you, but there wasn't the opportunity earlier on.'

Clearly not true, unless what he wanted to say was supposed to be kept secret from Wyndham or Vanessa. If that was so I wanted to hear it.

'Can we have a chat later, Nick?' the frizzy-haired woman asked.

'I'll be back,' Nick said curtly. He barely looked at her. Out of the corner of my eye I could see two more scavengers bearing down. A crop-haired blonde in black tights and a lavender shirt. At right angles to her a pudgy young man in a leather jacket, his bald head bobbing busily through the mob. Nick gripped my elbow and steered me in the opposite direction, towards the door.

'Let's go and have a quiet drink,' he said.

We passed through the lobby again, and, as they caught sight of Nick, a ripple went through the lines of waiting petitioners. Upstairs, on his desk, someone had placed a bottle of white wine and a small tray of sandwiches.

'You're doing all right,' I told him.

He gave me the smile I remembered. A tight grimace which came and went in a flash. That meant he was feeling a little more relaxed than he had been downstairs, and for a moment, I wondered whether his bringing me up here was merely an excuse to get away from the party.

'Tell me what's really going on,' he said.

'Wyndham's done that already,' I told him.

Nick sighed. He lay back in his chair and took a swallow from his glass of white wine. I could see the colour coming back into his cheeks, and his whole body seemed to swell a little, like a dried-up prune soaking in water.

'Bollocks,' he said. 'He told us what he thought we wanted to hear.' He grimaced. 'I've learnt a lot since I started this game. My first commission was a documentary about vigilantes. They were supposed to have a couple of guys who'd gone out and beaten up kids, ran people out of the district, the lot. Everytime I asked they told me everything was fine. I even saw this great interview they'd done. Graphic stuff. Then a week before the thing was due to go out, it turned out that it was all a hoax. Embarrassing or what?' He paused again, picked up a pen from his desk and tapped his nails with it. 'The thing is, I can't afford that sort of cock-up right now.'

Politics. While he talked I'd been remembering the rumours. Recently, the company had split responsibility for its documentary output. Nick's ratings had been slipping, and the company had appointed a younger newer whizz kid to commission factual programmes. They'd invented a new title for him, but he had become, in effect, the joint head of the department, and the gossip was that Nick only had a year to re-establish his status as head honcho. The grapevine said that the two men hated each other in any case, and that, right now, Nick was paranoic about the possibility of making a mistake.

'That's why I insisted that Wyndham take you on,' he continued. 'You're a cynical old bastard, and you know something about the people he's dealing with. You'll be able to spot whether someone's winding Wyndham up.'

We were about the same age, but I supposed that he was paying me a compliment. This was, also, a new version of how I'd come to be hired.

'What about Sarah? I thought this was her idea.'

He frowned.

'It was. Kind of. She was the one who originally sold me on the idea of this series, and when things started going a bit weird she suggested you. I'd have thought of you sooner or later, but that was helpful.'

'OK. I'm on board now. Why are you telling me this?'

The question embarrassed him. He fidgeted with the pen, then threw it back on to the desk.

'If there's no story there I need to know in good time. Doesn't mean I'll pull the plug. It might just be a matter of picking up on another line of enquiry or postponing the project. I can do that. What I don't want is to spend a couple of months fooling around, then be told at the last moment that I've got to do something. I need an early warning of any trouble.'

'Why don't you ask Wyndham? He's a good producer. You can sort things out with him.'

His forehead creased up again. He put his thumb to his mouth and pushed at his lips.

'Used to be. But there's a lot going on with Wyndham that makes me feel' – he felt for the word – 'insecure.'

I watched him for a few seconds, thinking about what to say. He hadn't mentioned Vanessa or Joan, but I guessed that they too were playing parts of some kind in Nick's overall plan.

'It's no good,' I told him, 'I'm not going to spy on Wyndham.'

'I'm not asking you to,' he said irritably. 'I just want to know that if I call a meeting about progress people are going to be frank with me. That's all.'

'Don't worry,' I told him, 'you've got it.'

I didn't know what I meant by that, and I couldn't tell what he thought I was saying, but the words seemed to reassure him.

'All right, then,' he said, 'that's good enough for me.'

10

I was tracking Wyndham's car back to Camden Town when I realised that there was another car following him. I'd noticed the battered green Escort when it pulled out behind Wyndham as we left the party. Then again when it overtook me and cut in behind the Jag as we swung into Tottenham Court Road. I lost him then, but at the next junction Wyndham raced through an amber signal, and the Escort whooshed past me and took the crossing a couple of seconds after the lights went red.

I pulled up and sat there watching the rear lights vanish. In normal times I'd have dismissed it as coincidence, but now I was suddenly convinced that the Escort was trailing Wyndham. As I slotted into the traffic headed for Camden Town, I thought furiously about what it meant, but for the moment I was at a loss. The simple job I'd taken on had become more complicated than I'd imagined possible. My conversation with Nick, for instance, had been unexpected and bizarre. He wasn't telling me all there was to know, I was sure of that, and the mystery, whatever it was, also involved Sarah. I'd played it cool, and I hadn't pressed him further about why he thought Wyndham had become a loose cannon, but I left his office in a state close to bewilderment.

When I'd got back downstairs the party seemed to be winding up, and as I went in I'd bumped into Wyndham coming out.

'Tickets,' he said loudly, poking his finger at my chest.

His face was red and shiny, the way it got when he'd had a couple of glasses too many, and, for a moment, I thought he was making a joke I didn't understand. Then I realised he was talking about the rail tickets for my journey the next day. Katrina had booked them and they'd arrived in the office that afternoon while we were with Nick and Vanessa. She'd tried to get us on the phone but we'd already left. A couple of feet away, Joan showed me a cold profile, and I wondered briefly why she hadn't simply brought the tickets. At the same time it struck me that she would have seen that as running errands, and she'd have found the mere idea humiliating. I looked at her steadily, as Wyndham talked, hoping that she'd loosen up and smile, but even though she must have felt my eyes on her, she didn't move. The woman with her, though, looked at me and returned my smile. There was something familiar about her face, and I was about to comment on it, when I realised that what I had recognised was a remarkable resemblance to Joan.

'This is Caroline,' Wyndham said. 'Joan's sister.'

We shook hands. Then we arranged to go back to Camden Town and pick up the tickets. I wanted an early start and didn't fancy hanging around in the morning till one of them turned up. Wyndham said he wanted to drop in at the office in any case, to see whether a fax had arrived, but I remembered that he'd always been hooked on working till halfway through the evening. Unless he'd changed a great deal, he wouldn't be going home till later on.

By the time I reached the side street where the entrance to the office was located, the Jag was parked at a meter nearby. There were a few empty spaces behind it, but I kept on going. I'd intended to circle the block until I found the Escort, but it was parked at the end of the street, close enough for the driver to see anyone coming in or out of Wyndham's office.

Upstairs, Wyndham was still in a genial mood.

'Where've you been?' he shouted. 'We got here five minutes ago.'

'I like to get where I'm going in one piece,' I told him.

At the other end of the room Caroline was perched on a desk, her feet planted on a chair, her coat falling away to show her long, round thighs. Joan sat in front of her, with her back to me, talking in a low voice.

Wyndham handed me an envelope. There were two rail tickets, and a wad of twenty-pound notes in it.

'Don't spend it all at once,' he said, 'and keep the receipts.'

I nodded absently. I knew this was banter, because we'd both been through the drill of dealing with expenses so many times before, but I was too preoccupied to reply in kind. My problem was whether to tell him about the green Escort and the man sitting in it outside his office.

In normal times I would have done so without hesitation, but something stopped me saying it within earshot of the two women. Maybe what I was feeling was sheer pique, because if these were normal times Wyndham would have suggested going out for a drink or dinner. It was obvious that he was about to do something of the sort with Joan and her sister, and it was equally obvious that no one wanted me along.

*

The Escort was still parked at the end of the street. I walked in the other direction, away from it, and circled round the block to where I'd left my car. Then I drove round the next block and back to the top of the street, from where I could see the Jag. As I pulled into the kerb the two sisters were just emerging on to the pavement, followed by Wyndham's long frame. They stood there for a few seconds, then one of the women put her arms round Wyndham's neck and they kissed. It wasn't a lingering movie kiss, but it wasn't a swift peck either. It was the sort of embrace a couple exchange at the stage when they've kissed often, but still enjoy the feel of it. The other woman must have felt excluded, because she shifted around and stared back up the road towards me. That gave me a good look at her and I realised that it was Caroline, which meant that Joan was the woman clutching Wyndham. That surprised me. Not that I was amazed to see Wyndham snogging one of the sisters, but after seeing all three of them together I would have put my money on Caroline.

I was wondering whether their relationship went further than kissing, when Joan dropped her arms, squeezed out of Wyndham's grasp, crossed the road and got into a black Golf. As she did so, Wyndham and Caroline climbed into the Jag. I hadn't counted on that, but it suddenly struck me that I didn't know for certain that the man in the Escort was actually following Wyndham. If his target was Joan, I'd find out soon enough.

The Golf took off and zipped round the corner in a couple of seconds, but the green car didn't stir. In a few more seconds Wyndham's car backed up, then pulled away at a more sedate pace, and as he took the corner, I saw the lights on the Escort glowing. By the time I got into gear and started moving, they were both out of sight.

I thought I'd lost them then, but they'd been halted by the lights in front of the tube station, and I got over the junction only three cars behind the Escort.

After that it was more or less plain sailing. We drove in procession past Kentish Town and round towards Archway. Halfway up the hill, Wyndham turned off and parked in one of the side streets in front of a small block of flats. As I drove past I could see him and his passenger unbuckling their seat belts.

The Escort drove on, and I realised that he was looking for a space in which to park. But the street was crowded with cars and we were a couple of blocks away before he pulled in and stopped. I went past him without looking, and eased round the next corner. By the time I'd parked and walked back, there was no one in the green car, but ahead of me I could see a man, walking slowly past the building which Wyndham and Caroline had entered.

I stopped, leaned against the back of the Escort and thought about the situation. I'd followed automatically, to satisfy my curiosity, and I had no idea what to do next. It all hinged on who the man was and why he was trailing Wyndham. Perhaps this was the nut who'd sent Wyndham the threatening letters. Perhaps it was Jill's murderer. Perhaps it was something to do with Caroline. The last idea started me thinking about what Wyndham was up to with the sisters, but I gave up the speculation as soon as it occurred to me. There were simply too many possibilities.

I looked around. It was halfway through the evening. It wasn't closing time, but it was late enough for the street to be more or less deserted. No one around. Simultaneously, a plan flashed into my head. It was one of those schemes which would look both stupid and reckless if you paused to give it a moment's thought, so without hesitating I took the keys out of my pocket, bent over and let all the air out of the nearest tyre.

I didn't realise it at that moment, but that was all the action I was going to see for the next hour and a half. During that time I went back to my own car and drove around the block twice before finding a slot from which I could see both the Escort and Wyndham's Jag. By then he was back behind the wheel. I guessed that he couldn't have noticed the flat tyre, because he was slumped motionless in his seat, waiting, I guessed, for Wyndham to make another move.

It didn't happen till close to midnight. The late-night stragglers had come and gone, slamming doors and calling out farewells. Now the street was silent, the houses mostly dark, except for the occasional blaze of light from an upper window. I was on the verge of falling asleep when the sound of an engine starting up shook me into wakefulness. It was Wyndham, and I must have been dozing off, because I hadn't seen him come out of the building and cross the pavement. As I fumbled for the keys the Jag cruised away smoothly, and, in another second, the Escort pulled out. But it didn't get very far before stopping short in the centre of the roadway, and, in a moment, the driver got out, looked at the rag of rubber on his rear wheel, and kicked it violently.

I waited for him to open the boot, take out the spare tyre and squat down to begin cranking up the jack. Then I switched the lights on, came up behind, got out, and walked over to him.

'Need any help?'

He'd looked round irritably as he heard my footsteps, but instead of replying he muttered something nasty under his breath. This was the first time I'd had a good look at him, and somehow I'd been expecting him to look bigger close up, but he was actually shorter than I'd realised when I caught glimpses of him behind the wheel. About thirty, with a pale, spotty round face, and collar-length brown hair, going thin on top. His clothes, a khaki-coloured anorak and scruffy blue trainers, weren't impressive either, and what I could see of his body had the pulpy look of too much soft flesh curdled over fragile bones.

'Don't be like that,' I said. 'I'm only trying to help.'

This time he looked up from the wheel nuts and stared at me for a moment.

'You wanna help? Piss off. All right?'

That was probably my best option, I thought, but by now I'd gone too far to walk off tamely. When I let his tyre down I'd had some idea of using it as an opportunity to strike up a conversation, but it was obvious now that there was no point in being indirect about what I wanted to know. If he hadn't been such a scruffy physical spec-imen I might have hesitated, but something about him gave me the impression that he was accustomed to being bullied.

'Why are you following the geezer in the Jag, then?'

His back was bent to screw off the last nut, and he froze in the same posture as if he'd been seized by a trance. Then, just as suddenly, he moved again, finished unscrewing the nut, and turned towards me.

'What am I doing? I'm stuck on my arse changing a tyre. See any fucking Jags here? I ain't following nobody. So whyn't you fuck off?'

He'd propped the spare tyre against the rear bumper, and I bent down, found the valve, stuck a key in it and let him hear the hiss of air escaping. He straightened up abruptly, and came at me brandishing the big spanner. I'd been waiting for this and, with a shove of both hands,

I rolled the tyre at him. By the time he realised what was happening it was too late to check his rush, and when the tyre caught him about the knees, he cried out angrily and went down with his legs in an awkward tangle. He was still holding the spanner and I stepped on his wrist until he let it go.

I leaned over so he could hear me, still pressing my weight on his wrist. He strained away from me, scrabbling at my foot.

'Listen to me,' I said, but he didn't stop struggling, instead he twisted round and screamed at the top of his voice.

'Fuck off, you bastard! Fuck off!'

I pressed harder on his wrist and leaned in closer.

'Shut up and listen,' I hissed urgently at him. That got through.

'All right,' he moaned. 'Fuck it. All right.'

Behind me I sensed the lights going on in the windows of the nearest house. I took my foot off his hand and squatted down next to him. He propped himself up on his elbow and began rubbing and feeling at his wrist.

'What I want to know,' I told him, 'is who sent you, and what you're doing following the Jag. If you don't tell me, I'm going to let the air out of all your tyres, then while you're working out what to do, I'll phone the police and tell them I followed you trailing along behind the Jag from the West End to Camden Town to here.'

'Piss off. That's not a crime.'

He was trying for a nasty sneering tone, but I could tell that he was worried. He had to be. Given the ease with which I'd put him down he wasn't hard, just a little man trying to sound tough.

'You're right,' I told him. 'But someone killed a girl working for the bloke you're following a couple of days ago. Stabbed her to death. So it's a murder investigation. He's had threatening letters and all sorts and you're following him up and down. They'll want to ask you questions you might not want to answer. You know what they're like. They haven't got a suspect, and they'll love to get their hands on you. Just tell me what I want to know and I'll leave you alone.'

It wouldn't have been much of an offer if he was the killer, but, looking at him, I couldn't believe that. On the other hand, he had the dodgy air of a man with a lot to hide.

'I'm a detective,' he said.

That shook me. My next thought was that he was jerking me around.

'A detective? You? Pull the other one.'

'Private.'

There was a hint of pride in the way he said it, as if he was engaged in a professional occupation his mum could boast about.

'Never,' I said. 'Who's hired you then?'

'His wife. Sarah. She wants to know what he's up to.'

It was hard to believe that Sarah had hired this scruffy little article to do anything.

'How come?' I asked him. 'I mean, do you work for a firm or what?'

The disbelief in my voice offended him. He sat up sharply and pulled his anorak round him.

'I've told you. All right? I'm going to change my tyre now.'

But he didn't move. I could sense he was setting himself in case I hit him again, and I was just about to ask him more about how Sarah had found him, when I heard a door slam open and a square of light lit up the scene. I stood up and looked around. A middle-aged white man in a stripy dressing gown was hustling down the path in front of the house beside us, his face alive with indignation. Behind him, framed in the open door, was a woman in a flowered nightdress, long dark hair streaming over her shoulders.

'I saw that!' the man shouted. He arrived at the gatepost and called out to Sarah's detective: 'Are you all right? Do you want the police?'

I straightened up and got back in the car, ignoring the vigilante. As I drove past I saw the driver of the Escort shrugging him off, and I wondered whether he could change the tyre fast enough to clear out before the police arrived. Thinking about it provoked a little spurt of sympathy for him, but it wasn't enough to make me go back and offer to help, and the feeling evaporated almost before I realised what it was.

11

I rang Sarah from a phone booth outside Kentish Town Station. I knew she wouldn't be asleep because her habit had always been to go to bed late and get up early. She picked up on the first ring, and I didn't beat around the bush.

'Why have you got a man following Wyndham?'

There was a long silence before she answered.

'I was worried about the threats. I want to make sure nothing happens to him.'

'I don't think so,' I told her. 'You can't believe that little git could protect Wyndham from anyone serious. What's the real story?'

Another silence.

'I don't want to talk about this now. Wyndham should be back any minute.'

'I have to talk about it now,' I told her. 'I'm off to the country tomorrow and I don't want to go chasing Amaryll Johnson around when I don't know what's really going on.'

'It's got no connection with what you're doing.'

'I don't know that. I had a talk with Nick tonight and

it seems that there's all kinds of connections I don't understand, and you seem to be concerned with most of them. If you don't tell me what's going on, I'll ask Wyndham, and if he doesn't tell me I'm packing this in.'

'Don't do that.'

'So talk to me.'

'Where are you now?'

I told her.

'I'll meet you at your place in about forty minutes,' she said.

She was five minutes early. She was wearing a raincoat over a cotton T-shirt which came halfway down her thighs, and she'd plaited her hair into a long rope which climbed down between her shoulders. It gave her an air which was domineering and aloof, but the expression on her face was strained and nervous, and when our eyes met she looked away quickly. I had the feeling that she'd got out of bed, pausing only to put on the raincoat and a pair of slippers before leaving the house.

Upstairs in the sitting room she took the coat off, slung it across the back of the sofa and threw herself on to the seat.

'Turn that bloody light off,' she said.

I switched off the light overhead, which left only the lamp on my desk. We could see each other, but the shadows in the room created a feeling of instant intimacy. The sounds of traffic from outside had faded, and for a moment I had the sense that we were cut off, isolated in a silent bubble somewhere underwater, the only two people alive in our world. Sarah was turned towards me, one arm trailing on the floor, her face buried in the surface of the sofa, her hip curving up in an arc which seemed to attract and focus all the light in the room.

'So what's going on then?'

'What exactly do you want to know?'

'You know that I don't have the right questions,' I said. 'But I'll tell you what's worrying me.'

'Tell me.'

I told her what had happened that night, from my conversation with Nick to the point where I'd left the driver of the Escort squatting in the road. At the end of it she stirred and her face made a half turn in my direction. One eye gleamed.

'It's nothing to do with anything else.'

'I still want to know.'

'It's Wyndham. Things have been going badly lately. For the last few years, I suppose. Since we went independent.' She paused, and the silence rushed in. She raised her head and looked at her watch. Then she started again. 'Well, I guess it started before that, except that we were too occupied to notice how bad it was. Some of it was boredom. Some of it was depression. He screwed a few women. I did some things, but we didn't really want to make too many changes. Better the devil you know. We weren't unhappy.'

She stopped. I waited. Then she sat up abruptly and hugged her knees.

'I'd calmed down a lot lately,' she said. 'I thought he was more relaxed. When he got this commission he was more cheerful than I'd seen him in a long time. I had the feeling he was fucking Joan, but I didn't want to know. I had no idea how I'd feel if I knew for certain.'

She swung her legs to the floor and sat on the edge of the sofa. She was wearing white bikini briefs. I hadn't been sure up to that point, because they were cut so high that they gave the illusion that there was nothing under the shirt. She leaned forward.

'Then all this stuff started happening, and I heard rumours.'

'What sort of rumours?'

'There's more than one player in this game. They commissioned another true-crime series round about the same time.'

'You're joking. Why would Nick do that?'

'He didn't. The other editor in the department came in with this series already in development. It's supposed to be completely different, and the official line is that whatever happens with one of them won't affect the other, but no one believes that. Personally I don't think there's a hope in hell of both of them getting on the screen. I think they'll both be fighting for the same slot, and if one of them screws up its schedule, or turns in a crap pilot, that's it.'

I thought it over. All this fitted in with what I'd heard about the company's office politics, and I knew that the networks routinely wrote off very much larger sums for similar reasons. Now I knew what lay behind Nick's intriguing. But I was still confused.

'But why are you checking on Wyndham?'

She laughed, with a touch of real amusement.

'I'm not. I just happened to pick an idiot. He's supposed to be following Joan.' She leaned back, a little of the tension going out of her body. 'The rumour was that Joan is chumming up with the producer of the other series.'

'You think she's sabotaging the project?'

'I wouldn't put it past the little cow.'

'Did you tell Wyndham?'

'Of course. He asked her about it, and she said she'd been out for a drink with the guy. He asked her, chatted her up and that was it.'

'Does Wyndham believe her?'

'He says he does.'

'But you don't.'

She shrugged and looked away from me.

'I don't know. It depends what kind of offer he's made her. It depends on what's going on between her and Hammie.' It was the first time in our recent conversations that she'd used her nickname for him, and in the context, it had a forlorn undertone. 'I wanted to know who she was meeting. I thought it might help.'

'Your man gave me the impression he was following Wyndham.'

'He was probably bullshitting you.'

'So why was he sitting around watching Wyndham?'

'You say he was with Caroline. Poor Jack probably had them mixed up. I said he was an idiot.'

'He didn't have to be an idiot to do that. I'd have got them mixed up myself.'

She smiled at me, and I grinned back at her, before I remembered that her explanation only accounted for part of the story.

'I can believe she's got a motive for slowing the project up, but I don't see her sending anonymous letters and knocking off researchers.'

Her face fell.

'I never said she did. Maybe that's just a series of accidents. I don't know. I'm just doing what I can.'

'So why not get a real detective or someone credible? Who is this guy anyway?'

'Nobody special. I met him when I was doing an article about community care. He said he was looking for a job and I thought, why not?'

She must have read what I was thinking.

'Well, why not? All I wanted was someone to follow her and tell me what she did. He was stable enough for that.'

112

I was inclined to doubt that, but there didn't seem much point in arguing about it. I had some more questions, but I could guess the answers to them, and somehow I seemed to have run out of steam. As if she knew the interrogation was over, Sarah lay back on the sofa, her eyes still fixed on me.

'This isn't the straightforward piece of work we talked about,' I told her.

'Nothing's changed,' she said.

I didn't bother to reply. I couldn't put my finger on it, but I could feel in my bones that she was wrong; that something had changed.

'Have you finished with the questions?'

I nodded. 'Yes.'

She rolled over on to her side, propped her chin up on the palm of her hand, but instead of getting up as I half expected, she gazed intently at me, an odd little smile coming and going on her face.

I stared back at her. 'What?' I asked her. 'What?'

'What do you think?' she said. 'Do you want to fuck now?'

I caught the train to Leeds round about nine in the morning. Katrina had got me first-class tickets, so I stretched out and began trying to doze off before we left King's Cross. In the usual run of things the rocking motion of the train would have sent me to sleep almost immediately, but this time I hovered halfway between sleeping and waking, a stream of images flowing through my mind, and every time I moved I was conscious of the erection which seemed to have been bulging in front of me from the time I'd opened my eyes and got out of bed.

I didn't know when Sarah had left, because I'd fallen asleep after a couple of hours. At one point I'd asked her how she would account to Wyndham for being out so late, and she said he'd assume she was with a friend. I had no way of telling what that meant, but, in any case, I wasn't worried about Wyndham, or about the prospect that he'd find out, or about what he'd think if he did. The problem that had been on my mind, and which still continued to puzzle me, was the question of what had happened to Sarah.

Back when we used to commit adultery on a regular basis, she'd been vigorous and enthusiastic in a conventional way. There'd never been much time, and she didn't tease or play games. We'd kiss or touch, then strip off our clothes before collapsing into bed, and, most of the time, our foreplay had been directed to establishing or heightening desire. Her body had been as eager and mobile as I wanted, but thinking back, it struck me that the way she'd gone about it had been passive, and the pattern of our lovemaking had been one in which she'd signal her readiness, then wait for me to take action. But the intervening years had changed all that.

We'd started in a familiar clinch, wrapped round each other on the sofa, but when I reached down and tried to touch her below the waist, she closed her thighs together, and with a grip that was surprisingly strong, pulled my hand away from her.

'Do you really want me?' she said. 'Or is this just fast food?'

A couple of inches away her grey eyes were huge and intense. Up to that point I'd been in two minds about that, but hearing the question seemed to resolve my doubts.

'I want you,' I said.

She smiled, squirmed away from me, sat up and straddled my legs. In the same moment I realised that somehow,

114

without my noticing, she'd unzipped me, found my penis, and was holding it in a tight squeeze.

'I want you to do something for me,' she said.

She rocked back and forth a little. Her face, looming above me, was set in sharp, hard planes, her mouth clamped into a thin line, her eyes narrowed and staring intently.

'Anything,' I told her.

Her fingers stroked me with a deliberate and agonising patience. I closed my eyes, and felt her bending over me to whisper.

'Tie me up. Make me helpless. Make me do what you want.'

My eyes snapped open.

'What?'

She let her full weight rest on my body. Her teeth closed on my ear and let go again. I heard her take in a sharp breath, then I felt the rush of air as she expelled it.

'Take what you want,' she whispered. 'Use me. Isn't that what you want?'

Seven hours later, with the train picking up speed through north London, I had closed my eyes against the bright dazzle of the morning sunlight, but the passionate sound of her whisper still seemed to be echoing in my head. I must have fallen asleep then, and I didn't claw my way back into consciousness until the train was pulling into the platform at East Retford.

Another magical transformation had taken place while I slept. Outside the station the sky was stained in grey and it was raining, a soft drenching drizzle which felt as if it had been going on forever. There was a taxi waiting in the corner of the station forecourt, and when I stepped out on to the pavement the driver started his engine and cruised up in front of me. He was wearing a grimy white cap back to front, and under it his face was lean and narrow, with a pale, grainy skin stretched tight over the cheekbones. He gave me an enquiring look, and I waited for him to wind the window down and ask me where I was going, but, instead, he jerked his thumb at the back of the car. I opened the door and climbed in gratefully out of the rain. He watched me in the driving mirror while I settled myself in.

'Just come up from London?'

The accent sounded like Yorkshire, which confused me a little, because I had the vague sense that I was actually in Lincolnshire or Nottinghamshire. I thought, for a moment, about asking the driver, but I wasn't sure whether or not he'd take it as some kind of insult, so I contented myself with reading him the address I'd found on the back of the envelope. He grunted something I didn't catch and took off, zipping out of the station yard and into the street so fast that I couldn't stop myself looking around to see whether we were going to hit something.

I needn't have worried. There was hardly any traffic going by, and when he turned off on to the other side of the railway tracks the streets seemed deserted, the rows of terraced cottages lined up in neat blocks beside them, as if some careless young giant had been playing house and forgotten to clear up.

'It used to be more lively,' the driver said, 'but since pit closed it's gone dead.'

I should have guessed. The decline of traditional industries, and the unemployment which went along with it, were reshaping landscapes all over the country. There'd been an edge of bitterness, too, in the driver's tone.

'You worked down the pit?'

'Yeah,' he said curtly, and I got the feeling that even though he'd raised the subject, he didn't want to talk about it any more. I took the hint and gazed around at the street, trying to extract some defining pattern from the sweating ochre walls of the houses. But I could feel him watching me in the driving mirror.

'Most men round here worked down pit,' he said suddenly.

'Is this what you do now?'

He snorted contemptuously.

'You couldn't make a living doing this. It helps keep us from starving. I'm really in show business. Took me redundancy and started last year.'

'What do you do?'

'Impersonator.'

'Who?'

I was ready to bet Elvis. I'd read somewhere that the clubs in this part of the world were full of Elvis impersonators.

'Madonna,' he said.

There was a touch of defiance in his tone, and he was watching me in the mirror, as if to check whether I was going to laugh.

'Must take a lot of practice,' I said. 'All that dancing.'

'You're telling me,' he said. 'Keeps me fit.'

'Must be expensive and all,' I continued. I was floundering, but I couldn't work out an inoffensive way to bring it to an end. 'The costumes must cost a bit.'

'Well, I used to do Elvis.' Suddenly, without a pause, he broke into song. 'Heartbreak Hotel'. *'Since ma baby left me ah found a noo place to dwell-ah.'*

He sounded like an Elvis impersonator, so I nodded appreciatively and said 'yeah'. He grinned happily.

117

'When I packed that in I still had the costumes and we used the material for the dresses. Beautiful stuff, velvet, silver lamé, rhinestones.'

He took his hands off the steering wheel and gestured languidly, and I noticed his long, shiny nails for the first time.

'At least I keep me hands clean now. When I worked down pit, it used to drive my missis mad, scrubbing them.'

I wasn't sure where to take the conversation next, but by the time I thought of a reply, he'd pulled up and stopped. We were in the middle of a street where the houses were like upturned boxes. Two up. Two down. The doors and windows flush with the pavement, as if the builders had been announcing a puritanical denial of any soft-headed notions about the inhabitants' need for their own territory.

I got out, asked Madonna to wait, crossed the pavement in one stride, and knocked on the nearest door. No answer. I tried again, and again with the same result.

'No one there,' the driver said. He'd wound his window down and when I looked round he leaned out and pointed at the window above me. The glass was dark and blank, but it took a moment before I twigged. Then I realised that every other window in the street was shaded by net curtains. Their absence was almost certainly an indication that the house was empty.

I swore aloud and ducked back into the car.

'Where do you want to go?'

He was watching me, eyebrows raised, a touch of something ironic about his expression, and I realised that I'd been sitting there for nearly a minute looking at the drab front of the empty house. Running through my head was the image of a blank wall. I'd been so certain that the address would lead me somewhere, that I hadn't pursued a single thought about what to do next.

118

'Back to the station?'

The driver's question nagged me into action. I took out the envelope and showed him the address.

'Is there anything around here that looks like that? Any other road it could be?'

He studied it carefully, turning it over in his hand and reading the front, then turning it round again. He looked up at me, his face expressionless.

'No. This is it.'

It had been a desperate hope, which I didn't expect to succeed. I nodded and told him to go back to the station, but, instead of starting the engine, he turned round and faced me.

'Who are you looking for?'

My first impulse was to tell him to mind his own business, but then it struck me that a taxi driver in a town this size would probably have an encyclopaedic knowledge of the people moving about in it. I gave him Amaryll's photograph and told him the name. He stared fixedly at it for a few seconds.

'What do you want him for? What's he done?'

Within the last minute I'd begun to anticipate the question, but I had the suspicion that he wouldn't tell me a thing if he thought I was a debt collector or some other kind of official chasing a man on the run.

'He's not done anything.' I laughed. 'That's the trouble. We do a bit of decorating and that in London. Things were slow the last few weeks. You know how it is.'

Our eyes met, and he grunted his assent.

'It's the same up here.'

'All right,' I said. 'He comes up here to see his auntie and the next day I get a job. Half a dozen houses in Haringey. Council job.' I guessed he'd have read about Haringey being loony, left wing and all the rest of it, and

I was betting it would strike a chord. 'So I tried the phone number. No answer. The job starts as soon as. I need a mate to do the work or we'll lose it. If I get somebody else he'll kill me. That's why I came up.'

His expression was sympathetic now, and I knew I'd convinced him. My desperation was the key. He knew all about that.

'Wait here,' he said. He opened the door, then turned and smiled at me. 'I don't know this Johnson, but I know a man who might.'

He scooted across the road, and I watched him closely to see whether there was anything about the way he moved that reminded me of Madonna, but there wasn't. On the other side he walked rapidly along the pavement, and a few houses before he got to the next junction he stopped and knocked at a door. It opened almost immediately, and he began talking to someone I couldn't see. Then he disappeared.

Left to myself, I peered out along the street. The rain was still coming down, a thin grey veil which bleached the colour out of everything I could see. Under it the houses were faceless, but I was willing to bet that there were a dozen eyes watching the car from behind the streaming windows. The door opened and the driver got in and slammed it behind him.

'No luck,' he said. 'She moved out a couple of months ago.'

'Moved?' I repeated stupidly.

'Aye. Moved. She were a nurse, that lady. Her husband worked down pit, and he died after it closed. So she moved.'

'Where's she gone?'

'Don't know. Sorry.'

12

The taxi driver's friend across the road had also been a miner. Now he was a student of leisure management. Between them they'd summed up everything there was to be known about Amaryll's auntie. She'd worked in a clinic nearby, but that had been shut down shortly after the mine went, so she'd wound up her affairs and left the town. Talk was that she'd gone to Manchester.

I rang Wyndham from the station, and told him the bad news.

'Go to Manchester then,' he said.

I told him I didn't have an address for Amaryll's aunt in Manchester, and that even if I could locate her I wasn't sure Amaryll would be there. He told me to stop moaning and take a look. He sounded like a desperate man. I told him it would probably be a useless trip.

'Give it your best shot,' he said.

I asked him to put me through to Katrina, and when she came on the line I gave her the name of Amaryll's auntie, Angie Boswell, and told her what I wanted her to do. Afterwards I rang Ida and told her I was on my way. She said she'd meet me at the station and when I protested, she said it was no trouble, so I told her what train I'd be on and went to change my tickets.

It was the late afternoon by the time the train pulled into Piccadilly. Ida was waiting by the barrier. I'd half expected her to be accompanied by two daughters, the way she always used to be, but she was alone, and it struck me that the girls would now be adults or very near it. Ida herself seemed to have aged more than I would have expected during the four years since I'd last seen her. She had the same round, pretty features, but she'd put on weight, and she was wearing spectacles.

'You're getting a little grey,' she said, inspecting me.

She sounded triumphant. Twenty years ago we'd been desultory lovers, and now we were better friends, but she'd never surrendered the sense that, somehow, I'd gone off and left her behind. As it happened, I thought she was right, but I didn't feel any guilt about it, because it had seemed obvious from the start that it couldn't last. Ida's parents had come from Barbados in the late fifties and she'd been born in Manchester. During the couple of years that I'd lived in the city, I'd always had the sense that I was passing through, while for Ida it was home, and, even then, I couldn't imagine her settling down anywhere else.

'You're not looking too bad for an old bag,' I told her, and she mimed a kick at my shins, then we hugged each other.

Back in the car I expected her to turn left towards St Peter's, but, instead, she drove straight on towards the city centre.

'Where are we going?' I asked her. 'Have you moved?'

She couldn't have, or she'd have sent me a card with her new address. That's how she was.

'No. I haven't moved. We're going to Princess Street. You didn't eat on the train, did you?'

I told her I hadn't, and she gave me a mocking smile, as if she'd known that I would be neglecting myself.

'I'm glad you've come,' she said, 'I want to talk to you.'

She turned a corner, parked, and we got out. We were in Chinatown. Everywhere I looked I could see big Chinese letters and garish electric colours, red, gold, green. Down the street a big red arch which transformed the look of the place, as if we'd stepped through a fold in space and emerged thousands of miles away. What made the impression even stranger was the fact that when I lived in the city, there were only one or two Chinese restaurants in the district. Now they seemed to have multiplied, spawning these bustling blooms of colour all over the narrow streets which led down to the city centre.

'I told you about getting divorced?' Ida asked.

We were in a long dark room with tables arranged in rows. The evening hadn't yet begun and the place was half empty. But there was a relaxed, cheerful feel about it. Right at the end there was a huge circular table with about a dozen Chinese men sitting round it, and every few minutes there was a burst of laughter.

'Businessmen,' Ida said. 'From Hong Kong or maybe Singapore. He gets a lot of those in here.'

Once she mentioned it I could see that they were carrying bags and purses, and they had the naughty look of serious men who were beginning to unbutton themselves for a night of fun.

'How do you know so much about it?'

'I delivered the manager's last baby,' she said. 'He's a really nice man, and every time he sees me, he insists that I come for a meal.' She must have seen the look of puzzlement on my face, because she frowned and

123

shook her head. 'I'm a midwife now. Remember? I wrote you.'

I remembered. She'd written me when she got married. I'd been just about to go abroad, and I'd sent a telegram and some flowers. A few months later she wrote to say that she was getting divorced, and giving up nursing so she could spend more time with her daughters.

'I remember about the divorce. But I didn't want to mention it. Sorry things didn't work out.'

She clicked her tongue, and shook her head again.

'It was worse than that, Sammy. That's what I wanted to tell you about, in case you said anything when you see the girls.'

Over the next half hour she told me about her marriage. He was a psychiatric nurse and she'd met him in the hospital when he came in with a patient who'd jumped out of a window. They got married soon after, bought a house in Whalley Range, and she was as happy as she expected to be for almost a year. Then, one day, she'd come home unexpectedly after a long shift, and found her husband lying on their bed with her older daughter Yvette. They were kissing passionately, but when she broke it up, he claimed that they'd just been fooling around. He'd been showing her how to kiss, he said, because she was self-conscious about her inexperience, and worried about being laughed at when she went out with boys. Ida had responded by locking him out of the house and beginning divorce proceedings.

'What did Yvette say?'

She shrugged. 'She told me the same story. I knew she was lying but there was nothing I could do. To this day she won't talk about it.'

She'd had the continuing fantasy, she said, that one

day Yvette would break down and tell her exactly what had been going on, then they could return to the intimacy of their previous relationship. But, although it had been nearly two years since, Yvette still maintained that when her mother saw her writhing on the bed with her stepfather, it had been a harmless bit of fun. The worst part of it, Ida told me, was that she had begun to doubt her own instincts, and she now found herself wondering whether she hadn't been in too much of a hurry to jump to conclusions. Perhaps the problem had been her own dirty mind.

'You did right,' I told her firmly. 'Even if it was the way he said it was, a man who thinks it's cool to teach his young stepdaughter French kissing is not going to stop there. Probably you just caught it in time. Give her a chance. She'll come round.'

'I hope so,' she said. Suddenly she slammed her fist on the table in front of her. 'Damn and blast that man. I'm sorry I ever saw him.'

'It's over now.'

'I dunno.' She turned and faced me. 'It's all this psychological stuff. You try to talk to anyone and it's like being back in college. If my mam was alive none of this would surprise her. She'd just say he was a man and the devil got up in him. It wasn't complicated. She thought sex was natural, like rain or thunder or something like that. It wasn't about power or hatred or insanity. You had to know what it was like and tame it or use it or enjoy it, but you couldn't explain it. I wish she'd been around. Whenever I tried talking to anybody about this all I'd get was questions about our relationship and what my daughters felt about me. I didn't want to hear all that shit. Family therapy.'

'Did you do therapy?'

'Nearly. But I didn't want anyone messing with my mind. I just started going to church again.' She laughed. 'Best thing when the devil's about.'

It wasn't until later that I got the chance to tell Ida why I'd come. By this time we were at her house. Yvette and Ismay had grown into bulky teenagers, who greeted me with a fairly distant friendliness, and Ida had ended the awkward moment by dragging me off to the kitchen, so that the girls could do their homework in peace. Peace sounded like Snoop Doggy Dog.

When the phone rang it was Katrina.

'I spent the whole afternoon on the telephone, checking nursing agencies, but I got her. She's working in Manchester.'

She gave me the name of the hospital.

'You're brilliant,' I told her. 'I owe you one.'

'You owe me more than one, dearie.'

In the kitchen Ida was watching the news, but she listened patiently while I brought her up to date.

'What are you going to do?'

'The first thing is to find out what she looks like.'

My plan sounded lame, but it was all I could think of on the spur of the moment. I was going to identify Angie Boswell, then follow her home, see whether Amaryll was there, and if he wasn't I'd think again. Ida frowned as she listened.

'Why bother with all that? What you need is to find out her address, then go and check it out.'

'How am I going to do that? I can't just go up to her and ask.'

Ida smiled.

'You can't, but I know a couple of women who can. I know people at that hospital. It won't be hard for them to find out.' She took in the expression on my face and laughed out loud. 'It's a small world here.'

I should have guessed. The health services were run by a network of women like Ida, and she'd been working in this town for twenty years. If the thing could be done she'd do it.

Half an hour later I had the address. Angie Boswell's flat was in a block off Moss Lane, on the other side of Hulme, about a mile away from where we were sitting.

13

The rain had followed me across the Pennines. It trickled down the back of my neck and squelched up over the tops of my shoes as I walked along Moss Lane. The address I'd been given was a newish block of flats near Alexandra Park. It was surrounded by flats and houses which had a box-like, miniaturised look about them. In the bad old days this had been the site where acres of slums festered like a mouthful of rotting teeth. The city fathers had replaced them with a rash of crumbling concrete which spread like a scummy grey lichen over the landscape, and from which the locals, who'd endured the slums for generations, had fled as if they were escaping the plague.

Behind me they were demolishing the huge prefabricated blocks of the Hulme estate, but the new wave of housing around it had the slapped together, temporary feel of a holiday development on the Mediterranean coast.

Angie Boswell lived on the second floor of the block. I hadn't had the time to think of anything subtle, and in any case, walking through the rain had put me in too much of a bad temper to bother, so I simply climbed the stairs and knocked on her door. Angie was working the night shift, according to Ida, and I'd calculated that if Amaryll was staying with her he'd show up sooner or later. There was no answer, which, as it turned out, was fortunate, because I had no idea what I'd say or do if Amaryll had appeared in front of me.

It was about ten o'clock. If the impression I had about the man was right, he could be out for most of the night. I nerved myself up to face the weather, and walked down to the nearest pub, out in Wilmslow Road. My memory of it was a barn-like room, dotted with battered furniture, and occupied by a cross section of grimy local prostitutes, tired hustlers and tattered students. Now the surfaces were covered with shiny blond wood and cushioned with red leatherette. I had the feeling that the clientele hadn't changed much, but the styles were different, and this time round it was hard to tell the students apart from the whores and the hustlers. I ordered a whisky, and sat at the bar, unsuccessfully, to spot a familiar face. But I'd been away too long, and I had the suspicion that most of the people I had known in this district would have died or moved on.

By closing time I'd had enough. Outside, the rain had eased to a desultory drizzle, but the wind had got up, and as I hurried along Wilmslow Road it kept throwing handfuls of freezing water at my face. When I got to Angie's flat I checked the pane of frosted glass above the door, hoping against hope, but it was still dark. I knocked anyway. No answer, and I settled down on the stairs to wait. The concrete step struck me with a chill that seemed to go right through to the bone, but after a few minutes I'd either become acclimatised, or my flesh was so numb that the cold didn't matter, and within the next hour I was dozing off.

In my half-conscious state I heard footsteps coming

129

and going on the floor below, but I wasn't disturbed until I woke suddenly, just in time to snatch my hand away from a pair of high heels clattering past me. At the same moment I caught a glimpse of mesh-covered thighs, and smelt a gust of perfume, accompanied by the woman's own hot, biological scent. When I looked up I saw the couple, a paunchy white man standing near the top of the stairs, and the woman, a dyed blonde in a black imitation fur coat.

'What d'you think you're fooking doing?' she shouted.

I shook my head to clear it. For a couple of seconds I hadn't been sure that I wasn't dreaming.

'Waiting for a friend,' I told her.

'Fook off or I'll ring the police.'

I let my eyes pass over her and stared at the man. He didn't seem interested, and when he saw me looking he turned his head away. People in this district had never been eager to involve the law in their affairs and I was sure that hadn't changed.

'Just mind your own business,' I told them, 'and you'll be all right.'

The man shifted a couple of steps away.

'Come on, chuck,' he said sharply. 'Come on.'

The woman stood her ground for a few seconds, then she turned and flounced off.

That was the end of the entertainment for a while, and I'd started to doze off again when Amaryll ran up the stairs and stood a few yards away on the landing below me, fiddling with his keys. I wouldn't have known him from the photograph, because he'd shaved off the moustache, and let his hair grow into a mass of corkscrew curls. He'd lost weight, too, and now he had a beaky, Arabic look which had rendered him unrecognisable. Somehow, even though I'd been waiting for so many hours, I wasn't prepared for the sight of him, close enough to touch, and I found myself standing up to greet him before I had time to think about what I was doing.

'Amaryll? Amaryll Johnson?' I asked.

I'd been startled out of sleep, so I'd made it louder and more abrupt than I intended, and I was equally unprepared for his reaction. I'd half expected him to be aggressive or to slam the door in my face. Instead, he turned and ran. Before I could move a muscle, he was halfway down the flight of stairs and picking up speed. For a moment I stood there, frozen in surprise, then I got myself in gear and ran after him.

If I'd had a chance to think about it I wouldn't have moved, because I was close to falling over for the first few steps, but once I'd got down to the bottom of the stairs my joints had begun to work again, and I was moving freely. By then Amaryll was fifty yards away, sprinting towards Wilmslow Road. I put on a burst of speed, pumping my legs and lifting my knees the way I used to when I was interval training, and the gap narrowed a little. Amaryll must have heard me coming, because he took a quick look over his shoulder as he dashed round the corner into the main road. At that point it struck me that this was a race. I had to keep him in sight or he'd disappear, but I had no idea how far I could run at this pace.

After about another hundred yards I was almost certain that I'd have to stop. Amaryll was still flashing along in front of me and I was beginning to gasp with the effort of keeping my legs moving. The other problem was that my feet felt flat and lifeless. I'd started out thrusting away from the surface of the pavement, springing on my toes, but within a few paces my muscles had refused, and now I was pounding along, lifting my feet one after the other, a pair of dead-weights. I slowed to a trot, and I noticed for the first time a familiar pain in my chest. By this time Amaryll had swung into Moss Lane and we were running down towards Princess Street.

It was now well past midnight, and the streets were empty except for an occasional knot of young men. Had it been earlier there might have been dozens of pubs or caffs open. Or perhaps a crowded shopping arcade that Amaryll could have nipped into and lost me. But at this time of the night there was nothing between us except for a few pedestrians. On Wilmslow Road we'd gone past a group of white boys, about five of them. They had the look of students out looking for late-night fast food, and seeing them gave me a sudden flash of memory back to the days when I used to be wandering down the same street at about the same hour, heading for the Somali caff, where the owner, Adam, served what the kids in the area had dubbed the wickedest biriani in the West.

Thinking about Adam distracted me from the desperate need to put a halt to the agony I was imposing on my body. I had slowed to a jog, but Amaryll wasn't moving much faster, and having come this far I was becoming more and more determined not to give up. Halfway down Moss Lane I had to swerve to avoid a couple of women in nightwalking uniform. Thigh-high boots, micro-skirts, tight sweaters.

'You don't have to chase him, duck!' one of them shouted. 'Not if you've got twenty pound.'

Up ahead the big sign loomed on the Harp Lager building. Up to this point I had been concentrating too hard to think about where Amaryll might be heading, but when I saw him shaping to make a diagonal run across Princess Street, it struck me that there was a maze of alleyways between the rows of houses and flats there.

Once he was in there he could jump over a fence and vanish within a few feet of me.

I forced myself into a slightly faster trot, and I had the illusion I was gaining on him, but as I was about to step off into the roadway the beam of a big motorbike hit me, and I sprang back just in time to avoid being run down. That was the end. I had stopped and I couldn't do any more running. Not even the sort of feeble jog which had got me to that spot. On the other side of the road Amaryll trotted steadily to the entrance of the alley opposite and disappeared.

I couldn't run but I could still walk. Driven on by the pointless anger which had been rising inside me for the last couple of miles, I followed him across the road, stumbling and swaying like a drunk. As I suspected, the alley was empty by the time I reached the entrance, but I kept on walking up it towards where the next path made a junction with it. I was nearly there when I heard the retching sounds and soft splashing of vomit, and when I rounded the corner I saw Amaryll resting on his hands and knees, throwing violently on to the base of a lamp post.

He'd fallen over a dustbin lying in the middle of the path, and after an evening of boozing and biriani, followed by the exhausting run, his stomach had revolted. Trying to ignore the smell, I leaned against the fence opposite, watching him heave his guts out on the path. Eventually he stopped, scuttled back from the pool of vomit and sat with his back against the fence.

'What the fuck do you want?' he said abruptly.

I felt like laughing, but I controlled myself, because I had the suspicion that if I did it would turn into a fit of coughing.

'You don't know what I want and you run all this way, man?'

He scowled at me.

'I don't know who the fuck you are,' he said. 'You got some business with me?'

I told him who I was and some of what I wanted. When I mentioned that I'd traced him through Linette he laughed scornfully.

'You've wasted your time,' he said eventually. 'I don't know nothing about that murder.'

'So who did you think I was? Why'd you run?'

I was playing for time.

'Thought you were the child support or something.'

I stared at him, trying to decide whether or not he was joking. The rain started again, a transparent lace which funnelled down the alleyway in stinging cobwebs of icy water. I helped Amaryll up and we began walking back towards his auntie's flat. A sharp wind had got up in the last quarter of an hour, but in a little while it seemed to die away, and as we walked along Wilmslow Road, the weather seemed almost normal for a wet night in Manchester.

I wasn't sure what his reaction would be if I started asking him about his relations with Helen and where he'd been that night, so I told him we wanted to talk to her friends about what she'd been like. He shrugged.

'She was all right,' he said.

I explained. We wanted to draw a portrait of her for the audience. Her neighbours and other casual acquaintances couldn't do it, but if he'd been a real friend, someone who'd sat and talked with her, he could show her as something more than a victim. He could describe how she walked and talked, what she cared about, what made her laugh, why he liked her.

Halfway through my spiel it struck me that during the last few hours I'd forgotten or suppressed my previous reservations, and now all I cared about was convincing him, making it happen, doing the job right. By the time I finished we had arrived back at Angie's building, but he didn't ask me up. Instead, he sprawled on the stairs, watching me, an unpleasant grin on his face.

'What do I get out of it?' he asked abruptly.

I considered the question.

'Well, for a start they'll pay you.'

'How much?'

This was difficult ground.

'I don't know. They won't pay all that much for an interview with you sitting there saying she was a nice girl. Depends on what you know, and how interesting what you've got to say is.'

'It's interesting.'

'Do you know who did it?'

His grin grew broader.

'I'm not telling you shit till I've got a deal.'

'Lemme explain something else,' I told him. 'I'm not ringing up these people and telling them that I've got this guy with interesting things to say, but I don't know what they are. You can forget that. The other thing you need to remember is that you're a suspect and all. You do this interview, you can tell your side of the story, because there's a lot of people used to see you creeping down Leon's flat when he was out, and they won't be slow to put the finger on you. You talk to us, it might save you being stitched up. You can explain why you left so suddenly, for a start.'

I wasn't really expecting him to fold up, but I thought that what I was hinting would sober him up. Instead he leaned back into a more comfortable posture and began laughing at me.

'I left because I fed up being hassled for money, man.

135

You borrow a few quid, people make a big deal out of it. And I'm not worried anyway. I don't give a shite what they say about me. I was somewhere else that night. There's about twenty witnesses. I'm right out of the frame.'

I stared at him. If this was true it meant that Wyndham's entire approach to the story was a waste of time. The problem was that I believed him. I knew enough about his type to be sure that his cockiness reflected his confidence in the truth of what he was saying. It would also explain why the police hadn't been interested in him.

'Where were you?'

He didn't reply. Instead he smirked at me, then held out his hand, palm upwards, and rubbed his fingers together.

'It's no good,' I told him. 'No one's going to pay just to hear your alibi. You're wasting my time.'

I wasn't bluffing either. I was willing to bet that if that was all he had to say there wouldn't be much point in going to the trouble of recording an interview.

'Keep your shirt on,' he said. He was still smiling. 'There's more to it. She was being threatened.'

'By her husband?'

'Nah.' His tone was contemptuous. 'He threatened her all right. But that was normal. This was different. Some nutter was after her.'

I had to give Amaryll some credit. He knew how to jerk you around.

'What? Why didn't you tell the police?'

'I did. They weren't interested.'

'They wouldn't be unless you could prove it.'

He laughed again.

'I can prove it. I've got the proof.'

'What is it?'

'Letters. Stuff through the letter box. I told the cops

136

about them, but they weren't bothered. Told me to stuff it.'

It was logical. The police would have focused on Leon from the beginning and if they were convinced about his guilt all their energies would have gone into building the background of their prosecution. Sherlock Holmes might have listened, but in the real world the investigation would have been directed towards making a watertight case. In that context Amaryll's story would have seemed like a dangerous irrelevance. On the other hand, I had the feeling that Wyndham would jump at it.

'Can I see these letters?'

He stopped grinning and his features twisted irritably.

'Fuck off. I'll show you the proof when it's all fixed, and I want a couple of grand up front before I open me mouth.'

'A couple of grand? Get real,' I told him.

He gave me a stony glare in reply.

'A couple of grand,' he repeated. 'Up front, and I'll do it tomorrow. I don't want to hang about.'

'Tomorrow's Sunday,' I told him. 'You can't get anything done tomorrow.'

'Oh yeah.' He thought it over. 'Monday then. After that I'm off. Let me know tomorrow.'

'Give me your number.'

He shook his head.

'Nah. Give me yours. I'll ring you first thing.'

I took a pen out of my pocket, wrote Ida's number on the back of an envelope, and gave it to him. He tucked it away carefully, stood up, clicked his fingers at me, and began walking away up the stairs. A couple of flights up he turned round.

'See yez tomorrow,' he said.

14

When I got back to Ida's she was waiting up. She'd made up a bed for me on the sofa in the sitting room, and I thought for a moment she was going to sit around talking the way we used to, but after I told her I'd found Amaryll and talked to him, she seemed to lose interest. Once she'd gone off to bed I rang Wyndham. Sarah answered. I said hello, asked for Wyndham, and he came on the line almost immediately. I told him I'd found our man, and followed on with what had been said. When I mentioned Amaryll's alibi he swore angrily.

'He would say that, wouldn't he?'

'I wouldn't bank on him lying about that,' I said. 'It was the one thing he wasn't worried about. He's really confident that he's in the clear.'

'What's this alibi, then?'

'He wouldn't tell me. Not till he had some kind of deal. There's something else as well.'

I told him Amaryll's story about a nutter threatening Helen, and he perked up immediately.

'Well, that's better,' he said. 'That gives us another option.'

'Not necessarily. He wants two grand.'

'Bloody hell! I can't do that.'

His reaction was about what I'd expected. Nick had approved the budget Wyndham wanted, but the costs had to be accounted for on a line by line basis. If a payment of two grand to an informant cropped up alarm bells would go off all over the place. Officially, the company would have to view it as an unethical practice, and if the case ever came to court, the evidence provided by a witness who'd been paid would be tainted.

'So what do I tell him?'

'Bargain with him,' Wyndham said. 'Haggle.'

'You really want to do it?'

'It will cause problems,' he said, 'but I can jiggle things about. Make it clear to him that whatever it is, we're talking expenses here. From now on this is informal stuff, you get me?'

'Suppose it comes to court? On appeal.'

'We'll worry about that later. If the thing gets on we'll be long gone by the time it happens.'

'So what do I tell him?'

'Beat him down as much as you can, but tell him the final word is up to me. And get him to London. We can't do this on the phone, and I can't get away.'

'That might be difficult.'

'Listen,' Wyndham said firmly. When he took that tone I could practically see the stubborn set of his jaw. 'Tell the bugger it's no pain no gain. Tell him we'll pay his fares and put him up at a five-star hotel.'

'You're kidding.'

'Of course I am. But once he's here, what's he going to do?'

That night I slept without any dreams that I could remember. When the telephone woke me I came to groaning, struggling reluctantly into a world full of sound

139

and fury. Somewhere in the house Ida was shouting at someone.

'We have to go back to London,' I told Amaryll.

He didn't like that, and he didn't like my hemming and hawing about how much he'd get paid up. In the end I guaranteed him that it would be less than two thousand and more than one. That left the business of going back to London, but after I'd mumbled some gibberish about luxury hotels and everything being paid for, he relaxed and graciously consented to accompany me.

By the time I'd finished with Amaryll, Ida seemed to have won the argument with her daughters. There was a knock on the door and she came in with a mug of tea. She was dressed to go out, and I guessed that all the shouting had been about getting the girls to go to church with her. I told her I'd be gone when she got back. She made a disappointed face.

'So soon? I don't see you for so long, and now you just blow in and blow out.'

I had the sense that her protests were rhetorical and obligatory. I played the game, swearing that I would have stayed longer if I could, but underneath it all I suspected that she regretted telling me as much as she had about her domestic problems, and now she was more or less relieved that I was going.

Before she left the house she ushered the girls in to say goodbye, as if to prove that she was in control and still able to teach them the right sort of manners. I did my best to act up to the role of the good old family friend, but Yvette's stony expression warned against indulging in any avuncular capers. At the door I told Ida that I'd be back soon, but I knew I wouldn't, and I had the feeling that she knew it too.

*

140

The train journey back to London was tense and uncomfortable. The only bright spot was that, once we were through the Midlands, the sun came out and lit up the fields through which the train was chuffing. Wyndham met us at the station. He greeted Amaryll like a long lost brother, and I could tell that they were going to get on like a house on fire. One of Wyndham's characteristics was the ease with which he could manufacture an atmosphere of friendliness with a variety of people. Amaryll had hardly spoken to me during the trip back, but, under the warmth of Wyndham's attention, he seemed to loosen up and expand. In the taxi he'd begun to raise the issue of money, but Wyndham refused to talk about it until he was settled into his hotel and had a drink inside him. At that point I half expected Amaryll to explode. Instead he put on a coyly judicious air and pointed out that Wyndham wasn't getting a word out of him until they'd done business. Wyndham responded by laughing appreciatively.

'Stop here,' I called out to the driver.

We'd only got as far as Great Portland Street, but I'd had enough.

'Not coming for a drink?' Wyndham asked. The question was for Amaryll's benefit, I guessed. If he'd really wanted me to stay, he'd have found a way of giving me a private signal. The fact that he hadn't probably meant that he wanted me to go.

'I'm knackered,' I told him. The taxi had stopped in front of the tube, so I said goodbye to Amaryll and climbed out into Euston Road.

Back in the flat the pigeons seemed to have gathered round the back window to coo their greetings. I figured they knew it was teatime, so I opened it and crumbled stale bread in a line along the sill. Over the roofs I could see the sun striking the tops of the trees along Park Lane. The perspective, the light and the way the window framed the trees and the buildings, gave the scene a bright, foreign look, like a picture postcard from another country.

The doorbell rang. I walked through the flat to the window at the front, looked out and saw Sarah. I dropped the curtain and pulled back against the wall. It wasn't that I didn't want to see her. In fact, the moment I recognised her I realised that she'd been somewhere in the back of my mind for the last two days, but I needed some time to think over what had happened, and the way she was now. As I started down the stairs I resolved to put her off somehow, but by the time I got to the bottom I'd changed my mind.

She was wearing a long rust-coloured tube in some kind of heavy fabric. Her hair was swinging loose and her eyes were hidden behind a big pair of tinted glasses. She gave me a quick smile and went ahead of me up the stairs. I followed her, watching the curves come and go in the back of the tube. In the flat she sprawled on the sofa. I leaned against the window, so that I could look away from her and watch the pigeons.

'So what happened? Wyndham said you'd found the guy.'

'Yes. I did.'

I told her the story of the last couple of days and she listened in silence, watching me intently, as if she was trying to read what was going through my mind.

'I knew you could do it,' she said eventually.

'Trouble is I don't know what I did,' I told her.

'Don't worry. Wyndham will sort it out.'

'If it was anything to do with me,' I said, 'it would worry me a lot putting all my eggs in Amaryll's basket.'

'Wyndham will sort something out,' she repeated.

142

I shrugged and she got up and came over to the window where I was standing.

'Nice view,' she said, but instead of looking at it, she put her arms round me, and we stood for a moment, pressing hard against each other.

'What do you want me to do?' she whispered.

'Use your imagination,' I said.

'No. You have to tell me.'

I told her, and immediately she sank to her knees, unzipped me and took me in her mouth. I leaned back against the window, supporting myself on my elbows. As if from far away I could hear the pigeons cooing. Down below in the mews a dog barked. The sound of my breath came and went like a ragged pounding in my ears. Suddenly Sarah made a long whining noise, stopped, and lay face down on the floor.

'Hit me,' she said quietly.

I cleared my throat.

'What?' I said stupidly.

She made a quick movement, hitched the skirt up over her hips and spread her thighs apart. Above the long wiry legs her buttocks had an unexpectedly full, ripe look to them.

'Hit me there. Hit me.'

I knelt beside her. Her toes were bent back and braced against the floor. The muscles in her thighs flexed and relaxed in a continuous ripple. Her hips bounced impatiently. I smacked her with my open palm. She gasped loudly.

'Again.'

I hit her again.

'Harder. Harder.'

I hit her harder a couple of times. She cried out and flattened herself against the floor. I stopped.

143

'Again. Again.'

I pulled away and sat with my back against the wall. The excitement I'd felt was ebbing fast.

'Keep this up,' I told her, 'and I'll be too knackered to do anything else.'

She rolled over, looked at me, pulled her skirt down and sat up, hugging her knees.

'What a wanker you are, Sammy,' she said. 'You've spoilt it now. Don't you fancy me nowadays?'

''Course I do. But this is your game. The least you can do is tell me what role I'm supposed to be playing. The way it is you're making me feel like a big dildo.'

She gave me a laugh which turned into a rueful smile.

'I didn't want to talk,' she said. 'I just wanted to do it.'

'I want to do it, too. It's just that I want to know what I'm doing.'

'Shit.' She shook her head irritably. 'What do you want to know?'

'I don't know. Anything you want to tell me. You've got to admit that you used to be pretty conventional. Something's changed.'

She stared at me, and for a few seconds I had the feeling that she was about to explode with rage, then her face relaxed into a smile.

'You want to hear about my adventures. Right? Talking turns you on.'

I didn't answer, because I wasn't sure whether or not she was right. She ran her tongue over her upper lip and I felt a little leap in my guts.

'All right then,' she said, 'let's go lie in your bed. I'll tell you everything you want to know.'

In bed she talked, lying with her head turned away from me, half buried in the pillow. I wrapped my legs

144

round her and stroked her, then, later on, she climbed up, straddled me, and, bent double, continued whispering into my ear as we rocked back and forth.

She hadn't had another affair, she said, for a long time after our relationship had ended, and she'd resolved to be good, to work at being married to Wyndham. But some bad things had happened, she didn't specify what they were and I didn't press her. After that she'd been desperate, and in a mood for something to happen, she didn't know what. Then she went to a conference in Grenoble. Some academic nonsense about broadcasting, but it was her turn to take a bit out of the conference budget and she'd gone. On the first morning there she'd bumped into a shy, middle-aged Dutchman with vivid blue eyes and had coffee with him. He wrote novels, taught semiology, and she had a vague sense that he was almost famous. He had delivered a paper on the semiotics of newsreaders' hairstyles during that first day, and after dinner took her for a walk in the grounds of the university. She was in a peculiar state of mind, and when he paused behind a tree and ordered her to strip, she obeyed without hesitation. This was only the beginning. For the next week she took his every wish as a command. Her submission and willingness to please excited him and he subjected her to increasingly extravagant demands. Sometimes he walked her through the town dressed only in a flimsy raincoat, pausing only to make her perform oral sex in a doorway or the lavatory of a restaurant. On the final night of the conference he made her walk, to his room, which was three floors away from her own, completely in the nude, carrying the thin leather belt with which he was to thrash her. She went past at least four broadcasters she knew, but, fortunately, they were East Europeans, and she'd never seen them again. To her amazement she discovered an overwhelming

145

delight in playing the submissive whore to the Dutchman's masterful dominance, and when they had to part she'd dissolved in tears. She'd only seen him one more time, when he passed through on his way to a conference in Winnipeg. He had summoned her to King's Cross, where he was changing trains, and fucked her without mercy in a back street behind the station.

Since then she had been, without shame, on the lookout for sexual experiences which would take her to the edge of abandon. Wyndham knew nothing about what had been going on, although she thought that sometimes he was suspicious. She laughed.

'And of course,' she said, 'he's always too busy fucking somebody else.'

'How come you're still together?'

She shrugged. She rolled away from me and turned her head to look.

'Don't talk about him.'

It was halfway through the night by the time she left, and the telephone rang a few seconds after she'd slammed the door behind her.

'Sorry about all that bullshit,' Wyndham's voice said. 'I had to schmooze him a little.'

For a moment I had the idea that he'd been standing across the road watching Sarah leave, but I knew that couldn't be true and I shrugged it off, and struggled to sound normal.

'Did you get anywhere?'

'Not bad. He has got an alibi, as it happens. The police stopped his car after he came out of a club in Tottenham. He refused the breath test and they took him down the station. He was sitting in a police station halfway across London when it happened.'

146

'That's why he was so cool about it.'

'Yep.'

'So what are you going to do?'

'Well, he's got a good story to tell, if it's true. He says that Helen was being stalked by some guy who sent her letters, flowers, presents. She told him she'd been followed and that someone tried to get into the flat more than once.'

'Why didn't he take this to the police?'

'The impression I get is that it's no skin off his nose Leon getting nicked for it. I don't think there's much love lost. He was her boyfriend. Know what I mean?'

'Yeah. Yeah.'

I thought about it. The story didn't seem likely somehow. Stalkers picked on movie stars and TV presenters, people like that. On the other hand, it was possible. Nowadays London seemed full of weird, sad men, with doomed eyes and angry voices, and I guessed that the drifters I saw on the tube and in the streets were only the tip of the iceberg. Anything could happen.

'I want you to help us out tomorrow,' Wyndham was saying. He sounded brisk and businesslike, which meant he was exuberant. 'Pick him up in the morning, make sure he's got some breakfast, and bring him to the studio. I want him to feel important. We'll do the interview first thing.'

He gave me the addresses. He didn't mention what kind of deal he'd made with Amaryll. I agreed, and he told me some more about their conversation. Amaryll had a lot to say about Helen. He'd known her for years, before she'd met Leon. She'd been brought up in care and come down to London from Salford when she was sixteen, lived on the streets for a while, did a bit of business round King's Cross, then cleaned herself up and got a job in the box office of a club in Camden, which was where she met Amaryll. She was a nice friendly girl, who loved her kids and couldn't read. She was twenty-four when she died.

By the time he got off the phone it was too late to go out and eat. I thought about ringing Sophie, then put the idea out of my mind. I was in no condition to talk to her, much less see her. Instead, I made myself a sandwich with some three-day-old bread and a bit of greasy cheddar cheese, but when I tasted it I gave up, threw it away and went to bed.

The phone woke me almost immediately, or that's what I thought until I looked at the clock beside the bed and saw that it was half past three. I drew the duvet around my ears and willed the ringing to stop, but it didn't. I fell out of bed, crawled across the floor and picked up the receiver. It was Wyndham.

'Sammy,' he said. 'We're well up shit creek. It's your man, Amaryll. They just rang me. He's in hospital, and he's in a coma.'

15

They had found Amaryll in a street in Neasden. He'd been run over, fracturing his skull, pelvis and one leg. The police had found Wyndham's phone number in his pocket, and rung up at three in the morning.

'What do you want me to do?'

Wyndham gave a peculiar little hoot.

'I don't know. I don't know what I'm going to do myself.'

He broke the connection. I listened to the tone for a couple of seconds, thinking about calling him back, then I gave up the idea and went back to bed.

The day began with a flurry of telephone calls. First my son. Then Sophie, followed by Wyndham again. He apologised for waking me up with the news about Amaryll.

'I might have salvaged something,' he said. 'I picked up his bag from his hotel room when I paid the bill. There was a letter in it that he showed me last night. A threatening letter that Helen received. It doesn't entirely work without him, but it's better than nothing. In any case, we can use the fact that he was ambushed just as he was about to tell all.'

I told him I was impressed at how well he was taking all this, and he swore.

'I've got no choice, have I?'

A little while later I found Sophie sitting on a bench at the top of Primrose Hill. It was a bright sunny morning, but it was still early enough for the dew to be spangling the grass. A few steps off the narrow strip of tarmac were enough to soak the hems of my trouser legs with a dark wet border, and, as I approached her up the hill, I could see the path she'd taken before me marked out in a long narrow lane of shiny green.

I sat down and told her about my trip and what had happened to Amaryll.

'Too much coincidence,' she said.

'I feel like that too, but it could be. The other thing is that he owed people money. Suppose one of them caught up with him?'

'They didn't know he was in London, and I figure he'd keep away from his enemies. They'd have had to spot him by accident, then catch up with a man who is ready to run like a wild dog when a pin drops. And the damage they did is too extreme. If he owed money they might hurt him a little, maybe hurt him a lot, but they would want him alive. They wouldn't just drive at him. There wouldn't be any guarantee that he'd survive to pay what he owed.'

I'd been thinking along the same lines, but it wasn't a comforting idea, because it narrowed the suspects down to the few people who knew he was in London, which, apart from me, meant Wyndham and Joan.

'Maybe it was a gang. Bunch of white kids. See a black man. Right place. Right time. They just run him down.'

'In Neasden?'

I nodded. In Neasden racist hooligans would probably

150

have better luck attacking an angry pit bull than an adult black man. The odds were that if I'd left Amaryll where he was none of this would have happened.

'You don't need this,' Sophie said. 'Leave them to it.'

'I can't,' I told her. 'Not now.'

I was home before noon. Sophie had a meeting at the mosque in Regent's Park and, after I dropped her off there, I couldn't think of anywhere else to go. I had a cup of coffee, fed the pigeons, watched the lunchtime traffic for a while, then I rang Wyndham.

'Who did you tell about Amaryll being back here?'

'Who would I tell? The crew, Joan. That's it. I don't see any of them working Amaryll over. That sounds more like the moneylending bunch, and I told the cops about them. The street where they picked him up was close to their stamping ground anyway.'

'Not really. They hang out in Kilburn.'

'Whatever.' His tone sharpened up. 'What I want you to do is check round the estate. See whether any other women have been followed or threatened. Peeping Toms. Anything like that. The cops make out that nothing special's been reported lately, but even if they're being straight with me, I reckon there's probably a lot of stuff I can use which they didn't record or which they think is too trivial to talk about. Try Jamie's mum. She can put you on to some of the other old bags. They sift every rumour in the place, and they love talking about it.'

He gave me the address and I agreed reluctantly. It wasn't a job I would have taken if he'd offered it in the first place, but in the circumstances I felt bad about telling him to stick it. Besides, I wanted to stay close and see what developed. If nothing else I wanted to be around when Amaryll came out of his coma.

I got out of the flat and drove down to the estate before I could change my mind. Jamie's mum lived on a second-floor flat in the tower facing the one where Helen's blood was still drying on the walls. Jamie opened the door when I knocked. The sullen gormlessness of his face didn't change when he saw me, but he managed to say hello, and I told him I wanted to see his mum.

'What for?'

'Some stuff she might be able to help with. Just tell her I'm here.'

He retreated, and I heard him speaking in a low voice. Then she came out. She wasn't exactly what I'd have described as an old bag, but I had the feeling she would be soon. She was a small woman with an incongruously plump round face, in her late thirties, dark-brown hair chopped short, a tight short black skirt and a tight sleeveless black sweater.

'What you want then?' she asked abruptly.

I told her I worked for Jamie's boss and I wanted to ask her some questions about life on the estate. Her expression lightened up a little. She peered past me in both directions along the corridor, and then she stood aside.

'Come in then.'

Over the next half hour she told me everything she knew about being a single mother on the estate. I kept on steering the conversation round to Peeping Toms, perverts and flashers, and eventually she obliged with a list which seemed to include half the men in the area. The problem was that the behaviour she described seemed about normal for that environment. I'd been waiting for a resonance which would play back the vibration of real obsession, but it never came. There had been one man, an old Jamaican, who roamed about the estate shouting his head off, but a month before the murder he'd jumped off a balcony on the top floor and killed himself. As far as she knew, the police had interviewed all the other known nutcases.

Jamie had left, banging the outer door loudly, halfway through this recital. Being alone in the flat with Sandra made me uneasy. She didn't say or do anything suggestive, but she had a jerky, unstable manner, and there was a touch of neurotic apprehension about the way she pulled her fingers away when she handed me my cup of tea, which made me feel like sitting as far away from her as possible and avoiding any sudden moves. I'd just about made up my mind to leave when she started talking about Helen. She didn't want to speak ill of the dead, she said, but that Helen was a dirty little bitch.

'That kid was never his,' she muttered spitefully.

'What?'

She elaborated. Leon had been inside for more than a year, and the baby was supposed to have been premature. But anyone who could count knew different. She laughed bitterly. No one around had been surprised by what happened.

For the rest of the afternoon I visited three more of Sandra's friends, who told me more or less the same things. By about four o'clock I'd had enough, and what I heard had begun to persuade me that this wasn't an angle that would stand up. At least that was what I told myself on the way home.

Back in the flat the answering machine played me a message from Sarah. She wanted me to call her as soon as I came in.

'I need to see you right now.'

'Why?'

'It's important. I don't want to come to your place. Can we meet somewhere nearby?'

I gave her the name of a Lebanese restaurant off Edgware Road.

'What do you want to talk about?'

'When I see you.'

Another mystery. I was beginning to feel burdened by my own doubts about what I was doing. None of this was any concern of mine, but the whole affair had crept up and wrapped its coils round me before I realised what was happening. Now I was up to my neck in it.

Mr Hamed greeted me like a brother, the way he did with all his regulars. I wasn't exactly a regular, but for several years I'd been dropping in for breakfast, or a late-night kebab, and sometimes, in the middle of the morning when the place was practically empty, we talked about Beirut and how it had been before the wars wiped out his former life. Mr Hamed looked like a middle-aged French professor and sometimes talked like one, but in Beirut he'd practised as an architect and designer, until a mortar shell had dropped into his living room, killing his wife and children in one go. Now he ran a café off the Edgware Road.

He brought a coffee pot and two cups to the table himself. At the next table four Arabs dressed in long striped robes were smoking a hookah. They looked up and nodded as I sat down. I had no idea who they were, but I knew them by sight because they always seemed to be there. Between them the table was choked with food. Glasses of tea, rolls, butter, pitta, humous subtly coloured with red-hot pepper sauce, little triangles of minced lamb wrapped in filo, olives and tomatoes crusted with herbs, pastries lambent with the smell of roses, two fat stuffed aubergines, cut melons decorated with slices of ginger and fresh dates. It looked like a banquet, but

154

it was actually their version of a mid afternoon snack. Later on they would stroll home and re-emerge close to midnight, dressed in European clothes and heading for the casino opposite.

I kicked things around with Mr Hamed for a while. He said he was going to visit Beirut in a couple of months to see whether he could rebuild his house. I said that sounded great, but I kept my eyes averted, because I didn't want him to see that I was thinking about his shattered family. Behind him I saw Sarah pushing at the glass doors. I stood up and recognised Jack Gold coming in with her. He was still wearing the same anorak, but now he had a wispy stubble all over his cheeks to go with the long hair.

Sarah sat down without looking around or greeting me. Mr Hamed smiled, nodded at me and strolled away.

'You know Jack,' she said.

I nodded. Jack sat down, his eyes darting about nervously. He smelled of alcohol and halitosis.

'I asked him to come,' she said, 'so he could tell you himself.'

'Tell me what?'

'Go on, tell him,' she said to Jack.

He gave me an uneasy look as if he wasn't certain of his audience, but he needn't have worried, because once he'd started I was hanging on his every word.

He'd been following Joan the night before, he said, and after she left the office, she'd gone home, then driven straight to the hotel where Amaryll was staying.

'What?'

The information seemed to deserve my astonishment. Sarah smiled nastily at my reaction. I ignored her and focused on Jack. Yes, he replied when I asked him, it was the black Golf he'd been following. Yes, it was the same woman who always drove it. Yes, it was the big hotel off Great Portland Street.

'Did you see her talking to anyone?'

He hesitated.

'No,' he said eventually. 'I waited outside.'

'When she came out, was she with anyone?'

He looked embarrassed.

'I didn't see her come out. I went down the gents. When I came back she was gone.'

I guessed that would have been in the pub next door, and he wouldn't have got back till he'd had a couple of pints. I gazed at him, lost for the moment in wondering whether or not he was telling the truth. Why would he lie? His watery green eyes slid away from mine and skittered round the restaurant.

'I've got to go,' he said to Sarah.

She smiled at him.

'All right. Keep in touch and thank you.'

She was being much more polite than I would have been, under the circumstances, which was a surprise because her usual manner was fairly curt.

'I don't know what to make of that man,' I said.

'Don't you? He kept on about wanting to work, so I thought of him. It wasn't a job that required a PhD.'

'That's fortunate.'

She shrugged, bored with the subject.

'I want you to tell Wyndham about Joan,' she said.

'Tell him what? That she was seen going into the same hotel? Maybe she was just having a drink or meeting someone else. Or she got caught short as she was going past. Come off it.'

She took a deep breath and frowned at me.

'All those things are possible, but it's a hell of a co-incidence. Wouldn't you say?'

156

'All right. If there's something there, why are you asking me? Tell him yourself.' I leaned forward and stared into her eyes. She stared back without blinking. The colour of her eyes seemed to change according to her moods. In the shaded light of the restaurant they were deeper and darker than I remembered, and looking into them, a stray memory hit me. As a child I had lived in a place where everyone I encountered had eyes which were brown or black. Until I came to live in Britain the only creatures I'd seen with eyes of such vivid colour were goats, and, sometimes, meeting the eyes of white people, I seemed to catch a whiff of the goat's fierce indifference.

'I came into this to do a specific job,' I said. 'I wouldn't have taken it if I'd known about all this, and I don't want to get in any deeper. Tell him yourself.'

'I can't very well tell him I've been having Joan followed. I really can't.'

I looked away, because it occurred to me that at any moment she might refer to what had been happening between us and I was shrinking away from the thought that she might use it to twist my arm.

'There's a very delicate balance in my relationship with Wyndham,' she said carefully. 'I don't want to disturb it. I suppose I will if I think I have to, but by the time that becomes apparent it might be too late. Whatever that bitch is planning would have happened. Don't do it for me. Do it for him.'

I rang Wyndham from the flat. It was gone six and I was hoping that he'd have left the office, but he answered immediately. I told him I wanted to see him and after a bit of hemming and hawing we arranged to meet at a pub near Camden Town. When I put the phone down I had just over an hour, which was enough time for what I had in mind.

I dressed carefully in a white shirt, a grey tie with blue diamonds, black shoes and the navy-blue pinstripe I kept for ceremonial occasions. The ensemble felt uncomfortable, but my plan required me to claim white-collar status, and a black man who was doing that, I thought, had better be wearing one.

I drove across Marylebone High Street, round the back of Broadcasting House, and pulled up in the small car park beside the hotel. It was a huge concrete oblong, with none of the kitsch style of the posher hotels in the area, like the Langham. In this place the lobby had the affluent anonymity of an airport lounge, but it was easy to imagine coachloads of tourists and Oriental businessmen pulling in for the night.

I crossed over to the reception desk, where a stocky man wearing a blazer with brass buttons, and a toothbrush moustache, was fiddling with a computer. I said good evening and asked to see the manager.

'I'm sorry, he's left for the day. Can I help?'

He didn't know what to make of me, and his tone was cautiously polite.

'Insurance,' I told him crisply.

I put the card down on the shiny metal surface with a snap. The copperplate script on it announced that George Hayman was an agent and financial consultant to a reputable firm. The man with the brass buttons picked it up and studied it intently. It was clean and new, and I hoped it was convincing. The way I'd got it was to be unwary enough to stop in Oxford Circus for a girl with beautiful legs and a cheeky smile, who said she was doing a survey. She'd taken my address and for the next six months I received a pile of junk mail every week. George Hayman had turned up in person and slipped his card through the letter box after I'd slammed the door behind him.

'We're fully covered,' Brass Buttons said.

I gave him a look which I hoped expressed dignified disdain.

'I'm an investigator,' I told him, 'not a salesman. I'm checking on some details about one of your guests from last night. Mr Amaryll Johnson. He suffered a serious accident.'

He was quick off the mark.

'We've got no liability. It didn't happen here. He was miles away.'

I grinned at him.

'I know you're not liable. This doesn't concern you. We're looking at a claim, and I just want to check a few facts you might be able to help me with. It's a formality. I talked to head office and they said you'd be glad to help.'

I flipped open the notebook I was carrying and went on without giving him a chance to interject.

'I've got a statement here from a Ms Foster who says that she was here last night to visit Mr Johnson, at which point he was fit and healthy. You can confirm that?'

'Yes. He did have a visitor before he went out. I think the name was Foster. Very possibly. They had a drink in the bar. He signed for it.'

I made a few marks in the notebook.

'Did they leave together?'

'No. She left after half an hour, and he went back to his room. I didn't see him go out.'

'Good. Good,' I muttered.

I snapped the book shut, thanked him and left before it occurred to him to ring someone and check up on me. I had what I wanted, which was evidence that Jack was telling the truth. Even so, I couldn't believe that Joan was involved in the accident which had happened to Amaryll. There had to be some explanation, and Wyndham was the man to winkle it out.

He was waiting for me in a pub near the canal. I could hear the music from outside, but when I pushed the door open and went in I was almost deafened by the sheer volume of the sound. Most of it was coming from the far corner, where I guessed the band was, hidden behind the sweating press of bodies. The music was some kind of Irish folk song, a twanging blare of violins and guitars vying with the clamorous shrilling of the singers. Adding to the tumult was the noise of several dozen people conducting conversations at the top of their voices.

Wyndham was leaning against the bar, bellowing at a woman next to him. I fought my way through the four feet between us and shouted his name, and when he turned round, I pointed to the door, and pushed my way back out of it. Outside, I sat at one of the tables ranged along the pavement. About a minute passed before Wyndham came out. He was carrying two pint glasses of Guinness.

'Bloody hell,' I said. 'Next time find somewhere with a bit of life.'

He grinned.

'There's a couple of guys in the band who were up at Oxford with me.'

I'd caught a glimpse of them on my way out. They had a hairy, shaggy, and reckless air, like men who'd spent too many nights round a campfire near Waterloo.

'They look like something out of *Ulysses*.'

'They are in a way. First time I met them they were

160

wearing tweed jackets and ties. One of them was studying to be a priest. Then they started reading.'

'I should have guessed.'

'Come off it,' he said airily. 'I love all this ethnic stuff. Even if most of it is bullshit.' He took a long pull on his Guinness and banged the glass down on the table. 'It's what London's all about.'

'It's great if you're one of the gang,' I told him. 'If you're not it's usually boring, and sometimes it's dangerous.'

He looked at me intently.

'You seem more than usually miserable tonight.'

'I'm surprised to find you so uppish. That's all.'

He laughed.

'I saw Nick and Vanessa today. You're not going to believe this, but they like the angle about Helen being threatened and stalked. Love it. I didn't get a chance to tell you, but over the last two years there's been three or maybe four unsolved cases in the area which are roughly similar. You're talking serial killer. We can't go too hard on that because it would be irresponsible, but the suggestion is enough. If we can find a few women to stand up and talk about the atmosphere of fear on the estate, we're home and dry. That's where you come in. Find me some sensational stuff.'

'Oh shit.'

'Come on, Sammy. I know they're assholes, but this is a way out. Once we've got the pilot done and they've commissioned the series we're in business, and then we can make some decent films.'

I didn't bother to remind him that most of the junk we both despised started in this sort of compromise, because he already knew that.

'Is there any evidence to link all these things?'

'Depends on what you mean by evidence.'

I could guess what that meant, and I also guessed that arguing about it would be a waste of time.

'I've got something to tell you,' I said.

I told him about Joan going to see Amaryll at his hotel. His face got longer and longer as he listened. He drained his glass and drummed his fingers on the table, and when I'd finished he looked away from me, over at the line of street lamps along the canal. I looked at the beak of his profile and waited. In the pub the band stopped and started up again.

'What are you telling me?'

'I don't have the first idea,' I said. 'But whatever it is I thought you should know about it.'

'All right.' He slapped his hand on the table, dismissing the subject. 'I'll talk to Joan.'

I nodded, and told him that I had to go. He didn't try to dissuade me, and when I walked over to the car he was still sitting there, the empty glass forgotten in front of him, gazing raptly into space.

16

The big table in Sophie's studio was strewn with bits of camera, sheets of black and white paper, packets of film, and strips of pictures in various stages of completion. She sat at one end of it with her feet propped up on the corner, studying the pages of an old atlas she'd bought in the market.

I lay back in the armchair gazing out through the glass ceiling and told her what I'd found out about Joan and what Wyndham's reaction had been. I left out Sarah's involvement. I wasn't sure how much I could tell her without getting into trouble.

'What do you know about this Joan?'

She pronounced the name hesitantly. Curiously, she still had difficulty with minor words. She had spoken English early, and she was fluent in the language even before she came to Britain, but certain sounds escaped her.

'Joan?'

I told her how we'd met.

'What I don't understand,' she said, 'is the reason why you find it so difficult to believe that she could do this. Is it because she's so respectable or something?'

I considered the question.

'It's not that so much. It's like life goes on in different compartments. Somebody you know does something that doesn't happen in your box, it's like breaking through a wall. It makes everything unsafe, so you'd rather not believe it.'

She put her atlas down on the table and looked over at me.

'If this thing of walls was true, you wouldn't be here in London. I wouldn't have been born in Argentina. There are no walls. It's possible that downstairs there's a man planning to kill his wife or a stranger. Anything can happen.'

'Usually it doesn't,' I told her. 'Usually people do more or less what you expect.'

She picked the atlas up and began turning the pages again.

'Maybe.'

I was feeling the slow burn of irritation she could bring out in me, as if at the flick of a switch, and I had the sense that we were at the beginning of a serious argument, the kind which might end in shouting and tears.

'All right,' I told her. 'Anything can happen, but there's usually some kind of history.'

'I'm going to bed,' she said.

'Now?'

I looked at the clock on the table. It wasn't yet nine o'clock. In other circumstances her announcement would have been an invitation, but this time I could tell that it was a signal for me to leave. For a moment I wondered whether she could sense what I was doing with Sarah. Then I remembered she'd been out on the hill at dawn that morning.

'I have to be up early,' she said, 'before the sun.'

*

164

I got back home in an irritable and frustrated mood. I'd been hoping that talking things over with Sophie would help me decide what to do, but our conversation had left me feeling isolated and uncertain. Perhaps I was trying to prove her wrong when I picked up the phone, and perhaps it was the sense of being dismissed by Wyndham which made me dial Gerry Turnbull's number. When I'd bumped into him a few months before, outside the big swing doors at Broadcasting House, he'd given me his card and urged me to ring him any time. I wasn't certain about whether or not he was being sincere, but I reckoned that he could hardly complain if I were to take advantage of his invitation.

The phone rang for a while and I was just about to give up when he answered. He sounded surprised and pleased when he recognised my voice, which gave me a lift. I'd always liked him, but I reined in my euphoria because a well-worn cynicism told me that this sort of response was part of his stock in trade.

Gerry was actually a minor legend among the independent producers. Right at the beginning, while Channel 4 was still a legislative nightmare, Gerry had resigned from a secure job as a BBC producer, mortgaged his house and borrowed as much as he could in order to start his own production house. Six years later he was a millionaire with a large slice of shares in one of the major network companies. I'd worked for him on and off for years before that and we'd got on well enough, although the higher he climbed the more difficult it was to meet as friends, and after a while it was impossible to pretend to social equality with someone who'd turned into one of the big bosses.

I wound him up a bit about how rich he'd become, and he lied about how hard he had to work, and after a while I asked him about Joan.

'I know she worked for you when she started,' I said. 'What did you think of her?'

His tone took on a note of caution.

'Why are you asking?'

'Seems she applied for a job,' I said. 'And someone rang me asking about her. The thing is, I know her, but I don't actually know her, if you see what I mean. I said I'd ask you.'

'I can't say I know her all that well.' I guessed this was a stock answer. 'I don't know much more than you do. Why don't you try Joss?'

'Joss Spring? The cameraman?'

'Yeah. Is he still around?'

'I saw him a few days ago.'

That prompted an enquiry about how Joss was keeping, and then we got on to some more people we both knew and it was a little while before I could bring the conversation back to what I was interested in.

'How come Joss knows so much about Joan?'

'They come from the same place. Norwich? Somewhere like that?'

Joss Spring's telephone was engaged, and after I tried dialling the number a couple of times I lost patience, and slammed out of the flat. It was less than fifteen minutes away by car to where Joss lived, and I guessed that I'd probably have more luck talking to him in person. I drove through gentrified Notting Hill, and through the fringe of expensive real estate separating it from Ladbroke Grove. The house was on the other side of Ladbroke Road, a few yards from where a tract of council property began. Opposite was a breaker's yard from which a succession of rusting vehicles came and went, belching bluish grey plumes of lead and carbon monoxide.

166

I rang the doorbell, but no one answered. Somewhere above me I could hear voices raised, so I tried again. Suddenly the door opened to reveal a boy with a tight crew cut, a voluminous plaid shirt and a mobile phone pressed to his ear. This had to be Eddie, the stepson. When Joss married Prue, Eddie had been safely tucked away at a boarding school in Berkshire. Since then he'd been expelled from two of these establishments, returning home to wage what Joss described as a 'terrorist campaign'. Eventually they'd given up the struggle and sent him to a crammer in Notting Hill, which he attended when he wasn't shattered from spending the night in one of the local clubs.

Eddie eyed me with all the sullen contempt of his sixteen years, and spoke without lowering the phone.

'Who do you want? Joss or the slapper?'

In the back of my head I rejoiced that he wasn't mine. 'Joss.'

He retreated a few steps into the hallway and yelled. Then he turned and brushed past me on the way out, the phone still clamped to his ear. I stayed where I was, and in a little while Joss came clattering down the stairs.

'I was passing,' I told him, 'and I wondered if you fancied a drink?'

'Good idea,' he said. 'Let's go.'

We walked down Ladbroke Road towards the nearest pub, and I asked him how Eddie was doing.

'Usual teenage monster shit. Prue thinks he's selling E. But I reckon the mobile phone is just for show. Impresses his mates and his therapist. What he really needs is a good kicking.'

I kept my thoughts to myself. I'd seen enough of the breed to know that in ten years' time the boy could wind up breaking their hearts. Alternatively he could have blossomed into a millionaire entrepreneur, a politician or media superstar. Half the young high flyers I met seemed to have emerged from the same stable as Eddie. Gifted with a rock-hard core of reptilian self-interest, their highest sentiment seemed to be ambition, and, just as if they'd been grafted with some batrachian gene, they always learnt just enough about the world to take them straight to the wet spot of their dreams.

We sat in a corner of the pub, surrounded by its curiously mixed clientele. Clumps of black dreadlocks, rubbing shoulders with grungy white kids dressed in half-conscious imitation. Between them a sprinkling of whites in smart office clothes who looked as if they were out slumming for the night.

Joss had been telling me about Eddie's exams and his battles to ensure that he read a book occasionally, so we were into the second pint before I got the chance to drop Joan's name into the conversation.

'Purely as a digression,' I said, 'I hear that you and Joan both come from Norwich.'

He was thrown for a moment.

'Yeah. That's right.'

'Did you know her there?'

'I didn't,' he said. 'For a start it's not like a village. Secondly, I grew up in a village outside Norwich. And thirdly, I'm at least ten years older. I was probably at UEA by the time she had her first day at school.' He took a pull at his beer and gave me a sly look. 'Why? Do you fancy her?'

'Dunno. She's fit.'

Joss made a disgusted sound.

'You'd be better off sticking your dick in a vacuum cleaner, mate. She's poison, and Wyndham's shagging her anyway.'

Up to then I hadn't been absolutely certain, but if anyone knew it would be Joss. Production teams became like little families with no chance of real privacy. Usually they kept their mouths shut about whatever was going on, but after a long hard day, gossiping about each other was one of the perks, and I was, in a manner of speaking, one of the family.

'I thought he was shagging the sister.'

'He's doing that too.'

'What?'

'Yeah. Fastest gun in our end of town, old Wyndham. What can I tell you? They're weird, the lot of them.'

'Do they both know?'

'Dunno about that. Probably. They've been into that since they were kids, those two.'

'I thought you never knew them in Norwich.'

'My brother went to the same school for a while. So I knew about them. They were famous for being weird. They weren't twins, Joan's a year and a bit older, but they looked alike, dressed alike, talked alike. They were always together, made out they could read each other's minds. That kind of bollocks.'

'Yeah. Yeah. What else?'

Joss shot an ironic look, eyebrows raised, and I realised that he thought I was getting a perverted kick out of the story. In that instant I had the urge to tell him that I had different reasons for asking, then I thought better of it.

'Well, this friend of my brother, kid named Colin, chatted Joan up, and went round her house one night. Her mother was a widow or a single mother, something like that, and she was out a lot, so they could have kids round. Colin reckoned she was a bit of a scrubber, but twenty years ago any mum in her thirties who wore lipstick and high heels was reckoned to be a scrubber. Know what I mean?'

I knew what he meant.

'So Colin does the business. Very nice. Then up pops Caroline and says he's got to do her too or she'll tell. Poor sod thought he was going for a ride and ended up running the marathon.'

He choked with laughter.

'So what happened?'

'That's the interesting bit. He started getting earache from his mum about it, or their mum, I can't remember, or he just got fed up. Anyway, he started going off with another girl. So these two charmers hired themselves three of the biggest thickos they could find in the rugby team.'

'Hired?'

'According to legend their payment was a wank-off in a nearby bus shelter. But whatever they did had the desired result. These three guys got hold of Colin and gave him a real going-over. Black eyes, missing teeth, the lot. They called it a playground fight, but he was off sick for a week.'

He eyed me thoughtfully.

'Those are bad girls. Know what I mean?'

'Kids' stuff,' I told him. 'They must have been, what, fifteen and fourteen? Kids do cruel things and grow out of it.'

That was precisely what he'd been saying about Eddie.

'Maybe,' he said. 'But I think they got into some kind of trouble later on.'

'What kind of trouble?'

'No idea. It was just some rumour.'

'Would your brother know?'

'He's in New Guinea. On a field trip.' I'd forgotten. His

brother was some kind of botanist. 'I'll ask him when he gets back if you like.'

It would be too late by then.

'Nah. Forget it. I was just curious.'

He gave me a smile which said that he didn't believe me. So I got him another pint and changed the subject.

It was close to midnight when I got back home. I lay on the sofa thinking through what Joss had told me and trying to weave it into the events of the previous week, but it didn't fit in anywhere. Eventually I went to sleep and had a dream in which I was rolling on the floor of Wyndham's office with Joan. Wyndham came in waving a machete, whacked it on the table and I woke up sweating and scared.

I got up, made a cup of tea to calm myself down and picked a video cassette from the top of the pile, which turned out to be a Rodgers and Hammerstein musical. In a little while the garish colours and strange expressions on the actors' faces began to seem like a clutch of flickering hallucinogenic visions drifting around inside my head, and before I knew it I was fast asleep, dreaming of technicoloured birds streaking through a sky of impossible blue.

When the phone woke me the sun was glinting off the rooftops, and the rush-hour traffic was crashing and grinding past in the street outside. I'd woken up to hear the pigeons fighting over the remnants of the previous night's crumbs, but then I'd gone back to sleep.

When I picked up the phone it was Katrina.

'Hope it's not too early for you,' she said, 'Wyndham wants you as soon as you can make it.'

17

I got to Camden Town round about ten o'clock. I gave Katrina a big hello, but she responded with a quiet smile, and pointed up the stairs to where I presumed Wyndham was waiting. In his office he was sitting in his swivel chair looking out of the window. Joan was sitting bolt upright at one corner of his desk, and it was obvious that they were waiting for me.

'Hey, have a seat,' Wyndham said, swivelling round towards me.

The casual tone didn't fool me. By now I knew for certain that something was up. I sat down and took the bull by the horns.

'What's up?'

I'll give him credit. Wyndham didn't fool around.

'You've been going around asking questions about Joan's background. What's that all about?'

I kept my eyes on him but I could just see Joan in my peripheral vision. Her face was white and set hard, her eyes moist and angry. Inwardly, I cursed Wyndham for putting me in this situation. At the same time I knew that I'd asked for it, which only made things worse.

'I told you last night.' I looked straight at him, but there was something hidden, almost furtive, about his expression. 'What I wanted to know was how come she managed to turn up at Amaryll's hotel.'

'It's none of your business,' Wyndham said. He sounded angry now. 'And anyway, I said I'd ask her.'

'Did you?'

'Yes, I did.' He gave me a sarky smile. 'And there's a good explanation.' He looked at her for the first time. 'Tell him.'

'I don't owe him any explanations,' Joan said. 'And I don't actually want to speak to him.'

'I want him to know,' Wyndham told her. Then his voice took on a note of real impatience. 'Just tell him, for Christ's sake.'

'I got a phone call,' Joan said. 'From someone who said he was Amaryll Johnson, and asked me to come to the hotel.'

'It was Sunday,' I interrupted. Joan came out with what sounded like a gasp of rage.

'We've got mobiles,' Wyndham broke in quickly. 'The numbers are on the answerphone.'

When Joan started again there was an undertone of triumph in her voice, as if she'd been vindicated by my mistake.

'I asked him why he'd called me, and he said he'd talked to Wyndham, but he wanted a second opinion before he did the interview, and he didn't trust you.' She gave this last statement a vicious bite, and she stared at me with an angry sneer before continuing. 'When I got to the hotel, he denied ringing me, but we had a conversation. He told me about the threats Helen had received, and we discussed the interview. Then I left.'

She stopped speaking and turned her face away from me. She didn't look at me again. I shrugged.

173

'OK. But all that sounds like yet another mysterious coincidence. It's getting ridiculous.'

'That's not the point,' Wyndham said. 'The point is I want you to pack it all in. We'll pay you for what you've done, but in any case we need to wind this up and we don't need you any more.'

For the last few days I'd been thinking about packing it in on my own account, but hearing him say it was a shock. Above all it was humiliating to be sacked from a petty job like this, by a man I'd known for so many years.

'If that's how you want it,' I said.

'No hard feelings.' Now it was all over he avoided my eyes. 'We're still mates.'

It wasn't until I was out of the office and back in the car that the rage I felt began coming to the surface. I stopped at Primrose Hill and knocked on Sophie's door but there was no answer, and I drove back up past the Lords round-about banging on the horn and accelerating recklessly to overtake any vehicle that got in front of me. By the time I got back to the flat I had calmed down a little. There was a message on the machine from Sarah, asking me to ring her, but I ignored it. She'd got me into this, and if I talked to her now I'd probably say things I'd regret.

Underneath the boiling heat of my mood I kept thinking about Joan and about what she was concealing. Either Turnbull or Joss must have mentioned that I'd asked about her, but my guess was that they'd have done it in a fairly casual style. In any case, I hadn't said anything which could account for the fury I'd seen in her eyes.

I rang Joss. Prue picked up the phone and said he was shooting exteriors on the estate. She gave me the number of his mobile and he answered immediately. I asked him whether he'd seen Joan that morning and he said he had.

He'd also told her that we'd met and talked about her the night before.

'What did you tell her?'

'Nothing special. I said we talked about Norwich. That's it.'

'Did she seem pissed off?'

'Don't know why she should be. But it's hard to tell with her.'

When I put the phone down I'd made a guess which was evolving into certainty. Joan had overreacted, and she'd done so because she was terrified at the mere idea that I might find out something about her life in Norwich. I couldn't figure out what the link with Wyndham's project might be, but the more I thought about it, the more convinced I was that there was some connection.

I forced myself out of the house and, before I could change my mind, I started threading my way through the traffic up to north London. It was now the middle of the day but the motorway was quiet and uncluttered.

When I got off it and took the A road past Newmarket the traffic had melted and I found myself motoring through a thick, silent wood, where the trees arched over the road, staining the sunshine a cool twilight green.

In the afternoon sun Norwich seemed sleepy and languid. I found the library, but it had been ravaged by fire, so the receptionist redirected me to the building where the newspaper collection was being held. It was nearly another hour before I settled down with the creaky machinery of the microfiche. I started going through the local paper from six years ago. Joan was in her late twenties and I guessed that she wouldn't be too concerned about anything that had happened much earlier, before she went off to college.

It was well into the evening and the library was about to close before I found what I was looking for, and then I nearly missed it because the news item was about Caroline rather than Joan. It was front-page news in the local paper under the headline 'BURNING LOVE'; accompanying the article was a smudgy photo of Caroline and another one of a man with a short haircut and a handlebar moustache.

I took in the story with a feeling of increasing tension. It ran to about a thousand words, which was excessive for the newspaper, but the length was probably symbolic of the excitement it caused in the town. The gist of it was that Caroline Foster '(19)' had pleaded guilty to attempted arson on the home of a local polytechnic lecturer, Simon Priestley '(42)'.

The rest of the article went into some detail about the background to the crime. The two had been lovers, but Priestley had tried to give up the relationship, and subsequently been harassed by Foster, who had written to him, followed him all over the town, scrawled graffiti on his walls, damaged his car, threatened his wife in a series of abusive phone calls, and finally tried to burn his house down. She'd been remanded in custody for psychiatric reports.

I scanned a few more papers to see what happened next, but there were no more references to the story, or at least I couldn't find any. By then the characters on the screen were dancing in front of my eyes, and I'd developed a raging headache. In any case, the library was about to close, so I switched off the machine and walked out.

I sat in the car wondering what to do next. I now knew more about Caroline but it didn't seem to help me with working out what had been going on. On the other hand, there were a number of familiar elements here. Stalking, sex and violence mixed up and reacting explosively. It was all too much of a coincidence for it to be completely unconnected.

I drove around trying to decide whether to stay or go. My instincts told me that there was some kind of answer here, but I had no idea how to get at it.

Eventually I found myself driving past the cathedral for the second time, so I stopped, parked, and found my way into a maze of gravel paths, bordered by tall green hedges and banks of flowers. The sun was slanting into the horizon, and the light which strayed into the close had a clean, shiny transparency about it. Somewhere out of sight someone was playing a piano. Satie. I sat on a bench, propped my face in my hands, and listened, letting the sound steal into my open head. When I heard the voice I didn't realise he was speaking to me, until he'd repeated himself a couple of times.

'Are you all right? Are you all right?'

I looked up and saw a grey-haired man in a dark-grey suit and a purple shirt watching me from a couple of paces away. To judge by the concern on his face, he must have taken the way I was sitting for a posture of despair. Perhaps, I thought at the time, he wouldn't have spoken to me if I'd been white, but black people were rare enough in these parts to be the subject of curiosity, and for a nice, liberal, ecclesiastical gent like this one, seeing me in that spot, my head bent and my hands clasped together, must have seemed like his big chance to do good.

The funny thing was that he had no way of knowing that his sudden appearance had struck me as an omen. This was something that, later on, I found hard to explain even to myself. If anyone had asked me I'd have said I was an atheist, but like any halfway respectable Caribbean

177

kid, my early years had been imbued with an almost superstitious reverence for the Church and the clergy. It was hard to shake it off, and in moments like this, when I felt that my back was against some kind of wall, I sometimes came within a whisker of praying for a miracle.

'I'm kind of in despair,' I told him.

I hadn't meant to say this. It just came out. A curious spasm rippled over his face, like a fast cloud going across the moon, then he looked at his watch. He actually looked at his watch. Then he pulled himself together and sat down next to me.

'Can you tell me about it?'

'If you've got five minutes,' I said.

He laughed, a touch uneasily, I thought.

'Yes. I've got five minutes.'

The piano stopped and a choir of boys' voices started singing something from Brahms. They stopped and started repeatedly, but it was a sweet sound.

'I'm a reporter, sort of, and I'm working on a story which is complicated and ambiguous. They've just sacked me, because I started checking on one of my bosses. I came up here to pursue the background of the woman who got me the sack, because I think it's probably the clue to what's been happening. The thing is I don't know whether I'm doing this for revenge, or because I'm obsessed, or because I can't think of anything else to do, or because I'm in selfless pursuit of the truth.'

He made an embarrassed sound, and the look on his face said that he wished he'd taken the Pharisaic option and passed by on the other side.

I reached into my pocket and showed him my ID.

'Don't worry, I'm not going to grab your wallet.'

'I didn't think that for an instant,' he said gently.

'You were going to ask me what is the truth,' I went

on. 'The thing is, I don't have the first idea. A number of things have happened which you could call crimes. Anybody could call them crimes. People have got hurt, and I've got a feeling that if I don't solve the puzzle more people are going to get hurt. But there's something about it I can't work out. Why me? It's really none of my business, you know, and similar things will happen next week and the week after. Does my interest, my fixation, mean I'm obsessed with scumbags and violence and vicious motives?'

'It doesn't have to mean that,' he said. 'Doctors and nurses and ambulance men cope with dilemmas like this every day. I think you ought to ask yourself why all this is giving you so much trouble.'

'You put your finger right on it,' I said. 'I was born in a place where the problems I'm looking at would seem like a luxury. You get sick with anything serious, you probably die. Dog bites you, you get rabies. Brush against a guy with sores and you wind up with leprosy. You see a kid with a fat belly, it means he's on the verge of starvation. People walking around with legs like big round hoops because they grew up malnourished. Happiness is getting enough to eat, or not being killed because you got in someone's way or had the wrong political opinions, or lived in a village where they decided one night to get rid of your kind.' I was exaggerating, but only a bit, and I figured he would know. 'I look at the TV and every night I see people exactly like me, except I live here and they live there, and they're starving, tortured, their kids are taken away or have disappeared. I see babies who could be me, or my own child in the last stages of desperation, breathing their last, and then I go out and deal with some asshole whose idea of distress is marital infidelity or not having a new car every year. Sometimes my life here gives me the sense that I'm in some kind of parallel universe, an almighty joke world, a glass bubble full of self-indulgent greedy toddlers, spilling their food on the floor and smashing each other's heads in so they can grab some toy they'll abandon after a minute. The thing is, life is more serious than this and I'm too good for this. That's what I think sometimes.'

'It seems to me,' he said, 'that you should do something else. Don't underestimate the power of prayer.'

The words were so predictable that I had to stifle the urge to laugh. That's what priests were for, I told myself, and suddenly I caught a picture of myself from the outside, sitting in the dark on a bench outside a church, pouring my soul out to a strange white man who probably thought I was nuts. What could he do except utter the sort of priestly cliché he turned out a hundred times a day? If I'd had any sense, I told myself, I would have been talking to Caroline's victim or boyfriend, or whatever he was.

'Simon Priestley,' I said aloud.

'What?'

He was giving me that look again, as if he was about to start shuffling away.

'You've solved one bit of the problem for me,' I told him.

We shook hands and I made a quick getaway before he could invite me into the church. Spurred on by my moment of revelation in the cathedral grounds, I checked into a hotel near the station, ate a bland and watery meal at a nearby Chinese restaurant, then went to bed.

I spent most of the next morning trying to locate Simon Priestley. The problem was that the polytechnic didn't exist any more, and its departments had all been merged with one university or the other, but eventually I found the faculty where Priestley taught. It was less than half an hour away from my hotel. The switchboard put me through to Dr Priestley's extension, and when there was no answer, rerouted me to the faculty secretary who said that he was teaching now, but he'd be free later. I said I represented a publisher and made an appointment for half past twelve.

The college building had a utilitarian look about it, the style and decor hovering somewhere between a government office and a secondary school. At that hour the corridors were dotted with students coming and going. Automatically, I looked about for the black students, but all I saw on my way to the fifth floor were two Africans and a small knot of Asian girls. This was no surprise. The student population had grown enormously in the last few years, but blacks and Asian students were mostly confined to the poorest universities in the inner cities.

I knocked on the door which announced – DR PRIESTLEY & MR CLARKE. Inside it was about the size of a small classroom, lined with books. There were two desks at opposite corners, and Priestley was standing behind the one at the far end. A puzzled expression crossed his face when he saw me, then he smiled and stuck his hand out. The gesture had a kind of elegance which went with his looks and which had nothing in common with the smudgy newspaper photograph I'd seen. His hair was black, with a streak going white in the front, and he had a thin, poetic sort of face, which gave him a sensitive, quizzical air. He was dressed in a dark suit with a white shirt open at the collar, and altogether the image he presented was nothing like the tweedy teacher I had imagined.

I shook his hand and told him my name, then I told him there'd been a slight misunderstanding because I didn't come from a publisher. He frowned, and I noticed that the corners of his eyes crinkled when his forehead creased up. It looked cute.

'In that case who are you?' he asked.

I told him I was a journalist and I'd come to talk to him about Caroline Foster, but as soon as I mentioned her name he stood up abruptly.

'Fuck off,' he said angrily. 'Just fuck off out of here.'

I stayed where I was. He was tall enough, but he had thin slack limbs and narrow shoulders. If he wanted me out he'd have to call the security staff.

'You don't have to lose your temper,' I said reproachfully, 'I didn't come to threaten you, or abuse you, and this isn't about anything which could be printed or broadcast. Your name doesn't come into it, anyway. All I want is some information about what she did to you.'

'But I don't want to talk about it.'

'Talking to me can stop people being harmed, and maybe it can stop Caroline destroying herself. I don't think you need to worry any more. She's probably moved on to another obsession, and the odds are that she won't bother you again. I don't care how it started or how it went on and I don't have any moral judgements to make. All I want to know is what she did and what happened to her and why. If you talk to me maybe I can stop something much, much worse happening to someone else.'

He stood stock-still for a few seconds, glaring at me, then he sat down and leaned back in his chair.

'Is she stalking you now?'

'Not me. The thing is that I work for the same company as her sister, Joan, and some things are happening which I suspect are connected to Caroline and her problems. I need to know more.'

He took a deep breath and let it out again noisily.

182

'I can't tell you much.' He pursed his lips and moved them around as if he was trying to get rid of a nasty taste. 'I had a relationship with her and when I broke it off she harassed me, endangered my family, and ruined my career. I would probably have been head of this faculty now. Instead, I'm a part-time lecturer. What else do you want to know?'

Actually, I wasn't sure.

'Do you think she'd kill someone?'

'*Kill*?'

The question seemed to startle him, which was odd, given what he'd just said about her. 'I suppose so. When I knew her she was out of control.' He gestured. 'It's a sort of illness. They refashion the world in the terms of their own longings. Tell them to piss off and they take it as a code for I love you. She tried to burn down my house because she imagined that if she got rid of my family we'd go away together and live happily ever after. Yes. She'd probably kill someone to get her way.'

'What did they do with her?'

'She went to a psychiatric hospital. She had other problems. When she got out I didn't hear anything for a couple of months, then it started again. She used to hang around the car park outside, and follow me. I'd moved, of course, and I had to spend hours every day shaking her off, before I could go home. Then she trashed my car with a sledge-hammer and turned up in one of the lecture rooms, screaming and shouting. She went away that time for much longer. When they released her she went to live in some sort of group home in London. She wrote to me several times a week for over a year. Then suddenly the letters stopped. I've been waiting for the other shoe to drop.'

'What kind of relationship did she have with her sister?'

'The sister?' He considered for a few seconds.

There was a knock on the door, then it opened and a tall girl with long fair hair and a pretty smile stuck her head in.

'Shall I wait, Simon?'

He gave her a stern look, and his eyes flicked sideways at me. I kept my face straight.

'I'll be a couple of minutes,' he said. The door closed. Outside I could hear people shuffling and muttering.

'I'm due to do some tutorials now,' he said, 'Is there anything else?'

'Her sister, Joan.'

'Oh yes. They had a peculiar relationship. She was dependent. She talked about Joan all the time. She was at Sussex and Caroline wanted to go there and live in Brighton. At one point she suggested going there for the weekend. She said her sister wanted to go to bed with me, and she wanted me to. She asked me more than once.'

He stood up, and came round from behind the desk, a signal that he'd had enough.

'By the way, Doc,' I said, 'what part of London was this group home?'

He sighed impatiently.

'Wait a minute. I've got the address somewhere.'

He turned back to the desk, opened a drawer and scrabbled in it. Then he produced an envelope which he handed to me. I turned it over and saw an address in west London. Neasden.

18

It was late in the afternoon by the time I got back to London. I didn't know much more about what was going on, except the fact that Joan's sister Caroline was obsessive and dangerous, but I felt as if I was going somewhere rather than simply stumbling around in the dark. When I thought about it, I had to admit that I had no idea where this piece of information led, but I still felt better about it all.

There were the usual messages on the answerphone. The last two on the tape were from Nick's office. He wanted to see me right away, a woman's voice told me. I guessed this was Sandy, his secretary. Both Nick and Vanessa were now too important to deliver their own messages. I rang the number she'd given me, and said I wanted to talk to Nick. She said he was in a meeting and she would tell him I rang. I gave her my name.

'Wait a minute,' she said quickly, 'he told me to interrupt him if you rang.'

A few seconds passed before Nick came on the line. His voice had a harassed, grumbling sound. He wanted to see me. Urgently.

'I don't know if I can help,' I replied. 'I'm not working on the project any more.'

'I know all about that. I still want to see you. When can you make it?'

I said I'd be there in the next half hour and put the phone down. I couldn't begin to guess what Nick wanted, but I had the feeling that whatever it was would fit in with my sense that the riddle was beginning to unravel.

Sandy was wearing a long baggy sweater this time, above a skirt which was so short as to be almost invisible, and I kept my gaze studiously above her waist. She smiled at me, showed me into Nick's presence, asked me whether I wanted tea or coffee, and when I said I didn't, she told him she was going home.

'Bad news,' Nick said as soon as she closed the door behind her. He reached into the top drawer of his desk, took out a letter and tossed it over to me.

It was written in anonymous type, and it said that Dave had been nowhere near Beulah Hill at the time when he claimed to have seen Leon. Instead he was 'at the dogs'. It was unsigned.

'I haven't shown this to anyone,' Nick said.

'Why are you showing it to me? Ask Wyndham. He can check it out.'

'I'll tell you what the situation is.' He rocked back in his chair, looked at the ceiling, then fixed his eyes on me. 'We've got a slot in a fortnight. Something else has fallen through, and this is an appropriate time to get the pilot on. Events have sort of overtaken me. I have to make some decisions right now. I'm inclined to get it on, because so far I like it. We've got a possible miscarriage of justice. We've got a few murders in the same area at the same time. We've got a couple of women who've had some trouble, and a tame social worker to rabbit on about the threats to women on the estate. We can even cast doubt on some of the forensics. If they cut it right it'll be OK.'

'What happens if you lose Dave?'

'That's the difficult bit. We've found several other white Ford Escorts on the estate which might have been in the relevant area at precisely that time, and even without Dave we can put Leon in south London earlier on that evening. But Dave's the only witness who is spot on and definite about what he saw and the timing. That makes him the most vulnerable. If he actually was somewhere else at exactly that time our whole case looks stupid. If the tabloids come out with a headline two days later which says our major witness was lying, and we know that he was lying, it looks even worse. It's kind of a Zen problem. Our strongest link is also our weakest.'

'So cut the bugger out.'

'That's my first choice, but' – he straightened up and pointed towards the door – 'there's a filing cabinet out there full of letters not unlike this, accusing producers of everything under the sun. Theft, rape, buggery, traffic offences. You name it. Some of it is true, mostly it's irrelevant. Taking action on the basis of an anonymous letter makes me feel like an idiot. If I'm going to ask Wyndham to do anything about it, I'll have to be heavy. They'll think that I'm either attacking their professional competence or their professional integrity, we could get into a confrontation, and to be frank with you, Sammy, I can't afford that at the moment unless I'm absolutely right. So I'd probably ignore this, if it wasn't for the fact that I don't want to risk ending up with being shat on over it. If there's the slightest chance that the guy is lying I want to know.'

'I don't know what I can do.'

187

He gave me a sneaky grin and, in a flash, it took me back to the days when we worked together. Nick used to be the one who organised all the office sweepstakes, plodding through the building with a notebook in hand, popping up in the glittering dark of the editing suite, his nerdish specs gleaming as he peered into corners looking for people to sign up. More often than not he'd have his own bet going on the winner, whether it was a football match or the Derby. In the days when they started showing American football on the telly, he was the only one of us who understood what words like 'spread' meant. A number of us had more of the lust for gambling than he did, but he was the only one who seemed to win more times than he lost.

'You found that other geezer, Sam. Just like that. And I have a suspicion that you know more than you're telling me about all this.' He held his hand up. 'I don't want to know. I just want you to have a go over the next couple of days. If there's no other way, talk to the guy, spring it on him. Make a judgement about whether or not he's lying. Bullshit him about perjury. A lot of people think a statement on camera has some kind of official status. Worst comes to the worst, offer him a few quid to tell you off the record.' He waved his hand. 'I don't have to tell you all this. I'd like to know for certain, but if you can't find out I'll take an educated guess.'

'You'll have to make it worth my while,' I told him. 'I'm not doing it for the daily rate.'

He spread his hands out and gave me a big grin.

'Would I insult you like that?'

Over the next few minutes we wrangled about the payment and the expenses. After a while we came to an agreement, he handed me the letter, I put it in my pocket, told him I would have a go, and then I left.

*

On the way home I began wondering what to do. I didn't think of myself as a talented investigator, but I'd been around long enough to know that you could find out anything if you ask the right people the right questions. In the past I'd worked with people who had an instinct which saved them time. My own technique was to keep on asking around till I got lucky. But there was a sense in which I felt that I'd already got lucky with this one. A few days before, Dave had tipped me off about the Flanagans, and I suspected that his anxiety to keep his name out of it had to be due to the fact that they knew him. If I was right they'd know something about his movements and his associates. If my guess was right, one of them would have been at the dog races right alongside Dave. I didn't know whether they'd tell me, but I also suspected that the old lady would show less compunction about shopping a small-time delinquent like Dave than she would about squashing a fly. If the price was right.

The street outside their house looked much the same, except that they'd added a beaten-up Toyota to the line-up of cars. I knocked on the door, and waited. Standing there I had the creepy feeling that I'd been observed from the moment I entered the close. There was a scurrying behind the door and it opened abruptly. This time there was only one of the brothers, but he blocked the entrance just as effectively.

'What are you after wanting now?'

'Can I speak to your mum, please?'

He stared at me for a moment, as if he was trying to work out whether or not I was being sarcastic, but I kept my face straight, and eventually he turned round and shouted into the hallway.

She waddled out and sat on the stairs, just as she had

the last time, and he let me in, a wet brown sneer splitting the stubble on his face. This time she'd left the children in the back room, and I could hear them banging about, like rats scurrying behind the wall.

I came straight to the point.

'There's something I need to find out.'

She wheezed, coughed and sniffed.

'How much?'

I told her it would depend. She blew her nose on a tissue, examined it carefully, folded it up and wiped her eyes, then put it down beside her.

'Go on then.'

I asked her whether she knew Dave, and the blubbery features writhed into a smile.

'It depends. What do you want him for?'

'I know where he is. This is something different. I want to know whether he was at Wembley on a certain night.'

Wembley was the nearest greyhound stadium in this part of town.

'Wembley?'

'The dogs.'

She started to laugh, then she wheezed, coughed, blew her nose, and wiped her eyes all over again.

'Do you hear that, Terry?' she called out. 'The dogs.' She squinted at me. 'What night?'

I told her.

'Fifty squid.' She held her hand out. 'Now.'

'Too much.'

'Sod off then.'

Her eyes had narrowed to slits. Somewhere deep inside them a couple of blue beads glinted.

I put my hand in my pocket and hesitated.

'How do I know it's worth it?'

She started to laugh, and I braced myself, but she

stopped short. I guessed that she'd remembered what came next.

'You've got no idea. I'll tell you this, you'll never find out otherwise.'

I gave her the money. She put it on the stair carpet beside her and told me to wait outside. I squeezed past Terry and he shut the door in my face. I looked at the picture of the snarling dog, and reflected that a photo of Mrs F. would probably have done just as well. The door opened again.

'Come on,' Terry said, 'you've got a car?'

We drove up Harrow Road towards Wembley. Terry smoked rollups which stank out the car, and gave me monosyllabic directions. When I signalled a right turn into the motorway slip road which led to the stadium, he grunted and told me to go straight on.

'We're not going to Wembley?'

He gave a wet snort.

I took my hand off the wheel and wiped it ostentatiously, which provoked another stutter of laughter.

'Ain't them kind of dogs.'

'What? What do you mean?'

Instead of replying he waved me into a left turn, and we drew up in front of a house on the end of a row. Terry told me to wait and got out. He knocked on the door and when it opened, stood talking for a few minutes to someone I couldn't see. Then the door closed. Terry turned, beckoned to me, and walked along the front of the bow windows to a tall gate which blocked the entrance to a passageway running beside the house.

As we walked along the passage I could hear dogs growling or barking, I wasn't sure which, but it sounded like an insane wet muttering, amplified a hundred times.

In the dying twilight the alleyway was suddenly shadowy and sinister. I stopped.

'What's going on?' I asked Terry.

'We're going to see a man about some dogs,' he said. He gave me that snort again and walked on ahead of me, with an air of being indifferent as to whether or not I followed.

The end of the passage gave out on to what would have been a suburban garden, except for the paraphernalia scattered around. A tangle of dog chains and leathers, a short, knotted whip, a pole cemented into the ground with a couple of ropes dangling from it, like a beaten-up version of a maypole. Along the fence were several cages, faced with steel mesh. Behind them the dogs growled and screamed and threw themselves about, creating a constant background of disturbingly enraged sound.

The man who stood by the cages had black hair, but in every other respect he looked like a clone of Terry's. Badly fitting dark suit, watery blue eyes, barbed-wire stubble.

'So you want to know about Dave,' he said. He had a thick, wet voice.

'It's twenty pound,' Terry said.

I looked around, wondering whether to object. One of the dogs caught my eye, made a sound like a tiny explosion of thunder and threw himself against the steel mesh. Mentally I shrugged. Nick would think it was cheap at the price. I reached into my pocket, felt around, picked out a twenty and gave it to the man.

He folded it into tiny squares and shoved it into his back pocket.

'Sure he was fighting his dog that night. I lost a few quid on it.'

He met my gaze without flinching. I had no way of

telling whether or not I was being conned, but I had the feeling that this was too elaborate. The old lady could have made up a convincing story on the spot and I'd have had to accept it. I couldn't believe that she'd go to this much trouble to achieve the same effect.

'Where was this?'

'You don't want to know that.'

'Was he alone?'

He mulled that over for a few seconds.

'The little darky was with him.'

As soon as he said it I guessed.

'Was his name Amaryll?'

'I wouldn't know his name.'

'Was he light skinned? Mixed?'

'He was that. Only half a black man.'

His eyes flickered at Terry. They were laughing at me. In the circumstances I couldn't blame them. I'd let myself in for it.

'What time was this?'

'About ten to twelve. Coulda been later.'

'Was this anywhere near Beulah Hill?'

He stared at me in surprise.

'Beulah Hill? You're barking up the wrong tree there, Paddy. It was this side of the river.'

I dropped Terry off on the estate and drove on towards Lords thinking about how to handle what I'd learned. I knew what to tell Nick, that was simple enough. As far as I could tell his bet was to make sure that Dave's testimony was abandoned. On the other hand, I had a nagging feeling of guilt about doing that behind Wyndham's back. In normal circumstances I'd have got on the phone to him immediately. I had no doubt that the black man with Dave had been Amaryll. I had no doubt, either, what

Amaryll's reaction would have been to finding out that Dave was claiming to be driving up Beulah Hill at the time when they were both in north London. My guess was that his next step would have been to confront Dave and demand a cut. Shortly afterwards he'd wound up under the wheels of a car. The anonymous letter suggested that there was someone involved, who knew about this, who knew the right levers to pull, and who had some malevolent intention in manipulating the situation.

My thoughts flew to Joan, and the aura of suppressed rage she carried around with her. I couldn't be sure whether or not she was lying about the phone call which had taken her to the hotel, but whatever the truth of it was, all this meant that Wyndham was deep in trouble, and I had the feeling that if he kept on going where Joan wanted to take him it would soon be over his head. In spite of what he'd said about still being friends, I had the suspicion that he wouldn't want to talk to me, but, somehow, knowing the horrors lurking round him had cleared out the resentment I had felt.

As I drove through the gathering dark along Regent's Park, I made up my mind. Whether he liked it or not, I had to make him listen.

19

I was still thinking over the problem of how to approach Wyndham when I knocked on Sophie's door. There was no answer, so I charged back down the stairs, feeling a renewal of the irritation I'd experienced the last time I saw her.

At the entrance to the block of flats I brushed past an Arab woman, veiled and robed. I guessed she might be going to see Sophie, and I wondered whether I should say something about her being out, but my mood wasn't particularly philanthropic right then, so I decided against it. I was swinging out to the car when I heard Sophie's voice calling my name. I turned round and saw her holding the veil back, a triumphant grin spreading from ear to ear.

'Got you,' she said. 'You didn't recognise me.'

Upstairs she told me that she'd started wearing the veil and the other clothes because it made life easier among her Muslim friends, and it helped the men to view her with respect. Up to now it hadn't occurred to me that on this job she was probably mixing with men, and oddly enough the idea hit me with a little spike of jealousy.

'Next thing you know you'll be reading the Koran,' I told her, 'and eating sheep's eyeballs.'

'I am reading the Koran,' she said stiffly, 'and it's not funny.'

'So when are you going for the circumcision?'

It came out nasty, although I hadn't meant it to sound that way. Later on it struck me that this was the point at which the evening started to go wrong. At first she didn't react at all, as if she hadn't heard what I'd said. Then she sat down, and looked at me, frowning.

'I thought you would understand,' she said. 'I like these people I'm working with, and I have to understand them. Some of them look like me. A few look like you. When I hear people talk about them in the stupid way they do I feel angry. You understand?'

'I understand that,' I told her, 'but it doesn't make me want to be like them.'

'I don't know if I want to be like them either, but I know I don't want to see them from inside the mind of a European. I don't want to walk around radiating scepticism, hands off me. I want to know how it feels to be what they are.'

'Maybe it's not possible, and all this' – I gestured at her clothes – 'comes over as some kind of game.'

She turned away and began unpinning the turban, separating it from her hair.

'I was brought up to be a good Catholic. You can't understand the feeling when you go to the Mass a child of faith. The magnificence of the mystery, the power with which the spirit absorbs you. Imagine standing on the seashore late in the afternoon gazing out to sea. Or late at night seeing the waves come ashore. Your body goes hollow and weak, your knees tremble, you can have no resistance, only a kind of fear mixed up with admiration at the power of God. This is where real religion begins. It's never a game.'

This was a new side to her. I wasn't sure that I liked it.

'What are you trying to tell me? Are you being converted or something?'

She clicked her tongue with annoyance.

'No. When I got old enough to give myself permission I stopped believing. This is just more interesting than anything else I can think of right now.'

I didn't have a reply to that, and I listened while she talked some more about wearing the veil, and how difficult all the things she experienced every day looked from behind it. She loved the sense, she said, of being invisible. Western women, she said, strained and agonised continually over the contradictions of calling attention to their sexuality, while at the same time resisting the attentions it provoked. The veil was cool, she said. To wear it was like being on holiday. Eventually she ran out of steam and asked me what I'd been doing since she saw me last, but the way she said it gave me the feeling that hearing about my day wasn't top of her list of priorities.

I told her about going to Norwich, about the job I had to do for Nick and about Dave's story being phony.

'What do you think?' I asked her.

'Who's the woman?' she asked.

'What do you mean?'

She looked straight at me.

'There's a woman. I can feel that you don't want to be with me and it's not just the job. Some of this you're not telling me because you don't want me to know, and I don't want to know either.'

I sat still, somehow knowing what she was going to say.

197

'I can't do this right now. I need to focus and this disturbs me too much. Come and see me when this thing is over. Then we can talk about it.'

Driving home later on, I felt a kind of relief. I hadn't been looking forward to talking with Sophie about Sarah, and the way things were I'd known that I'd have to sooner or later. This way I could postpone the decisions I had to make.

There were two more messages on the machine from my son. I sat down and rang him. I got his mother and we talked politely for nearly a minute before he came on the line.

'You OK, Dad? I rang, you weren't in. Where've you been?'

I told him. He grunted, and told me the suspense of waiting to hear from the university was killing him. I told him I'd been through the same thing and when it was over he'd forget how bad it had been. He sounded incredulous.

'That was years ago, Dad. Things were different then.'

I nearly shouted at him, then I realised he was winding me up. I put the phone down smiling, and in that moment of lightness, fell asleep.

I woke up thinking about Wyndham. On TV the news droned out the inevitable list of dead and wounded in Eastern Europe and Bosnia. Another item gave details of a suburban murder, followed by a prison suicide. I gave up, went out to buy a newspaper, walked over to Hyde Park and sat on a bench reading. When I got back I rang Nick. I was expecting Sandy's voice but he answered the phone himself, and for a second I felt oddly dislocated. I glanced at my watch. Half past nine. She probably wouldn't be in the office till ten.

'Hey. Sammy.' He sounded excited about it. 'Didn't expect to hear from you so soon. So what's the word?'

I told him, but I could tell that I wasn't making his day.

'Oh bugger,' he said. He paused, working himself up to it. 'It'll be easier if I tell Wyndham this is coming from you. Do you mind?'

He knew damn well I minded. At the same time the logic was irrefutable.

'Go ahead,' I told him. 'I'll talk to him later.'

'Give me half an hour.'

I rang Wyndham half an hour later. He sounded disgruntled. At least.

'What can I do for you?'

'Got some things to tell you.'

'I heard about Dave. From Nick. Thanks a bunch for letting me know.'

'Nick doesn't know about this. It's nothing to do with him, but I think you ought to hear it. Straight up.'

'Christ. I don't have time for this, Sammy. I've just got off the phone to Nick. I've got a matter of days to do a cut, and I'm just about to get into blue-assed fly mode. Gimme a break.'

'This is no bullshit, man. You want to hear this.'

'What is it?'

'Not on the phone.'

It might have been the onset of paranoia, but if anyone in the office was listening I didn't want them hearing what I had to say.

'Meet you in half an hour.'

He named a café off the High Street and hung up.

I got there in twenty-five minutes, but he was late and it was nearly eleven when he showed up. He stalked in tight legged, with that wired look he had when he was working hard.

'So what's up?'

I told him about going to Norwich and what I'd found out about Caroline, and he listened with a half smile which made me nervous.

'Did Sarah put you up to this?'

'Put me up to what?'

'Checking on Joan and Caroline. Digging up the dirt.'

'Nope. It was my own idea.'

'Getting back at me?'

This wasn't going the way I'd hoped.

'You can believe that if you want to,' I said. 'But I was trying to help. I wanted to find out more about what was going on, and Joan is an obvious candidate.'

'Tell you something.' He was leaning forward, the coffee in front of him forgotten, his face red, his eyes glittering angrily. 'I knew about all this. Joan told me. Caroline talked to me about it. It was a neurotic episode which she regrets.' He sat back, and pushed the coffee cup away from him. 'Go tell Nick if that's the kind of stuff he wants to know, but don't waste my time any more.'

He got up and walked out without another word. I sat watching him go. Up to that point I'd been carried along by the thrust of curiosity and the sense that I was about to uncover secret designs which might hurt my friends. Now he'd made me feel like an interfering busybody and I'd find that hard to forgive.

An hour later I wasn't feeling much better. I'd been sitting in front of the window, watching the pigeons, brooding and ignoring the phone. But when it rang three times in a row I turned up the volume on the answering machine, heard Sarah's voice and picked it up.

'What have you done to Wyndham?'

'Why?'

'He rang me a little while ago, shouting about you and Caroline and Nick. He seemed to think I was to blame. What's it all about?'

I suspected that she already had a pretty good idea, but I told her anyway. When I was finished, the line went silent for a few seconds, then, unexpectedly, she giggled.

'I knew it,' she said. 'I knew there was something. Did you pick up anything about Joan?'

The way she put it stung me, but I controlled my irritation.

'No.'

'Pity. The sister may be mad, but she's the real bitch. I'll bet anything she's at the bottom of it all.'

She went on like this for a while before I interrupted her and said I was busy. She said we should have a drink later on, and I told her I had a job which would take all day. Then I cut her off, and took the phone off the hook.

20

I spent most of the day mooching around and dozing off. I'd put the phone back on the hook after a while, and it rang several times, but I ignored it. The light outside had almost gone before I obeyed the impulse to answer.

'Mr Dean?'

It was a woman's voice. Pleasant, but hesitant about addressing a stranger on the phone. I said I was Mr Dean.

'Angela Boswell.'

It took me a few seconds, but then the recognition shocked me awake. This was Amaryll's aunt.

'I called the number the police gave me, but they said to ring you. They said he'd come down from Manchester with you.'

That must have been Katrina or Joan. Probably Joan. In the circumstances it had the authentic tang of malice.

She told me that she'd come down to London to see him, although he was still in a coma, and she thought that being a friend of his, I'd like to come to the hospital and see him. I ummed and aahed, but agreed in the end. I wasn't sure why. I hadn't been to see Amaryll because

I didn't want to, and I'd assumed that the hospital would discourage visitors in any case. On the other hand, I had a tickle of guilt at the back of my mind about what had happened to him, and if I went down there and played nice guy with his aunt, Angela, my conscience would be clear. That was one motive. I preferred not to think about the others. The phone didn't ring again, and I sat in front of the telly watching a football match, until I drifted into a dark pit of uneasy dreams.

The telephone woke me. On the screen a long-haired boy with a guitar was jumping around while the audience shook their fists at him. I turned the sound down and picked the phone up. It was Sarah's voice. She sounded close to tears.

'Can you come, Sammy?'

'What's wrong?'

'Someone tried to burn the house down tonight.'

'Did you call the police?'

'They're here.'

'What about Wyndham?'

'I don't know. I've tried, but I can't reach him. Can you come?'

I thought quickly, picturing the street where they lived. It was on the fringe of Highgate, and you could see the top of Alexandra Palace from their garden.

'I'll be about three-quarters of an hour.'

It was well past midnight, but there was still a stream of traffic rumbling down Edgware Road from Marble Arch. I ran on down to Camden Town, then through Kentish Town towards Highgate. The street was in quiet suburban darkness, but lights were blazing all over their house, and a police car was parked in the drive. Sarah must have been listening for me, because she opened the door before I could ring. She grabbed for me and hugged me in a convulsive grip, then took my hand and led me into the sitting room. A couple of uniformed police, a man and a woman, were standing there and she introduced me to them. Her manner was slightly absent, but she did it with a granite politeness, as if this was a social occasion, with nothing out of the ordinary about it. Taking their cue from her the uniforms nodded and mumbled their greetings, but they eyed me with a steely alertness, like guard dogs pacing behind a fence. I had the feeling that they were thrown by my presence, and I suspected that in other circumstances they would have started asking me where I'd been for the last hour. On the other hand, Sarah was operating in her best middle-class householder mode, half of which would have been enough to put the coppers back in their box.

'He'll stay with me till my husband gets here,' she told them firmly.

'We'll be going now, then,' the policewoman said. She gave me a last lingering look, before Sarah ushered them out. In the hallway I could hear them talking in low, important voices, issuing some last-minute instructions or advice.

'What happened?' I asked her when she came back from the door.

'Come and see.'

I followed her across the hallway into the room opposite. This was identical to the one we'd just left, except that the glass of the French window had a hole about halfway up, and below it, there was a pile of wet ashes in the middle of a patch of charred carpet. In the room there was an insistent reek of petrol, and I realised that I'd been smelling it since I'd stepped in the door.

'I'm glad I was in the house,' Sarah said, 'but I keep thinking that I could have been burnt to death.'

She put her arms round me, her entire body trembling.

'Let's have a drink,' I said.

She poured two glasses of brandy, and told me what had happened. She'd been upstairs reading when she heard the glass break. By the time she'd got downstairs, there was a fire going on the carpet. She'd grabbed the fire extinguisher, put it out and then dialled 999.

'Good thing I was awake,' she said moodily. She drained the glass. 'You know what I'm thinking. Don't you?'

'Caroline?'

She nodded.

'Did you tell the police?'

'No. There's a detective coming in the morning. I might mention it then. I don't know.' She turned the glass round and round in her fingers. 'It's tricky, isn't it?' She stood up abruptly. 'I can't stand the smell any more. Let's get out of here. Get some fresh air.'

I gestured at the broken window.

'What about that?'

That stopped her for a few seconds, then she suggested that we shifted an antique rolltop to cover the hole.

When we'd done so, she stood back looking at it for a moment. She laughed. The sound was high and nervy, which fitted in with her fast, jerky movements and rapid changes of mood.

'If anyone wants to break in past that tonight, he's welcome to it. I've had enough.'

We drove down to Alexandra Palace in my car. By now the streets were deserted and when we got to the palace, it had the dark and brooding look in which monuments wrapped themselves at night. Before the fire which half

205

destroyed it, the walls used to be covered with decoration, gargoyles, carved stonework, Art-Nouveau metal. Now its surface had the plain brick dreariness of a municipal building, but its bulk and shape still possessed the power to impose. As a boy I loved walking in the massive park which surrounded it, but getting close to the building at night was scary, and even now, the feeling that it was crouching behind me, like some vast wounded behemoth, sent an uneasy thrill shooting through my nerve ends.

I parked in the open space in front of the building, and we walked down the wide slope of the hill towards where the racecourse used to be. Up ahead the stars were bright against their dark navy-blue background. Hemmed on the horizon a bank of soft clouds drifted sweetly. Down below us the half-moon climbed closer. It was one hell of a night.

'This was the only racetrack in London.' I pointed out where it used to be. 'I saw Scobie Breasley ride here, when he was coming to the end of his time, and Piggott was a flash young geezer winning on top of any old donkey.'

Thirty years must have passed, but I could remember it vividly, myself standing on tiptoe clutching the rail, the horses flashing past, like an unbelievably powerful group of muscles rippling, the motion over before I could let my breath out. For a couple of seconds I was transported, but Sarah's voice brought me back.

'Tell me again. About Caroline. Everything you found out.'

I told her again. Then I told her about Dave and Amaryll being together miles away from Beulah Hill where Dave claimed to have seen Leon.

When I'd finished, I waited for her response, but what she heard had silenced her for the moment.

'They're stitching him up somehow,' she said. 'But you'll have to convince him. He won't listen to me.'

'Why not? You're his wife. In any case, going by today, I'm probably the last person he trusts.'

She stopped walking, moved a few paces, and leaned back against the tree we'd just gone past. Something fluttered up above. In that moment I found the noise spooky, but Sarah didn't seem to notice. She was staring away towards the horizon.

'We're splitting up,' she muttered.

In spite of everything I knew about both of them, I was shocked by this piece of news.

'He told me. Weeks ago. He's fucking the stupid little cow, and he wants to leave. Sell the house, buy me out of the company. I said I'd go quietly if he still felt the same way in another couple of months. It's been hell.'

'I thought you'd both come to terms with things.'

She took her eyes off the horizon. Her teeth flashed in the moonlight.

'Is that what you thought?'

'Yes.'

'Maybe we have,' she said. 'I told him last night that I'd changed my mind. That I'd take the house and the company away from him. He wasn't exactly pleased.'

The implications of this startled me, against all reason.

'I don't believe that he'd do that. Not with you in the house. He may have gone bonkers, but he's not stupid.'

'Oh, I don't know,' she said. 'I don't believe it either. It's just that you get crazy ideas in situations like this.'

She held her arms out and draped herself round me.

I patted her soothingly, and I felt her body heave. I was about to say something sympathetic when she bit me on the neck and pulled away, laughing. Another mood swing.

'What was that for?'

'You are a dirty bastard, you really are. All the time you were supposed to be comforting me, a distressed maiden, you had a whacking great erection. I could feel it poking up every time I hugged you.' She squeezed the front of my trousers. 'And it hasn't gone away.'

'Well, it did,' I told her modestly. 'Only it had a good think about things and decided to come back.'

'Let's do it now,' she whispered.

'I'm supposed to be comforting you.'

'Right now,' she said. 'You can comfort me pretty good with that.'

She squeezed me again. I looked around.

'Here?'

'You want me to beg?'

She dropped to her knees, unzipped me smoothly and took out my penis.

'Please,' she muttered. 'Please.'

'Stand up,' I ordered.

She stood up. As she did so her skirt fell away and made a pool round her feet. She shrugged her coat off, turned around and embraced the tree. All she wore now was a T-shirt, and below it the smooth skin on her hips and thighs gleamed white in the moonlight. I had started to hear a high, impossibly loud, humming sound, and as I covered her body from behind I realised that this was the noise I could feel vibrating somewhere beneath my hands. I gripped her breasts harder and felt her whole body beginning a squirmy, rippling movement. Her buttocks thrust blindly back at me. Once, twice, and I slipped easily into her.

After we were done she leaned back against the tree, and pulled her clothes on.

'How're you doing?' I asked her.

In reply she gave me a cheerful grin.

'Not bad,' she said. 'Not bad. At least tonight hasn't been a complete waste of time.'

21

When I arrived Linette Holder was sitting in the waiting room with Angie Boswell, Amaryll's auntie. For some reason I'd been assuming that she was mixed race too, but the woman with Linette was white. She had greying brown hair, pleasant, even features, and sharp hazel eyes, glinting behind a pair of gold-rimmed glasses. She was wearing a fawn-coloured skirt, a black jacket and highly polished black walking shoes. She looked like a social worker or the nurse that she was, and, for a few seconds, I felt a sense of dislocation as I struggled to put this woman together with Amaryll.

She shook hands firmly, after I'd greeted Linette. The doctor was with Amaryll, and afterwards, perhaps, we could see him.

'Are you a friend of his?'

Look where you could end up with friends like me, I thought.

'In a way,' I told her.

She frowned.

'What do you mean? In a way?'

I told her I worked for a TV programme on which

Amaryll was due to appear, and that we'd got to know each other in the course of preparing it. I watched Linette out of the corner of my eye, but if she noticed the discrepancies she didn't react. In any case, this wasn't too far from the story I'd originally told her.

Mrs Boswell lapped it up. Of course. Mention working on the telly and everyone perks up. To do Angie justice, I also had the feeling that it was a long time since she'd heard someone say anything good about Amaryll, and now it was happening she felt her heart swelling in vindication. She asked me what he'd been about to do on TV, and I told her he'd been a friend of a murder victim, and that he'd shown a lot of courage in volunteering information which might help catch the killer.

She pressed her hand to her mouth. I had an idea she was beginning to wonder whether there was a connection with her nephew being run over, but I didn't want to encourage her to think along those lines.

'He's got a good heart,' she said. 'He's had a lot of trouble, but underneath he was a good boy.'

I nodded soberly, wondering how a woman who seemed so sensible could deceive herself so dreadfully. Then my thoughts threw up a picture of my son. Whatever he did with his life, I thought, I'd probably find some reason to love him, and if I couldn't, I'd love him anyway.

'Did he live with you?'

A tear ran down the side of her nose. She reached into her bag for a tissue, took her glasses off, wiped her face, and blew her nose. She did all this with a matter-of-fact no-nonsense air, as if she'd noticed a smudge in the mirror, which didn't merit a second look.

'Most of the time,' she said. 'He was in care for a bit, after his mum died.'

I should have guessed. Putting a kid into care was

usually a recipe for disaster. She didn't say why he'd been in care, but I supposed it didn't matter. By the time she and her husband, Ernie, got him, Amaryll had made some bad friends and acquired worse habits. He played truant and messed about with drugs. He got into serious trouble. She pursed her lips and shook her head. Reading between the lines, I guessed that he'd been nicked and sent down. Later on he'd had a breakdown. First they sent him away, then they sent him back, and he'd had to take his pills regularly and attend therapy sessions. By this time Ernie was almost an invalid, and all the disturbance didn't help. When Amaryll went off to London she was relieved, and he seemed to be doing so well. He'd written her letters about the house he lived in, and his therapy group. He'd even sent her photos of himself and his friends.

'Mrs Boswell?'

The interruption was a nurse at the door. Angie stood up, smoothed her skirt, clipped her handbag shut, and followed the nurse down the corridor.

I turned to Linette.

'Did you know all this?'

She pursed her lips and shook her head in an unconscious echo of Angie's gesture.

'So how comes you're here? I thought you didn't want to see him again.'

'She rang me,' she said. 'He told her I was his girlfriend and he was putting some money together for a new flat.'

And Angie would have had to contribute most of it, I guessed.

'Maybe he was,' I told her.

'And pigs could fly,' she replied, a note of venom sharpening her voice. 'I only came because of her, and they reckon he ain't gonna wake up again.'

She gestured ruefully, as if apologising for the fact that

she wasn't as hard as she wanted to be. Then we sat in silence till we heard Angie making her way back along the corridor, her heels banging steadily towards us.

'You can come now,' she said.

'You go,' I told Linette, 'I'll wait here.'

Angie eyed me sternly.

'You'd better come now,' she said. 'You may not get another chance to see him.'

She turned on her heel and led the way.

Amaryll was isolated in a small room at the end of a larger ward. He was swathed in bandages, like the invisible man. One of his legs was stuck up in the air, and the rest of him was cradled in a spider's web of pulleys, straps and tubes. Only a small patch of his features could be seen. His skin looked waxy and dead. In fact, the only evidence that he was alive came from the movements of shiny green dots and squiggles on the screen of the machine behind his bed.

Angie didn't touch him, but she stood by the bedside for a couple of seconds, looking at him, then she began to sob into her handkerchief.

Beside me, Linette started sniffling, and I reached out and put my arm round her. We stood like this for a while, then a couple of nurses came in and one of them put her arm round Angie and whispered to her.

She nodded, and began pulling herself together.

'We've got to go now.'

I breathed easier outside the hospital. In my youth hospitals used to smell of disinfectant and give off an aura of forbidding cleanliness. Nowadays I was uneasily conscious that hospitals were a hotbed of disease, the focus of terrifying mutations and exotic bacteria. The contradiction

213

frightened me a little. I had enough contradictions in my life.

I offered Angie a lift, and she said she was staying with a friend in Kentish Town. Linette said she was meeting someone in Notting Hill, and then going to pick up her baby. As she hurried off I had the feeling she was relieved to get away.

On the way over to Kentish Town, I pumped Angie, as delicately as I could manage, for whatever she knew about Amaryll's friends and habits. She knew nothing about his friendship with Dave or his acquaintance with Helen, but he'd written her quite a lot about the people in his therapy group.

'What sort of therapy was it?'

She thought it was a discussion group, under the supervision of a doctor or a psychotherapist. Amaryll thought it was useless, but he kept on going, partly because it was a condition of his probation, partly for the company and the chance to talk. He had to be careful sometimes, he'd told her, because some of them weren't just disturbed. They were stark, staring mad. One man claimed to be a hitman, and said he was going to be a mercenary so he could kill people. Another man would get down on the floor when he was angry, and bark like a dog. It was the old story, she told me. If people took their medication regularly they could keep their problems under control. But they never did. Even so, in the photos Amaryll had sent her, they mostly looked all right.

'Photos?'

'Yes. I brought some of them.'

She'd been thinking, she said, that they might be useful. Sometimes you could bring people out of a coma by talking to them, or playing their favourite music, or describing scenes they knew. She'd brought Amaryll's letters and photos in the hope that they might help, but he was too far gone for that. Her voice thickened, and I knew without looking that she was crying again.

'The photos,' I said. 'Could I take a look?'

'When we get there.'

Coming off the High Street in Kentish Town I got trapped in the one-way system, but Angie directed me to the right street with a surprising coolness.

'Amazing sense of direction you've got,' I said. 'Or have you lived in London before?'

She laughed, tickled by the compliment.

'Neither. This is just the way that Linette brought me yesterday. She picked me up at the station.'

'Linette?'

I had got the impression that she didn't have a car. Come to think of it, I'd had the impression that she didn't possess two pennies to rub together.

'Yes. She's got a nice car. A Toyota, I think.'

I'd been had. Angie read the expression on my face.

'Is something wrong?'

'Nothing much. Just wishing I could afford a better car.'

She smiled uncertainly, but I didn't have to elaborate because I was just pulling up outside the address she'd given me. She asked me in, but I said I was in a hurry and I merely wanted a quick peek at the photos. You never knew what might help. I had no idea what I meant, but she didn't question it. Instead, she opened her purse and handed me an envelope crammed with a thick sheaf of photos.

'I left the album at home,' she said.

I skipped through them in silence. I didn't know what I was looking for, and matters were complicated by the fact that she'd brought several photos of Amaryll as a small boy, and as a sullen youth standing in the back garden in Retford. My attention was beginning to wander when it was caught and held by a picture of Amaryll and Dave. She peered over my shoulder at the snap I was holding.

'There's a couple of the group just below that.'

And so there was. Amaryll stood in the middle of half a dozen other people. Dave stood on his right. To his left was Caroline Foster, and next to her, his face creased in a determined scowl, was Jack Gold.

22

Sarah opened the door and gave me a big smile, but I wasn't in the mood to play games with her, so I got straight to the point.

'I've just seen a photo of your man Jack with Dave and Amaryll and Caroline. These guys were all in some therapy group together. You must have known. So what's up?'

Her smile faded, but instead of replying she turned and walked back into the sitting room. I followed her through the French windows and into the garden. It was a big garden for this part of the world, more than the width of the house, and half as long again as a cricket pitch. Up the middle ran a neat lawn, bordered by long rows of flower beds. Against the fence at the back a riot of begonias sprouted. She'd been working in the flower beds close to the house when I interrupted her, and now she pulled on a pair of gloves and resumed what she'd been doing, taking some growing shoots one by one out of their pots and spading them into the earth. She looked healthy and wholesome, like a woman who went to sleep and dreamed of roses.

'I didn't know that,' she said thoughtfully. She sat on the path beside the flower bed and looked directly at me. 'And I don't see why you assumed that I did.'

I shrugged. I'd thought there was something odd about her connection with Jack to begin with, and, somehow, the conclusion that she'd been deceiving me was irresistible.

'It explains a lot, though,' she continued. 'I first got on to him because he was a contact someone gave me when I was doing a story about homelessness. He was supposed to be tracing runaways and he knew a lot about where they went and what happened to them. Then I forgot about him, the way you do, until he rang me up a few weeks ago when Wyndham started on this story.'

He'd said that he knew what the company was doing and he knew the estate, perhaps he could help in the investigation. This didn't surprise her because, by now, the researchers' door-knocking had made the film common knowledge in the district. In addition, she'd paid Jack small fees on previous occasions for his information, and she guessed that he assumed there was more where that came from. She'd explained that although Wyndham was her husband she was nothing to do with the project and so she couldn't do anything for him. But she'd promised to speak to Wyndham on his behalf. Wyndham wasn't interested but Jack had kept ringing, and she'd been on the verge of ignoring his calls, when she had the bright idea of using him to keep an eye on Joan.

'That's it,' she said. 'But now you tell me this I suspect that he had his own motives for wanting to be involved. Working for me would have been a good cover for keeping an eye on everyone, including me. Instead of storming

218

in here confronting me, you could ask yourself whether this was something to do with Caroline. If he knew her, he must have known she was crazy, and he never said a word.'

It seemed a reasonable conclusion.

'Do you know how to reach him?'

'No. All I've got is his telephone number. He rings me when there's something to report. If I want to reach him I'll call and leave a message.'

'Do me a favour,' I said, 'ring him now and tell him to meet you later at my place.'

'I'm waiting to see Wyndham. I can't leave here for a while.'

'I don't want you to. But if you tell him I want to see him he might not come.'

'Right.'

I waited, but she didn't move.

'Can you do it now?'

She flashed an irritated look at me, but she got up without speaking, and began stripping off her gloves. We went back into the house and she dialled Jack's number. Then she put her hand over the mouthpiece.

'It's the machine. Suppose he doesn't get the message till tomorrow or something?'

'Tell him, if he can't make it tonight, to come tomorrow morning.'

She did what I asked and went back into the garden. There didn't seem much to say then, so when she put her gloves on and bent over her pots, I left. The way she said goodbye wasn't unfriendly, but she turned away with a detachment that told me she hadn't forgiven the aggressive style of my arrival.

*

Back at my flat I waited for Jack and filled up the time opening the bills which had arrived in the last week and been lying on the floor inside the door since then. I was looking at the final threatening demand from the water company and working myself into a rage about it, when something struck me about the telephone bill. I took another look. The calls were itemised, with the long-distance numbers given in full. I hadn't been sure why that was important when I looked, but suddenly it struck me that I'd missed a trick at Amaryll's hotel. They'd have a record of his calls.

I dithered for a while, wondering about whether or not Jack would arrive as soon as I left, but in the end I couldn't resist.

I shaved, suited up, and got there in less than a quarter of an hour. It was about ten and the lobby was quiet. I found the night manager in his office behind the reception and he greeted me with a practised and slightly oily civility. I wasn't surprised. He worked at night, so, from his point of view, going to the trouble of checking up on me would have required more effort than it was worth. Being suspicious now would have been to admit that he was wrong the first time, and he wasn't about to do that. Instead he'd convinced himself that I was the genuine article.

'Mr Hayman,' he said. He threw his arm out and looked at his watch. 'You fellas are on the job all hours.'

I winked at him.

'The early bird catches the worm.'

He laughed appreciatively, and we kicked around another few rounds of witticisms of more or less the same quality. Then I told him what I wanted and he said he couldn't do it. It was more than his job was worth to show an outsider confidential documents. It was a question of the guests' privacy. I said I understood and fell back on Plan B, which was to show him a list of numbers and get him to tick the ones that Amaryll had called that night. He balked a bit, but eventually he agreed.

Amaryll had been a busy boy. He'd phoned Wyndham, Dave, Jack and Linette. There were also a couple of numbers which weren't on my list, but there was nothing I could do about them. Linette's number had been the surprise package that I was pondering over as I settled down again to wait for Jack. She'd told me that she hadn't had any recent contact with Amaryll, but, according to the hotel records he'd phoned her and talked for five minutes. There could have been any number of reasons for her lying to me, but my guess was that it was something to do with her ownership of a new motor. Buying any kind of car was an expensive business, even an old banger like mine, and when I first met Linette there'd been nothing to suggest that she could afford it.

Sometime around midnight I must have fallen asleep, and when I woke up the morning sun was fingering the carpet. I picked up the phone and dialled Wyndham's number. Sarah answered. I said hello and she asked what time it was and when I told her it was almost eight, she groaned. I asked her whether she'd heard from Jack. She said no and cut me off.

I rang Linette next, but when she answered I changed my mind and put the phone down. What I wanted to do would stand more chance of success face to face.

With any luck, Jack would turn up sometime, but it seemed a certainty that he wasn't the sort to make early morning calls, and I figured that I had at least until ten o'clock.

*

221

When Linette opened the door she looked surprised to see me, then she scowled, a gleam of anger in her eyes.

'What do you want?'

I told her I wanted to talk and she said she had to get the baby down to the minder, because she had to get to work. I asked her where she worked because I could give her a lift. She said it was Safeways and it was only a few minutes away. She could walk.

'But I forgot,' I said, 'you've got a car, haven't you? Where did you get it?'

'None of your business.'

Now she was getting ready to slam the door in my face. I pushed a bit closer.

'Maybe it's not my business, but did you tell Amaryll when he rang you the other night, or were you too busy setting him up? A lot of people would like to know how a checkout girl at Safeways got herself a Toyota a short time after Amaryll nearly got himself knocked off.'

I was guessing, but her jaw dropped, her lips quivered, and she looked past me involuntarily, her eyes searching the street behind me. She was frightened. That much was certain.

'Let's go inside,' I said gently.

She stared at me dumbly, the fight gone out of her, then she turned and led the way upstairs in silence. As if catching something about his mother's mood, the baby began to scream. He'd been sitting in a high chair in the sitting room, and I clucked at him while she got him down and, automatically, began wiping his face and hands, and changing him out of his pyjamas.

'So what happened?' I asked her.

She didn't reply. She was bent over the baby, busy fiddling with his clothes. I couldn't see her face, and for the moment I couldn't tell whether or not she'd heard me, and I geared myself up to make my last attempt to persuade her.

'Whatever it is,' I said, 'it can't be that bad. If you cover up, you could find yourself being stitched up. If you tell me maybe I can keep your name out of it. Nobody has to know about the phone call if I don't tell them. No one has to know what you did.'

'Can you do that? Keep me out of it?'

'Yes,' I lied firmly.

She sat back on her heels, clasping the baby to her. He squirmed and tried to escape, but she held him tight, as if fearful of letting him loose to crawl around near me.

'I didn't do anything,' she said, 'only the money for the car, and he owed me anyway.'

'What money?'

'The money he left here that night he got done.'

'Wait a minute,' I said. 'Tell me the whole story.'

She took a firm grip on the baby and hurried through it.

At first when he'd rung her that evening she'd told him to get lost, but he said that he had something for her and the baby and eventually she said he could come round. She'd given him a hard time for disappearing without trace, and he'd explained why he'd had to go. The story was that he'd done a jeweller's shop with Dave. He hadn't wanted to, but Dave was a mad bastard and he knew he'd get into trouble if there was no one to look after him.

'Oh yeah,' I interjected. I couldn't resist it. 'Did you believe that?'

She shrugged, but I had the feeling that she was embarrassed by that part of the story. Amaryll had taken the stuff up north with him to sell it off bit by bit, she went on, and he'd made nearly two grand. He had it with him and he showed it to her, a big pile of fifty- and twenty-pound notes. He'd been going to split it with Dave, he told her, but then he'd heard something which made him change his mind. The TV people had told him that Dave was saying that he'd seen Leon up Beulah Hill. Amaryll had known that wasn't true, and he couldn't understand what the game was. So he'd rung Dave, but when he asked what was going on, the only answer he got was that the guy wanted to be on TV, and this was his only chance. It sounded mad but Amaryll believed it, because Dave had always been obsessed with getting on TV. He'd also been a compulsive liar. Like he couldn't help it.

'There was something else,' she said.

The baby gave a wail and she shushed him rapidly before going on. Amaryll had always suspected that Dave was the one who'd sent the anonymous letters to Helen; and when he accused him point-blank Dave had admitted it. Boasted about the letters and about stalking her. When Amaryll asked why, Dave had said he'd done it to get her attention. This had been the last straw. Amaryll knew that Dave hadn't done anything more than threaten Helen, but it had pissed him off completely, he told Linette, to think that Dave had not only terrified the woman while she was alive, but now she was dead, he was so screwed up that he'd do anything to stay in touch with her and her affairs. It couldn't be right, Amaryll said. The guy was so fucked up he'd even go on telly to give an alibi to the man who most likely killed her.

'So Amaryll had a go at him, told him he was a dick-head, and it was like raping her after she was dead, and then he said he was finished with him and he was keeping all the dosh.'

I suppressed the thought that Amaryll's indignation had been pretty convenient.

224

'Wasn't he worried about Dave turning nasty?'

She shrugged again and the baby started screaming. This time he didn't seem about to stop.

'He did turn a bit nasty,' she said, raising her voice. 'But Amaryll wasn't bothered. He knew too much about him. You know what I mean?'

I knew what she meant. But Amaryll had ended up in hospital, which meant that he'd got it wrong.

'What happened to the money?'

Her eyes shifted away from me.

'He took some of it with him. He said I could have the rest.'

This was the first statement she'd made that I didn't believe. I'd have bet anything that Amaryll had intended to come back for his dosh. But thinking about the fact that Amaryll hadn't come back started me off on another track. I took the letter Nick had received out of my pocket and showed it to her.

'You wrote this, didn't you? The postmark's just up the road.'

She nodded reluctantly.

'I didn't want him to get away with it.'

'That's if it was him that ran Amaryll over.'

She considered this for a moment, and finally she screwed her face up and clicked her tongue in disgust.

'He's lying anyway.'

Nothing to be gained by pursuing the question, so I changed direction.

'Where does Jack come into all this?'

'I don't know,' she said. 'I don't know who he is. I've got to go. I don't know any more.'

She got up, and put the baby down while she crossed the room and fetched his buggy. He began struggling to his feet in anticipation of being strapped into it. I got up and waved to them from the top of the stairs. She paused in the middle of lifting the child into the buggy.

'I never said anything,' she told me.

'Don't worry,' I said, 'I don't think anyone will bother you.'

23

I waited until the early afternoon before telephoning Sarah. She hadn't heard from Jack, so she didn't know whether or not he'd got the message. If he'd turned up while I was out he'd have rung her to find out what was going on. She was sure of that. I asked her how she was and she said she was fine but she had things to do. Then she cut me off.

By now I'd given up on Jack. I had the feeling that he hadn't come, because, whatever he was up to, he didn't need Sarah any more. But that thought reinforced my growing conviction that he would have the answer to all the riddles which seemed to surround the production. Since my conversation with Linette, I believed that I knew the reasons why Dave had lied, and I could make a shrewd guess about why Amaryll was in a hospital bed. What I couldn't figure out was whether Joan and Caroline were connected to all this, and if they were, just what the connection was. I couldn't understand, either, how Jill's stabbing fitted in, or why Wyndham had been getting anonymous threats.

I was certain that all these events were part of some

process which was moving towards a climax, and there seemed to be no way I could intervene unless I knew what the process was and why it had been set in motion. Talking to the police had crossed my mind, but I'd rejected the idea immediately. I had no evidence for any of the things I knew. Most of it was guesswork, based on various individuals' past behaviour, or the fact that they'd once known each other. I was on more solid ground with Dave and Amaryll, but I had no doubt that, faced with the cops, Linette would deny what she'd said; and I didn't want to wish on her the trouble that the interest of the police might represent. Not without a very good reason, and I wasn't sure that I had one. In any case, every instinct I possessed told me to keep away from the police. Almost every encounter I'd ever had with them, once it got beyond the superficial, hummed with the suppressed tensions of racial anger, and the encounter with the pair of uniforms at Sarah's house had reminded me what they could be like. It was odds-on that they'd greet me with hostility and suspicion. It wouldn't help, either, that I'd been connected with Wyndham's project. Like everyone else, the police were convinced about the importance of TV. But, from their point of view, what mattered about TV was how much good it did them. So they viewed the nightly procession of crime fictions with contemptuous affection. Their contempt was for the upright morality of the TV cops which had nothing to do with the atmosphere in which they worked. Their affection had to do with the fact that the stories on the screen were invariably good public relations for them. Money couldn't buy it. For much the same sort of reasons, they approved wholeheartedly of the TV programmes which focused on appeals for information, and they loved the images of themselves on the screen, grave and busy, presiding over reconstructions of robberies and murders, fiddling with glowing computers, global warriors in the endless fight against crime. On the other hand, they hated with an equal passion the merest hint that anything they'd done was incompetent, corrupt or futile. Asking them to go over an investigation they had wrapped up would be a difficult and risky business.

I was, more or less, back where I started, but now the pressure was off. I'd done the job for which I'd been hired, and everyone concerned wanted me out of the equation. Whatever was going to happen could happen without me. It was about time to see Sophie, I thought, and straighten things out.

That was the thought in my head when I started out. Later on I was never able to put my finger on the reason why it turned out differently. Perhaps it was my anger at the thought of defeat, perhaps it was some kind of obstinacy that I couldn't control, perhaps my attention wandered at a crucial moment and the car locked into some subliminal command. Whatever it was, I found myself driving into the estate down the slip road which ran along behind Dave's flat. I parked, switched off the engine and pretended, for a few minutes, that I was thinking the matter over, but my mind was already made up.

Dave opened the door after I'd knocked a few times.

'What do you want?'

Somewhere in the background the dog let loose with a volley of ferocious growls.

'I want some information.'

'Piss off.'

I put my foot in the door. Dave looked at it and sneered.

'You don't want to do that.'

229

'You and Amaryll robbed a jeweller's. He went off with the money. He told you he was going to keep it. A few hours later he's in hospital. On top of that Helen gave him the letters you wrote her, and he's given them to me.' I was lying with all the confidence I could command, and I reckoned I had nothing to lose, so I raised the stakes. I raised my voice too. 'You can talk to me or you can talk to the cops. I don't give a shit.'

Dave stood there for a moment, his face and body frozen in shock. Then he pushed past me and looked up and down the corridor. The gesture seemed to be a reflex, and in similar circumstances I might have done the same. Instead, I moved closer, trapping him between the door-frame and my body, and spoke to him quietly.

'You talk to me, and I'll tell you where the money is, and give you back the letters.'

We stood eye to eye. I could smell the beer belching up from his insides. There were little red spots round his mouth and chin, as if he'd been drooling some kind of bile and it had left a mark on his flesh. His eyes dropped.

'All right. Come in.'

'Is that dog locked up?'

He told me he was and we walked into the flat. He sat on one of the upright chairs in the sitting room, but when he waved me to a seat opposite him, I shook my head and stayed standing.

'What's going on then, Dave?'

'I dunno what you're talking about,' he said.

'Pull the other one,' I said. 'Look. I'm doing my best here. Right now they probably think it's hit and run, and I would guess he never saw what hit him. So the investigation's bollocks. They're not digging around his friends and that, so they don't know anything, and you got away with it. But if they know about you and him, how long do you reckon it will take them to pull you in? Even if you didn't do it, you'll be well stitched up.'

Dave didn't react as I'd hoped. Now he was back in the flat he seemed to have regained a measure of confidence, and his sneering manner had begun to return.

'You want to be careful, mate,' he said. 'Accusations like that could get you into trouble. You know what I mean?'

I laughed scornfully and shook my head. Actually, for a second or two, I was stymied. Then something about Dave's eyes sparked off a memory from the playground. This was a kid who always wanted to be hard, but never quite made it. Over the years he'd developed a convincing façade, and if you put him in a group of fellow nutters on the football terraces or a back alley, he'd be dangerous. But the fact that he'd hung out with Amaryll meant that his skinhead look didn't go all the way through, and his stalking of Helen pointed to some kind of sexual screw-up, which would translate into a fear of being hurt. Catch him all on his own, and he'd be a pussy cat. So I lost my temper. I grabbed the chair in front of me and flung it to one side. Down the hallway the dog began to bark furiously and scrabble at the door.

'Fuck me!' I shouted. 'You wanna go at me?' I flared my nostrils, widened my eyes and breathed hard, inflating my chest, puffing myself up and squaring up to him. He got up quickly and faced me. 'I ain't no girl!' I yelled. 'I'll smash your fucking face in. Then I'll go down the nick. I swear.'

We stood like this for a few seconds, his face a glaring, twisted reflection of my own. Then he turned away, and slumped back into his chair.

'Ah. Fuck it,' he said. 'I never touched him. I was here. Wasn't I?'

'Then who done it?'

He stirred uneasily, refusing to look at me. But looking at him brought back the image of the group in the photograph I'd seen, and the answer burst into my head.

'It was Jack. Wasn't it? You sent Jack.'

The look he gave me confirmed my guess.

'I never sent him,' he said.

'So why'd he do it?'

'He's a nutter. He reckons he's a hitman. A mercenary, like. He said he'd teach Amaryll a lesson. I never knew what he was going to do. I told you he was a nutter.'

Angie had mentioned Amaryll describing someone like this. That made Dave's story credible, but it didn't explain anything else.

'So what does Caroline have to do with Jack and what he's doing?'

He made a show of puzzlement.

'Caroline?'

'Yes. Caroline.' I was losing patience again. 'Don't make out you're stupid. I know you were all in therapy together. Sat around telling each other your problems. You know exactly who I mean, and you know she's Joan Foster's sister. They look alike and she's been around often enough. Don't piss me about.'

'I'm not,' he said resentfully. 'I know her, but she ain't got nothing to do with Jack.'

'All right,' I said, 'just tell me how you got involved.'

Little by little I coaxed what he knew out of him. He'd met Caroline, Amaryll and Jack a couple of years before, when they'd all been outpatients together. He'd become mates with Amaryll, and he saw Jack occasionally, although generally they'd kept away from the guy because he liked playing with guns and knives, and you never knew what he'd do next. Caroline had been posh, a different class, and he hadn't met her outside of the group sessions he attended. When Helen was murdered, everyone on the estate had been talking about it, especially during Leon's trial and conviction. During one conversation with Jamie's mum, Sandra, he'd mentioned seeing Leon up Beulah Hill, fiddling with his car. He hadn't said it was the day of the murder, but she'd got hold of the wrong end of the stick. At this point his eyes widened and he gave me a straightforward, innocent look, which I guessed to be a signal that he was lying.

'I believe you,' I said encouragingly. 'Don't know their arse from a hole in the ground, that lot.'

He almost smiled. Then he went on without being prompted. The next thing he knew, a TV girl was knocking on his door. At first he'd denied seeing Leon, but she insisted. Her information was that he'd said it. So, in the end, he'd agreed. After this, Jack had got in touch, took him out for a drink and asked him a lot of questions about what the TV was doing, and what kind of film they were making. One night he'd told Jack about Amaryll and the money, and Jack had warned him that Amaryll was dodgy and not to be trusted. When Amaryll told him he was going to cheat him out of his share, he'd rung Jack.

'So you ring a guy who said he was a hitman,' I asked him, 'and you don't reckon he'll do anything serious? You kidding?'

'I thought he was bullshitting,' he said. 'He reckoned he had a contract on one of the TV people. I just thought it was bollocks.'

'One of the researchers got killed last week. Right in your flat. What do you think that was?'

He shook his head vigorously.

'No. That wasn't him. He hasn't done it yet. He told me.'

'Are you sure? He's got a contract on someone and he hasn't done it yet?'

Dave nodded. He screwed up his face impatiently.

'Yeah.'

I took him over it a couple of times, and I couldn't shake his story. In the process I got an address where he said Jack stayed sometimes, but it wasn't too long before the point arrived at which I could sense him making up his mind to stop answering my questions, and to ask a question on his own account.

'Where's the money, then? And them letters.'

'I don't know,' I told him. 'I haven't got them. It was all lies, mate.'

It took a while to sink in, then he went berserk.

'Fucking black bastard!' he shouted. He got up, and I braced myself, but all he did was to shout some more. 'Bastard! Bastard!'

His pet had started up again, an ugly chorus of deep-chested growls. I retreated rapidly down the hallway, taking care not to turn my back on him, and I yanked the outer door open before he could unlock the room where the dog was confined.

As I stepped outside he shouted after me.

'I lied and all, you stupid git! I lied! It was all bollocks! All bollocks!'

This time, though, I didn't believe him. He might have exaggerated and modified some things, but remembering what he'd said about Jack and his contract to kill someone in the production, I felt a prickle of instinct which convinced me that he was telling the absolute truth.

24

I thought I had it worked out now, but the result didn't make me any happier. If my guess was right, whatever Wyndham was up to with the sisters had triggered another round of obsession. Jack would be the instrument of their revenge, or whatever it was. All of them were too unstable to predict, and anything could happen. In any case, it was clear that Sarah was in danger, and the same probably applied to Wyndham.

I geed the car up through the evening rush hour round Camden Town and headed for Highgate. It was a fine spring evening. It hadn't rained for a while and the traffic was moving fluently. Occasionally I caught a glimpse of the sky, a pale duck-egg blue, with white-gold streaks running across its horizons. In different circumstances I would have felt moderately cheerful, but now my mind was occupied with what I had to tell Sarah and how she would take it.

She was gardening again, as if she hadn't stopped in the twenty-four hours since I'd left her. She was warmer this time, smiling at me and going to put the kettle on for a cup of tea. When she came back, we sat in front of the big windows watching the sky.

'I'm sorry about yesterday,' she said. 'I was pissed off.'

'Doesn't matter,' I told her, 'I've got something to tell you.'

I told her what Dave had said and what I thought about Jack's intentions. She took it well, frowning a little. Then she grimaced and did an exaggerated shudder.

'I can't believe it,' she said. 'The number of times I've talked to him. It makes my flesh creep.'

'Maybe he's not after you.'

'If it's true.' She paused, thinking it out. 'If it is true, he might be after Wyndham.'

'It's possible.'

'What about the police? Shouldn't we call them?'

'And tell them what?'

'What you've told me.'

'What happens next is Dave denies it. They talk to Jack, if they take it that far, and they can locate him, and he says this is rubbish, I've got a simple explanation. We'll look like idiots.'

'So what do we do?'

'I don't know. Warn Wyndham. See what he says. When is he getting back?'

'He's not. He's in Paris. He won't be back till tomorrow.'

He'd gone over there to show a French company a cut of the film, she explained, because he was hoping to sell them a modified version of the series.

'What time's he getting back?'

She turned away from me. She was frowning again.

'I don't know.' She made a resigned gesture. 'He's moved out. When he gets back he won't be coming here. I don't know where he'll be. I'll ring his office tomorrow. He'll be there. I'm going there to see him in the evening. He said he wants to talk to me, and someone from the office rang and made an appointment. Would you believe? An appointment.'

I said I'd ring him at the office in the morning, and then we sat looking at the sky in silence. I had nothing to say, partly because I couldn't think what to do next. In a sense I'd done about all that anyone might expect. Now it was up to Sarah or Wyndham to decide what to do with the information I'd gathered. But, even while I was telling myself this, I knew that either they wouldn't act, or if they did, it would be too late by the time they'd made up their minds.

'Stay with me tonight,' Sarah said.

I looked over at her, trying to gauge her intent.

'I don't know,' I told her. 'Suppose Wyndham comes back.'

'I've told you where he is,' she said. 'He won't be back, and I'm not suggesting that you sleep with me. You've just said that a man might be trying to kill me. How do you think I feel? I want someone here in the house tonight. I think Wyndham would understand that, even if he turned up, which he won't, and even if I gave a shit what he thinks, which I don't.'

As she spoke, her voice rose louder and higher, and I could feel her tension vibrating in the room.

'All right,' I said. 'I'll be your bodyguard tonight, but after tonight what are you going to do?'

'I'll go stay with my uncle for a while. He won't notice, and I can get back here in an hour. Till things get sorted out.'

Her parents were both dead, and Uncle Will was the only surviving relative I'd ever heard her mention. He lived in a big house near Hove. It seemed appropriate.

The rest of the evening was dull and restless. We gossiped, idly, about what the next political scandal would be, about how long the government would last, and about how fecund the ladybirds had been this year. She told me about the house they'd bought in France. It was an old farmhouse standing on the side of a hill in Normandy, surrounded by a cherry orchard. At the weekends you could hear the farmers blasting off their shotguns in the fields. No one came up the lane, except for the other English couples who lived nearby. She had stayed there one weekend, she said, with three Italian students she had met on the ferry. They were obsessed with football and spoke only a few words of English, but they'd also been randy, tireless as only boys can be, and deeply grateful. After they left, she'd been exhausted, and she stayed an extra day, sleeping and lazing around, gazing out at the sunlit fields, and listening to Elgar. When she heard the first bars of 'Chanson de Matin', she had burst into tears.

'We have to sell it,' she said, 'because I don't want it any more, and I can't stand the thought of Wyndham staying there with anyone else.'

Later on she telephoned a local restaurant. When it came the food was fish, heavily spiced and dotted with hot red peppers. Sarah produced two bottles of wine, and we ate round the kitchen table. By the time we finished we'd got through both bottles, and started on another.

'Lately,' she said, 'I've been wondering about what happens next. Two Jehovah's Witnesses came to the door last week. They don't believe in evolution. Did you know that? I find that an impossible hurdle. I told them that their concept of the universe was inadequate. We had a nice chat. They said that what looked like chaos was really God's order. I told them that what looked like chaos was really chaos.'

We sat in front of the television, with a bottle of brandy. She told me that in the restaurants in the town near their house in France they put a blob of apple sorbet in a glass and drowned it in this brandy, and it was delicious. We didn't have any apple sorbet, but I drank the brandy and tried to imagine it. After a while the sound of the television seemed to go away.

'I should be comatose,' she said, 'but this doesn't seem to be having any effect on me.'

I agreed, then I lay on the carpet and laughed. I seemed to be losing my grip on time. I dozed off, and she shook me awake, said it was about midnight, and led me to the spare room.

I stripped my clothes off and dropped them on the floor, then I lay back in the bed and looked at the ceiling, which seemed to be spinning slowly, but when I closed my eyes the bed started going round. I buried my face in the pillow and clung on for dear life.

When I woke up it was still dark and someone seemed to be moving around downstairs. I got up, looked around for my shoes and socks, found them, then gave up the idea, because it seemed like too much trouble to put them on. There was nothing in the bedroom, either, that I could use as a weapon. So I wrapped myself in a blanket, and went down the stairs slowly, trying not to make a noise, clinging to the banister rail to stay upright.

The sitting room was dim, lit only by the flashing reflections from the images on the TV. I peered round and made out Sarah lying on her stomach on the rug in front of the television, her head cradled in her arms. She was wearing a short white towelling robe, which left her hips and thighs bare, flaring out in a tulip shape around her.

I stumbled into the room, got down on my knees and ended up partly on top of her, part of my weight resting on the floor. Against my skin, her flesh felt cool and soft,

239

and, as if by some magic command I was erect, nudging involuntarily against her. She stirred sleepily, and in a little while she turned around, reversing our positions. She climbed on to my body, sat up and guided me into her. Then she bent all the way down to rest her cheek against mine, hitching the blanket up around her, and we went off into a haze, rocking slowly inside the flickering glow of the screen.

25

I rang Wyndham's office as soon as I got back home, and Katrina answered. She said he wasn't in yet, but she was expecting him after lunch, and I left a message asking him to ring me. I had a feeling that he wouldn't, but he surprised me, because it was only an hour later when the phone rang. He asked me how I was doing, and I said I was fine, but I had to see him urgently.

'What's it about?'

'I don't want to discuss it on the phone,' I said. 'I'll tell you when I see you.'

His voice turned weary.

'I don't know, Sammy. Today's a bad day.'

'Come on, man. I've got to talk to you.'

He made up his mind.

'OK. I'm showing a cut to Nick and Vanessa later on in the evening. Meet me there, about half past six. We'll have half an hour, beforehand. You can stay and see it too. Should be interesting.'

The successful negotiation of my meeting with Wyndham gave me the sense that I'd brought my involvement with the project to an end. In the cold

241

light of day, the fantasies of violence and death which had flooded my mind the night before had disappeared. Once I'd talked to Wyndham, I thought, I'd pack it in, and leave them to it. Sarah was another matter altogether. Cutting myself away from her would be more than difficult. Thinking about her, I remembered that she'd been asleep when I left, and I hadn't found out what her plans were, or when she intended to leave for Brighton. I was about to reach for the telephone when the doorbell rang.

My son was standing on the pavement, staring up at the window, an impatient look on his face. I ran down and let him in.

'What's going on, Dad? I rang you late, but you weren't in. I was expecting you to ring back.'

I hadn't listened to my messages or I'd have known.

'Sorry. I was out. I didn't hear the message.'

'Where did you go?'

'See some friends.'

'Who?'

'You don't know them.'

He was pursuing the details of my life in the way that he usually did when he saw me, but I had the sense that he wasn't really interested. There was an abstracted look about him which told me there was something he wanted to talk about urgently.

'When I leave university,' he said abruptly, 'I'm getting out of this country for good.'

It was like a flash of lightning in the dark. For an instant his eyes told me everything. In that fierce light I could read the pages of my own childhood as they turned.

'How come? The last few years you've been telling me you're English.'

He stared at me moodily.

242

'Well, I'm not. Am I? Anyway, whatever I am they're not going to give me a chance.'

'What's happened?'

I was looking at him carefully. If he'd been beaten up I couldn't see any bruises.

'Nothing.'

He couldn't have been arrested or he'd have said. A kind of relief flooded through me.

'Come on,' I said, 'something must have happened.'

He told me then. He'd been up to the university for an interview. It had gone well, but before meeting the lecturers he'd spent the morning looking around with some other candidates.

'One of these guys kept on at me, man. He was like from some place where they'd never seen any black people except on TV, and he started talking to me like he was out of the Desmonds. I mean, he couldn't get it right, and he kept on kind of sticking in bits of rap. And he kept coming up, every time I was trying to talk to somebody else, going on and on about black music, and hip hop and Spike Lee, like some idiot. In the end he started going on about Bob Marley and Kingston, Jamaica. So I said I didn't give a shit about Bob Marley and I'd been brought up in Camden Town, so I didn't know anything about Jamaica or South Central LA. He just looked amazed.'

'I'd have told him to fuck off.'

'I did. But he just laughed like I was joking. I had to start getting mad, before he left me alone. Then later on I was talking to this girl, and he came up and said, careful, he's a militant. I nearly punched his face in.'

'You've met that kind of fool before.'

'But it's not like London. They're all like that out there. They look at you like you've showed up in the wrong

243

place. And when you talk to them they can't seem to have an ordinary conversation with you. It's not that they're trying to be unfriendly. It's like they can't conceive of a person like me having the same interests or intelligence or ambitions as them. I mean, they're talking about A levels and books and that, and when I come up they start asking me about drugs.'

'They're not all going to be like that. Anyway, you know it doesn't matter what they think. You're going there for yourself.'

'Yeah. But, Dad. This is a university. I thought it was going to be different from school. The students are supposed to be intelligent. It puts you right off. I mean, I've only been outside of this country twice, but by the end of the day the only people I could talk to were the foreign students.'

His eyes lurked with a temper which made me feel frightened for him. I thought furiously. Perhaps this would be one of those turning points when whatever I said would make a difference. But all I could think of to say was that it had been this way for me too.

'I wouldn't mind so much,' he said, 'if they were trying to be offensive or something. At least that would mean they thought I was a person with feelings and thoughts of my own. The way they are is like they've got some picture of a black person in their heads, something they've seen in the movies or on TV, and they can't believe I'm not like that. It's like the way I am, the way you are, my granny and my cousins and my uncles and my aunts, all of that, it's like it doesn't exist as far as they're concerned, because it's not what they've seen on TV.'

I felt a spurt of impatience.

'Well, to them it doesn't. Your whole life I've been telling you about racism. It's more than people shouting

244

nasty names, or trying to beat you up. It's the way that they construct our lives in their heads. What we are is what they're comfortable with, so they prefer to forget that you're real. But the important thing is to decide for yourself who you're going to be or how you feel about yourself.'

'That's easy for you to say, Dad. In your day it was all out in the open. You never expected anything from them, so you didn't care. But this is my country. All of them looked like people I'd grown up with. You couldn't tell them apart from my cousins. It shouldn't be like that.'

'Let's go for a walk,' I said.

I listened to him talk for the next hour, and replied with platitudes of one kind and another. After all this time, I thought, I still hadn't worked out how to cope with what he felt about his experiences. Of course, I'd talked to him at length about who we were and what that meant, but when he came to me like this, his head full of rage, I froze. What I feared most was the thought of teaching him my own despair.

I got to the TV company's office early, for a change, and I sat among the petitioners waiting for Wyndham to show. When he arrived and saw me his eyebrows lifted in surprise.

'You're on time.'

We went to a pub nearby, which was full of office workers on the way home. Wyndham ordered whisky without asking me, and I guessed that he was nervous about the viewing.

'About the other day,' he said, before I could start, 'I was pissed off. Forget what I said.'

'Doesn't matter,' I told him. 'Something's come up though.'

I told him about my conversation with Dave, and what he'd said about Jack having a contract on someone in the production, but as I spoke his expression grew more and more incredulous. Eventually he began to laugh.

'You've lost it, Sammy,' he said. 'You've gone troppo. You know that?'

'You don't believe what I'm saying?'

'I think you've been conned. Can't you see? I'll tell you what I know. Neither Caroline nor Joan had anything to do with the fire at my house, because I was with both of them at the time. Secondly, Dave tells you Jack is a nutter, which might well be true, but you've forgotten that they met in an institution. Dave is a congenital liar. He can't help it. Right?'

I nodded reluctantly.

'Right. What makes you think he's telling the truth, and even if he is, what makes you think that Jack was telling him the truth when he told him what he did? This is what these guys do. They live in a fantasy world. Believe me, Dave is convincing, but the next thing you know he'll be telling you that he's getting messages through the telly.'

'You've changed your tune. A few days ago you were basing a whole programme on Dave's testimony.'

He shrugged.

'I know better now,' he said. 'Thanks to you.'

'How can you be so certain?'

He grinned. This was a question for which he was prepared.

'I'm in the business. Remember? You take some facts, stitch them together, embroider them with a veil of speculation and you've got a moving tapestry of horror. People love sitting at home panicking about criminal conspiracies, serial killers, drug-crazed hitmen. So it's an industry.

246

Writers, producers, directors. We're all playing the game. But it's like romance. The way it happens in the movies, two people meet, have a vicious row, next thing you know they're in bed together. Try that in real life.'

'You're saying these things don't happen?'

'Of course they happen.' For some reason he was enjoying this. 'But we impose a coherent narrative, invent motives, telescope events, the way Dave is doing with you. It's a story, man. That's why it's so convincing. But the reason real life is so much more terrifying is because anything can happen for the most trivial of motives, and it doesn't make sense. A researcher is standing near a block of flats thinking about what she's going to do that evening. Three young girls come up and ask her for a cigarette. She says she hasn't got one. They tell her to hand over her bag. She says no and they have a struggle. One of the girls stabs her, and they run away. When the police arrest them they say they only wanted a fag. The cops understand that shit. That's why they're cops and we're only TV wankers.'

He stared at me, his eyes serious now.

'You're talking about Jill?'

'Yeah. The police arrested the girls who did it yesterday. One of them confessed. There was no mystery about it. Cops went from door to door and found a wheelchair pensioner who saw them running away.'

'Bloody hell.'

Wyndham drained his glass and signalled for more drink.

'Did you tell Sarah about this hitman stuff?'

'Yes.'

He gave me a moody look.

'I wish you hadn't done that. The state she's in is bad enough without making it worse.'

'That's not exactly my fault. She's in a state about you leaving. Bit sudden, wasn't it?'

He looked away from me and for a moment I thought he wasn't going to reply.

'It wasn't sudden at all,' he said impatiently. 'It was coming a long time. Years. She's at the time of life when women go crazy.'

'She's not old enough.'

'Nothing to do with it.' He drained his glass and waved to the barman again. I put my hand over mine. I'd barely finished the first drink. He lowered his voice. 'It's this crazy thing about babies. We were trying to have one.'

'And you couldn't.'

'That wasn't the problem. She got pregnant, but the amniocentesis said it was going to be a mongol.'

'Down's syndrome.'

'A fucking mongol. That wasn't what we wanted.'

'What did she think?'

'At first she wanted to keep it. Then we talked it over. It was impossible. For the sake of the child.'

I didn't doubt his honesty, but I couldn't believe that it had been a simple decision for Sarah.

'She was obsessed with trying again. But I'd had enough. It ruined things. I lived with this pressure for years. Enough is enough.'

I couldn't meet his eyes, or take the pain I saw there.

'So what are you going to do?'

He came closer, his head almost touching mine.

'This is between us.'

'Sure.'

'The thing is, Joan's pregnant.'

Suddenly he was smiling. A curl of triumph on his lips. I thought about Sarah standing in the garden fiddling with her plants and I felt a stab of something like anguish.

'Does Sarah know this?'

'I had to tell her. It wasn't easy.'

When we got back, the receptionist directed us to a viewing room where Nick and Vanessa were sitting in front of a huge telly. Nick looked as relaxed as he was ever likely to, but Vanessa was tapping a pen irritably on her writing pad, and when she saw me coming in behind Wyndham she pursed her lips and looked away before she said hello.

'Joan had an appointment,' Nick said, 'so she decided not to wait. You've just missed her.'

Wyndham grunted an acknowledgement, but I could see from the way he moved that he was too wired to care one way or the other.

'Well, let's get on with it,' Vanessa said, 'I haven't got long. Time I went home.'

Wyndham put the cassette in. They hadn't yet had the time to put the titles on, but it started with a wide shot of the estate, followed by the camera tracking along one of the paths at night. The scene looked moody and mysterious, like the opening sequence of a detective series. On the soundtrack there was a pounding reggae rhythm with half a dozen voices rapping above it. Then the screen went blank.

'We've got the titles here and a bit of studio presentation,' Wyndham said.

When the picture came back it was a reconstruction of Helen's murder, done in the same dramatic style. Even though I knew it was a reproduction of real events I had the sense that I was watching a slick succession of clichés. The terrified blonde, the unseen killer, the screams in the uncaring night. To do the director credit, the scene pulsated with tension and fear. I glanced sideways at Wyndham and noted that there was a faint smile on his face.

After the final scream faded out over a long shot of a lighted window, the presenter came on and gave a brief account of the murder and the subsequent trial. He was a well-known reporter. He wore a double-breasted Boss suit, and spoke in the hushed but urgent tones which commanded attention. 'Was the wrong man convicted?' he asked. 'And is there still a killer lurking in the area?'

The next passage featured a number of Leon's friends and relatives who maintained that although he was the size of a ten-ton truck he was a gentle giant who would not hurt a fly. This was followed by three witnesses who had seen him in different places at different times of the night. After this the presenter hinted that there were other, more convincing explanations for the murder. That was the end of Part One.

Part Two kicked off with a number of interviews testifying to the presence of crack dealers on the estate. These cut back and forth between some shadowy footage, from a hidden camera, of various young men lurking around and apparently doing deals. Unremarkably, they were all black. Jamie's mum, Sandra, came on next and said that Helen was in the habit of receiving a stream of mysterious callers. After her the screen jumped to a close-up of the presenter's worried expression.

'The couple,' he said, 'were part of the murky world of drugs. Was this a drug deal gone wrong?' He paused, his concern deepening. 'Or was it something with even more alarming implications?'

This was the signal for a montage of headlines and photographs of young women. I counted four women, although the images were so speedy and abrupt that it might have been more, or less.

'In the last three years,' the presenter intoned solemnly, 'there have been several unsolved murders of young women in the vicinity, all of them were in their twenties, all of them were attractive.'

I guessed what was coming next. The serial-killer theory. They did it with the same combination of carefully chosen fact and reckless speculation. Various women, including Sandra, testified to having been peered at, stalked or molested in some way. The threats against Helen were quoted, and a copy of an anonymous letter Helen had received scrolled down the screen, the flat angry obscenities unravelling in time with the cadence of the presenter's voice.

When he appeared again he was framed within the entrance to one of the blocks.

'Are these the words of a killer on the loose?' he asked, before pacing slowly past the camera and out of the shot.

The screen went blank, and everyone in the room was silent for a few seconds.

Nick was the first to speak.

'So what do you think, Sammy?'

It was a lashed-up load of manipulative tosh, I thought. This was the sort of programme, I thought, which would probably embarrass the hell out of Wyndham if he ever got up the nerve to look at it again. While this went through my mind I could feel them all looking at me.

'It'll be OK,' I said. I looked at Wyndham. His face was impassive, and I couldn't read what he was thinking. But I was certain he wouldn't want the truth. Not in front of Nick, if ever. 'The story could have been stronger, but I don't suppose you had much choice.'

He looked over at Vanessa.

'What did you think?'

'It should be all right,' she said briskly. 'It moves along,

251

and it makes the point that women are in danger there. Not bad. They certainly won't switch off.' She peered past us at Nick. 'There's a couple of points I'll talk to you about tomorrow after I've had a think.'

He nodded, and she got up, gave Wyndham a quick smile and left the room.

'We need to talk,' Nick told Wyndham. 'There's a little cleaning up to do. It's too long for a start. Let's meet in the morning.'

I looked at the digital timer. It had run to almost half an hour. They'd need to chop some of it out to bring it down to the right length for a broadcast half hour.

'Right,' Wyndham said. He sounded relieved, but not much pleased. 'How about a drink?'

'Give me five minutes,' Nick said. 'I need to make a call. I'll meet you down in the lobby.'

The moment Nick closed the door, I asked Wyndham the question which had been running through my mind. I'd decided not to, but, somehow, I couldn't resist.

'So you think Leon is innocent? I mean, do you believe that yourself?'

He shrugged. 'That's not the point. Is it?'

'To me it is,' I told him. 'You haven't come up with one bit of convincing evidence for it. All you've done is spread a little confusion around, man.'

He smiled.

'It's not our job to award guilt or innocence. That's for judges and juries. We're just raising questions to be answered.'

'How come it's our job to do that?'

He grunted impatiently.

'Come off it, Sammy. Advocacy's escaped from the courtroom. We've become part of the process. We tell everyone the man's been found guilty in the first place,

252

and they believe it because it's on the news. A little doubt isn't going to hurt.'

He still hadn't answered my question.

'I knocked myself out looking for a hint that the guy was innocent and I didn't find it.' As I said this I remembered that Amaryll's anger with Dave had been triggered by his belief that the Beulah Hill alibi could result in Helen's killer getting off the hook. From that point on I'd been convinced. 'If I had to swear I'd probably say guilty. What I want to know is what you think.'

He grinned at me, amused by my irritation.

'You're reacting like a punter,' he said. 'Every night they switch on the telly and reassure themselves with a few episodes in the story of good against evil, disorder tidied up, chaos tamed. They need to know who to blame, even if it's the wrong person. But they know that in real life the cops get it wrong sometimes. On the other hand, we're on the job, questioning the system, putting things right in the court of public opinion. They need us to do that so they can keep believing in the story. That's what they're paying me for. Whether he's guilty or not isn't the issue. I don't know. It's not my problem.' He stood up and stretched his arms out. He was beginning to relax, calmed by the knowledge that the job was practically done. 'Let's go get a drink. If we're going to talk about this I need some refreshment.'

Something surfaced from the back of my mind. Nick had mentioned an appointment.

'I thought you were going back to the office,' I said. 'Sarah told me she was meeting you.'

He frowned.

'No. I'm not planning on seeing her tonight.'

'Are you sure? She said someone in your office made an appointment.'

He shrugged.

'No. Must be a mistake. I'm not going back there tonight. I haven't had much sleep and I need to eat and drink. That's what I'm doing tonight.'

I stared at him, lost in thought for a couple of seconds. I was sure that I hadn't misunderstood what Sarah had said, but if Wyndham hadn't made the appointment someone else had. All of a sudden I felt a rush of apprehension. I opened my mouth to blurt out the idea that had flashed into my mind, but then I remembered Wyndham's reaction earlier on, and I shut it again.

'I'll hold you to that drink another time,' I told Wyndham. 'I just remembered. There's something I have to do.'

26

What I had to do was find out what was happening to Sarah. I rang her from the lobby, but there was no answer. I rang Wyndham's office with the same result. I ran for the car, and by the time I got to it I was sweating, all the forebodings of the night before hardening into certainty. At the back of my mind I'd been so relieved that Joan hadn't been at the meeting that I hadn't thought about how odd that was. At that moment it had seemed logical because she'd have seen the film more than once during the afternoon, but she had just as much at stake as Wyndham did. She'd have wanted to be there.

The rush hour was over but the traffic along Euston Road was still heavy enough to slow me down to a crawl, and it was nearly half an hour before I got to Camden Town. I pulled round and parked in the alleyway which ran past the front of the building. The big doors were closed, but there was a row of bells by the side of it flanking the plate of an entryphone speaker. I peered at it, and picked out the names 'Davies' and 'Foster' on the third button from the bottom. I pressed it and waited. Nothing. I pressed it again. Still nothing. I felt a kind of relief. If there was no one there I could wash my hands of the matter. Sarah would ring me from Brighton the next day or the day after or whenever she felt like it, and I'd tell her that she'd had me worried for a little while.

I started walking back to the car, but the closer I got to it, the more I was nagged by the sense that there was some detail I'd forgotten. Suddenly it hit me. There'd been a black Golf parked at the top of the alleyway. I hurried up to it, then realised that I couldn't remember the number. One black Golf looked much like another and it was a fairly common car. I circled round it and peered in the windows, but there was nothing to tell me whether or not it was Joan's car.

After a minute I gave up, walked back and looked up at the building. The lights on the first floor were on, but I couldn't decide whether or not that was significant. There were lights behind several of the windows. On the other hand, I had the feeling that some of them were on an automatic timer or were left on all the time to discourage intruders. As I looked, I thought I caught a flicker of something moving. I kept looking. It didn't happen again, and I couldn't be sure that it wasn't my imagination, but it was as if that little flash of something had thrown a switch in my head. I walked back, pressed on the bell again, and kept my finger down. When nothing happened I started on the other bells, working from the top.

The third bell brought a man's voice.

'Hello,' the speaker barked abruptly.

'Bike!' I shouted. 'Bike!'

'You're bloody late,' the voice grumbled, but the buzzer went and I pushed in before it stopped. The stairs were wide and curving. Easy to climb, and I took them three at a time. The door to Wyndham's office was locked, and

I rang the bell, then banged on it, but there was still no response. I was about to turn away when I smelled the smoke. It was faint but there was no mistaking it. I banged on the door again.

'Oi,' a voice shouted behind me. I looked round. A middle-aged white man in shirt sleeves was leaning his paunch on the banisters and looking down at me. 'What do you want? They've gone home!' he bellowed.

The aggression was predictable and I almost smiled, but at that moment I couldn't spare the time to assuage his fears.

'Come down here!' I shouted back.

He took half a step backwards.

'What?'

'There's a fire. Can't you smell it?'

He came down reluctantly. I ignored him and kicked at the door. It didn't give an inch.

'Have you got a key?' I asked him.

He shook his head.

'I'll ring 999,' he said and scuttled back up the stairs.

I looked around. There was a fire extinguisher in the angle of the stairs. I grabbed it and began battering the lock. I must have hit it four or five times before I felt it shift, but after that it was quick. By then a tendril of smoke was escaping from under the door. A few more strokes and it flew open.

A cloud of smoke poured out. Black, a choking brown, greyish-white strands curling wickedly through it. It was laced with fumes, bitter and acrid, potent enough to throw me back against the wall, coughing, gasping and spluttering, eyes streaming, like a raging sniff out of some insane devil's lungs. Somewhere in the middle two tongues of flame licked out and weaved. Behind the dark cloud inhuman voices growled and sang.

I ripped at the front of my shirt and tore off a big enough piece to wrap round my face, then I banged on the top of the fire extinguisher, releasing the catch and spraying it in front of me, I forced my feet back to the door. The torrential outflow of smoke had made it seem worse than it was. The scene was covered in a thick brown mist, but through it I could make out that one side of the room, to the left of the door, was a wall of flame, and the computers were alight, but the stairs leading up to Wyndham's room were intact. I shouted Sarah's name, and waited for a second but there was no reply. In any case, she probably couldn't have heard me.

I retreated a few steps to build up my momentum, and before I could change my mind I ran through the door, holding my breath and heading for the stairs, the foam from the extinguisher still gushing round me, like an aura of dirty soap suds. Halfway up I slipped and fell to my knees. Behind the mask I gasped for breath and felt the smoke cutting into my lungs, a hot, angry stabbing pain. I held my breath again, choked, and felt the pain knifing through my chest. I crawled up as rapidly as I could, dragging the dribbling metal tube behind me. It must have taken seconds, but it felt longer. At the top I brushed through the open door and reeled, bent double, across the room to the window. I swung the extinguisher at it, and the glass exploded outwards. I put my face to the hole and hauled cool air into my lungs, but almost immediately I seemed to be smothered in the rush of smoke pouring past my head.

At the same time I recalled something about creating draughts, and I had an instant picture of the fire smashing its way up the stairs and through the room to get to the window. I looked round desperately. It was too high to jump and I'd have to go back down those stairs. The room was empty. I'd made that much out on my way to the window. I began nerving myself up for the rush back downstairs, then I remembered the toilet, which was just outside Wyndham's door at the head of the stairs. Water. There'd still be water in there. I ran for it, and hurled myself against the door. It moved, but I had to give it several shoves before it came all the way open. The smoke was a shade lighter there and I slammed the door shut before bending over to look down at the floor. A woman's body was huddled there. I'd pushed her over against the wall, and she was face down, her arms stretched out beside her. I shouted Sarah's name, bent over to pull her up, and, out of sheer astonishment, nearly dropped her again when I saw her face. In the dark, I hadn't noticed that her hair was dark rather than Sarah's blonde, and I'd had to get close up before I realised that the woman I'd dragged off the floor was Joan.

27

In the end I was grateful to find myself in hospital. I had used the plastic bin in the toilet to soak myself and Joan with water, wrapped my face in my shirt, covered hers with a towel, and then hoisted her over my shoulder in a fireman's lift for the journey downstairs. We'd only just made it, and I'd finished by crawling out on my hands and knees dragging her behind me. I had collapsed then, and half conscious, saw the man from upstairs bending over Joan as she lay flat out on the floor giving her the kiss of life, and pressing her chest clumsily. The only thing wrong with the picture was that her blouse and her bra had been ripped off, so that she looked like part of an erotic frieze, lying half nude and supine under his ministrations. In any case, I was too weak to protest, and it seemed like only a couple of heartbeats before the ambulance were clamping masks to our faces.

The oxygen, or whatever it was, got me going surprisingly quickly, and once in the ambulance, I sat up and had a look at Joan. She was still unconscious, but she was breathing easily through the mask. They said she'd be all right, and I relaxed. The odd thing was that, although

I knew that once she'd recovered, our relations would be as cold as ever, I felt a kind of pride in her survival and a strong sense of anxiety about how she was doing.

I'd only suffered some superficial burns, on my hands and face. They smeared me with antiseptic cream, bandaged one of my hands, and told me to come back in a couple of days or to see my GP. A uniformed policeman was waiting to interview me. I told him I'd gone over to the office to meet a friend and I'd seen movement behind the window, so I'd gone up and smelt the smoke.

'Good job you did,' he said. 'You saved her life.'

Underneath my fatigue the words gave me a little thrill and I smiled at him. In the wake of the euphoria I nearly began talking about Caroline and Jack, and the real reason I'd gone up to Camden Town, but as soon as the temptation surfaced I suppressed it. He took my address and phone number in case they wanted another statement, and went off.

I went looking for Joan, but I didn't get very far, because Wyndham and Caroline were sitting together in the waiting area down the corridor. They were holding hands like a couple of lost babes. When he saw me Wyndham got up and reached me in a few quick strides of his long legs. He tried to put his arms round me, but I fended him off.

'Careful, man. I'm fragile.'

He held my wrists tightly.

'I heard what you did. Thanks. I can't tell you how grateful I am.'

'Don't be so soft,' I told him. 'Pull yourself together, man.'

He laughed. Caroline emerged from behind him and rested her fingers lightly on my shoulder.

'You're a hero,' she said. 'You really are.'

She looked softer, more vulnerable than Joan, and if someone had asked me to guess I'd probably have said that, of the two sisters, she had the more equable temperament. Looking at her I found it hard to figure out why I'd thought it possible to mistake them for each other. I found it hard, also, to continue thinking of her as a nutter, bitter and twisted underneath her smile.

'How's Joan?' I asked Wyndham.

'Fine,' he said. 'They're keeping her in but she'll be OK. We're waiting to see her.'

'Do they know how it started?'

'No. They haven't had time to investigate. Something electrical would be my guess. The shit I'm going to get into with the insurance doesn't bear thinking about.'

A moody expression crossed his face.

'How did you come to be there?'

'I was passing.'

He gave me a peculiar look but before he could pursue it I turned to Caroline.

'Can I talk to you for a minute while you're waiting?'

Wyndham frowned. I guessed that he was remembering some of the things I'd said. His eyes locked in on mine.

'Let's not get into all that now, Sammy.'

'I don't want to get into anything,' I told him. 'I just want to talk to her.'

'What about?'

'I can speak for myself, Wyndham,' Caroline said. She grinned at him. 'I'm a big girl now.' She pushed his arm gently. 'You go and sit down. I'll go with Sammy and find some coffee.'

We found a machine on the ground floor near the lobby. It was close to midnight, and the hospital seemed to have emptied itself for the night, so that our footsteps echoed along the wide corridors. The machine was old and battered, but it worked. I turned down the offer of a coffee, because I wasn't sure I could face putting a hot drink to my lips. Instead, I chose a can of synthetic orange.

'I wanted to ask you about Jack,' I said. 'What's your connection with him?'

She frowned. Puzzled.

'Who's he?'

'He's a guy you met at the day centre. About three years ago? I'm not sure about the time, but I've seen a picture of you with him and Dave and Amaryll. You do know them.'

She stared at me, startled at the mention of the day centre and the photo.

'What's he look like?'

I described him and she thought for half a minute.

'Yes,' she said. 'I think I remember him. Funny thing. I've seen him around a couple of times recently, but I couldn't place him. I wasn't thinking very clearly when we met.'

'You haven't spoken to him lately?'

'No. We didn't speak much then either. What's this all about?'

I braced myself.

'I think the fire might have been arson, and if it was I think it might have been Jack.'

Her face creased up in bewilderment.

'But why would he do that?'

A thought struck her then, and she frowned at me.

'And you think I had something to do with it?'

'Not exactly,' I hedged, 'but you know all these people. I thought you might have an idea what was going on.'

She was gazing straight into my eyes now.

'Why would you think that?'

263

'I talked to Simon Priestley,' I told her.

'Ah,' she said. It sounded a bit like a moan she'd been holding in for a longish while. She swung away from me abruptly, and faced the machine. She put her hand out tentatively and traced a pattern on its surface with her forefinger. She swung back round to fix her eyes on me. 'I was round the bend when I did those things. I wouldn't do them again, but I'm not sorry. He screwed me up good. I don't suppose he told you that. He had me whenever he wanted but he wasn't content with that. He dominated me, then he dumped me. I know I did it because I wasn't well but I still think he deserved it. I wouldn't do anything like that to anyone else. I wouldn't do it even to him nowadays.' She paused. 'I didn't have anything to do with that fire. That's my sister up there. You may find it hard to understand, but that time when I wasn't well, I had a motive. Without a motive I'm safe.'

She grinned suddenly, as if sharing the joke, and it crossed my mind that I liked her as much as I disliked her sister.

'What about Wyndham?'

She shook her head.

'No. When I went with Wyndham it was a bit of fun. Then he got serious with Joan. It wasn't a problem. She's my sister.'

'Not all sisters would see it like that.'

She gestured the idea away.

'That's their problem. I'd do anything for her. She saved me.'

If she was lying I couldn't see it.

'Someone phoned Sarah and made an appointment for tonight. It could be that she was meant to be the one stuck up there.'

'It wouldn't be anything to do with either of us,'

Caroline said. 'I was supposed to meet her there. If I hadn't been late you'd have had two people to rescue.' She paused, and gestured. 'Believe me. Joan wouldn't hurt Sarah. She felt bad enough about the whole situation.'

'Bit late.'

She grimaced.

'Oh, all right. You've known them a long time. I didn't know her. We've met once. It wasn't something I thought about until I heard Wyndham was leaving. With Joan it just happened, and she does feel bad about it.'

Down the corridor the lift wheezed and whirred, and Wyndham walked towards us.

'We can go in now,' he said to Caroline. He looked at me. 'Why don't you come and see her?'

'Maybe tomorrow,' I told him. 'Right now I could do with being on my own.'

He nodded, then reached out and touched me on the forearm.

'You're a star,' he said.

'A pretty dim one,' I told him.

He laughed dutifully, but I knew that he didn't get it, for which I didn't blame him, because I was only just beginning to realise how far off the right track I'd been.

28

I woke up later than I intended. I'd slept through the noise of the pigeons, and the swelling roar of the rush hour, and the sun lancing through the slit in the curtains. It was past noon. The phone rang, but it stopped before I could psych myself up to go and answer it. My body ached in every bone, so I fell back on the pillow and let sleep take me where it willed.

It was rush hour again when I woke up, but I must have been thinking hard while I was asleep because I awoke with my mind set and determined about what I would do next. Coming home in the early hours of the morning I'd been thinking about the fire, and the fact that I'd believed everything Caroline said. At first I'd wondered whether she too was an expert and indecipherable liar, but what she said had made sense and it felt right. The problem was that I'd lined up Caroline as the brain behind Jack's actions, but if I ruled her out, it was possible that there was some other motive, which had nothing to do with Wyndham's love life. I couldn't imagine why Jack would have sent Wyndham the threats or tried to burn down his house and his office on his own account, so he had to be following some kind of direction. I hadn't a clue what that might be, or where it was coming from, but it was clear that if I wanted to know I had to find Jack and squeeze it out of him somehow.

I got dressed painfully, and set out for the address Dave had given me. It was a hotel in Bayswater, a short-stay, one-night-stand kind of place, as I figured out the minute I stepped into the lobby. It was daubed in the kind of paint which looked as if it had come from a job lot which had fallen off the back of a council lorry. Dusty green and brown, slapped rudely over peeling plaster.

Behind a makeshift desk in one corner of the room was a bald-headed man with sharp black eyes and a greying stubble. I told him I was looking for Jack Gold, and he shook his head, his deep-set round eyes darting past me and then back to look me up and down.

'He's gone.'

Three blond boys came down the stairs and one of them started talking to the baldhead in a strong German accent. He said that the room was filthy and the washbasin didn't work. The man shrugged and said it had been all right this morning but he'd send someone to have a look.

'When?' the German boy asked loudly, pressing closer.

The baldhead swung to stare into the street.

'Soon as he comes in, mate.'

He didn't say who 'he' was, but the boys seemed satisfied and they moved away, muttering to each other.

I started again.

'Do you know where he's gone?'

The man shrugged without answering. I reached into my pocket, took out a fiver and laid it on the desk.

'I dunno. He said he fancied somewhere cheaper.'

'Where?'

'Dunno. There's hundreds.'

267

'Did you recommend anything?'

This was like pulling teeth.

'I told him about a few.'

'Which ones?'

He picked up the note and put it in his pocket, then he gave me the names of about half a dozen hotels and I wrote them down.

'You reckon he's at one of these?'

'How would I know?'

I gave up then and headed for the door. On the stairs I looked back to see whether he had picked up the phone, but he was still sitting there behind his desk, motionless as a lizard on a rock.

The hotel in King's Cross was the fourth that I tried. All the others had been of the same species as the one in Bayswater, a few notches down on the evolutionary scale. I parked on a single yellow line, looked around for traffic wardens, and when I didn't see any, I crossed my fingers, and walked up the stairs behind a Somali woman holding a baby and leading a toddler by the hand. Something tugged inside me when I saw her because she made me think of my mother, not that my mother looked like this woman. It was simply that when I thought of her arriving in England, this was how I saw her, tired and dispirited, but erect and composed, clutching her children protectively by the hand.

The man at the desk seemed like the spitting image of the one I'd left behind at Bayswater, but when I looked closer I saw that he had long straggling black hair and a blue stubble. I asked him about Jack, and he said they didn't give out information. I laughed with genuine amusement.

'Is he here?'

'No.'

I thought about bribing him, but I had no way of knowing whether he was lying or whether the man who'd given the addresses in the first place had been conning me, so I let it go and walked out.

I was standing on the pavement, trying to think of how to tackle the problem of finding a needle in the haystack of the city, when someone called out softly behind me.

'Oi, mister.'

I turned round. It was a girl, fourteen or fifteen, dressed in jeans, boots and a jacket which had once belonged to a man. A twist of greasy brown hair emerged from the cap she wore and climbed down her neck. In one hand she was holding a rope tied round a big mongrel's neck. I'd caught a glimpse of her in the lobby, and she must have followed me out.

'I can tell you about that bloke you were asking about,' she said.

'Is he there?'

'Give us some change,' she said.

I gave her a pound coin.

'He's dead,' she told me. 'He got shot last night, just round the corner. They stuck him in an ambulance, but he'd had it by the time they got here.'

She started walking off.

'What time was that?'

She turned around, and screwed her face up.

'Dunno. Just after midnight.'

'Do they know who did it?'

'No. Probably dealers.'

I walked back into the hotel and leaned over the receptionist. Then I swayed backwards as the beery fumes of breath caught me in the face.

'What do you want?'

'Why'd you lie about Gold stopping here?'

He looked up, and gave me what he thought was a threatening glare.

'Fuck off,' he said, standing up abruptly.

I reached for my wallet and showed him the card across which I'd printed PRESS in big letters on one of the machines in W.H. Smiths.

'I'm not interested in you,' I told him. 'I just want to know about this guy.' I grinned at him. 'Murder. It's news.'

He sat down again. The sight of the card had sobered him up, as I hoped it would.

'No. They don't like reporters round here. Can't help you.'

'Have a drink on me,' I said. I handed him my last fiver. He took it with a movement like a snake striking. 'I want to look in his room. See what he's left.'

'There's nothing there, mate. Cops took most of it. What's there is rubbish waiting for the cleaners.'

'Let's have a look anyway. Ten minutes.'

He took a key down and handed it to me.

'First floor. You want to be quick. The cops will be back any minute.'

The room was tiny, large enough for a single bed, a washbasin, and a wardrobe, with just enough carpet space in between to provide a clear passage between them. On the floor there was a clump of clothes, some of them with the pockets turned inside out. The little metal dustbin had been turned upside down, and its contents scattered over the floor. The pitiful remains of a desperately shabby week, a few spaghetti tins, a few sheets of newspaper stained with tea leaves, an empty carton of takeaway foil, a couple of used condoms. I caught myself wondering what the inside of my dustbin would look like, and dismissed the thought. The man downstairs had been right, the police had been thorough, and there was nothing left but rubbish. The whole place stank, as if something feral had been caged there. I kicked idly at the newspaper.

A waste of five pounds, I thought. Petrol money down the drain. I turned to go, but some reluctant impulse made me push the door of the wardrobe wide open for a quick peek.

For the first time I saw the photograph pasted behind the door. It was a small square snap, taken somewhere in the room. I could recognise the dingy striped wallpaper. The light had been dim, too, as it always must have been in this room, so that the picture itself had come out a dark maroon. It wasn't so dark, though, that I couldn't recognise the subject of the photograph immediately. It was Sarah, one hand poised behind her head, and her eyes downcast in a pose which was, at the same time, both withdrawn and provocative.

29

She'd changed her mind about going to her uncle's she said; and when she heard about the fire she'd stuck around, waiting to hear from me. I asked her if she could meet me at Mr Hamed's restaurant, in an hour, then I put the phone down and drove up to Highgate. I got there in about half an hour and parked round the corner till her car came past me gathering speed. Then I got out and walked up the other way. I knew how I was going to get in. Most of the houses had a gate closing off the path which went from the street to their gardens. The house backing on to Sarah's had its lights on, but it was dark next door. I clambered over the gate, wincing as I took the weight on my bandaged hand, then tiptoed down the path, hoping that there wasn't a pit bull lurking in the gloom. But this wasn't the district for it, and the only animal I encountered was a snooty cat who gave me one look and scooted away with its tail lifted.

At the end of the garden I scrambled over two walls, and I was in Sarah's garden. The shed loomed up in front of me, and I tried the door but it was locked. There were big glass windows along the sides, and I punched a hole in the corner of one of them with a stone figure of a frog that I found lying nearby. Inside the shed was a neat assemblage of gardening tools, flanked by rows of pots full of compost and growing plants. Above them was a line of cupboards bolted to the wall. In the first one I opened was a can, wrapped in a swaddling of rags and half full of petrol. She hadn't bothered, I thought, to destroy the evidence. If I was right it had to be Sarah who'd set her own sitting room alight. I'd found it strange from the beginning that the intruder had left nothing behind and skipped off at short notice without being seen. Sticking burning rags into a letter box would have been easy enough for a casual vandal, but getting into this garden took considerably more effort.

I picked out a trowel and small fork and went down the garden to the flower beds near the house. Jack had been shot and I had the feeling that if Sarah had a gun handy, she'd have hidden it somewhere like this. As I spaded over the ground I thought about what she'd been up to. It was the photograph which had set me off. If it had been taken anywhere else I'd have assumed that Jack had simply sneaked a snap of Sarah to feed his obsessions. But, when I asked, she'd told me that she didn't know where he lived. As soon as I realised that she'd been lying about that, everything else fell into place.

The problem was that I'd been trying to fit everything together into one coherent pattern. As it was, Sarah must have simply seized the opportunities that came along. She'd made sure I'd been brought into the project because of our relationship, and she must have been certain that she could use me to spread around the facts about Caroline's background. The anonymous letters had been set up to bring me in. The search for Amaryll had been convenient and suitably confusing for all concerned, and

I had no doubt that she could have planted the idea of running him over in Jack's mind. The fires hadn't happened until I'd found out about the sisters' past and told a couple of people. Setting her own place alight had been another diversion to suggest that she was the target. Everything else, Jill's death, Dave's stories, and Jack's crazy fantasies, had all been incidental and convenient. Poor Jack must have set the fire at Wyndham's office, imagining that what he was doing would put her in his power, and I didn't think his death would turn out to be a coincidence.

My spade chinked against something, and I dug for it eagerly, but when it came up it was only a stone. I swore quietly and threw it away.

'This is what you're looking for.'

She'd come up through the house without my hearing her and now she flipped a switch and flooded the garden with light. She was wearing a short black skirt and a white silk blouse. Her face was tired but severe. She was holding a stubby black pistol in her hand. She looked beautiful and not at all crazy.

'I came back,' she said, 'because I still had this in the car, and I was going to leave it here.'

I stood up and she turned and went back into the house. I didn't think she would shoot me, but my only alternative would have been to leg it through the garden and I guessed that if she wanted she'd probably get me before I was halfway to the wall. When I went in she was already sitting down. She gestured towards me with the whisky bottle in her hand, and I nodded. While she poured I looked for the gun. It was lying on the floor in front of her.

'Oh, sit down,' she said. 'I'm not going to shoot you.'

For a moment, I didn't know whether or not to believe

it. Then something about the phrase she'd used set off a memory of the time when I'd first started working for her. She'd sent me to record a short interview with an American writer who was passing through on his way to a conference, and everything had gone wrong. I was late, and on my way back I discovered that something had gone wrong with the tape recorder, and all I'd picked up was a garbled mishmash of sound. They'd dropped the item, and Sarah's annoyance had been obvious. At the end of the day she'd asked me to come and see her, and I'd hovered around in front of her desk, thinking that my slender career as a broadcaster was about to come to an end. Suddenly, she'd looked up and smiled.

'Sit down,' she'd said. 'I'm not going to bite you.'

That was the point at which I knew I wanted to sleep with her.

Remembering the occasion I blinked, trying to flatten out the peak of dislocation I was experiencing. It was hard to believe that this was the same woman.

'You sent Wyndham the threatening letters,' I accused.

'Yes. It started as a bit of a joke. I kept trying to think up blood-curdling threats, but I wasn't very good at it.'

'What about Amaryll? What was the point of that?'

She frowned, and shook her head.

'That was nothing to do with me. The thing is, Jack was a bit mad. He followed Joan to the hotel and saw Amaryll come out. He had some grudge against him. Amaryll insulted him, he said, during a group session they had years ago. Called him a lying little git, I believe. He's never forgotten it. Besides, Amaryll tried to cheat his mate Dave. He was doing Dave a favour.' She laughed. 'He wasn't exactly a stable personality. He gave me the gun, you know. Told me all about it. It's a nine-millimetre Beretta. Standard issue for the Americans or the police,

I forget which, and he bought it in Kilburn. He was very proud of it. It was the most precious thing he had to give.'

'Did you shoot him?'

She smiled, and raised her eyebrows at me over the rim of her glass.

'Probably.'

'Jesus, Sarah,' I said. 'Do you realise what you've done? It's serious.'

She laughed the way she did when she was really amused, and watching her I felt the urge to laugh with her, as if that would make it all right.

'I thought I knew you,' I said. 'Why all this? It's ridiculous.'

'I know,' she said, 'but you get started. I wanted to ruin Wyndham, and kill his girlfriend. I still do. But that's all over. It didn't work. I'm sorry I had to bring you into it, but it seemed a good idea at the time. Jack saw Caroline with Wyndham and the crew, and recognised her from the day centre they went to. So he telephoned me. I suppose he thought that would get him into my good books, which it did, but I wanted someone else, someone we all trusted, to find out about Caroline and expose her. The idea was for both of them to have an accident for which Caroline would get the blame. It could have worked if I'd kept it simple. I shouldn't have told you I was going to meet Wyndham at the office. But I thought you'd assume they'd tried to set me up and got caught in their own trap. I left Joan a message saying I had information about the murder on the estate, and that I'd come to the office. I called myself Vicky.' She laughed uproariously. 'Then I left a message for Caroline asking her to meet Joan. They were both supposed to be there, you see. But I think Jack timed it wrong, and the whole thing went up before Caroline arrived. He was incompetent.'

'But what made you do any of it?' It couldn't be because Wyndham screwed other women, I thought, but I didn't want to be the one to say it. 'Was it the baby?'

She looked over at me sharply.

'He told you?'

'Yes.'

She sighed.

'I suppose that was it. It was a couple of months ago that he told me about Joan being pregnant. Something broke. The thing is, it was our baby's anniversary. It would have been his birthday, and he didn't even remember. Something just went.'

She stared at me, her eyes demanding my understanding.

'I can understand how you felt,' I said feebly. 'But you can't just kill people.'

She nodded.

'I know,' she said. 'I'm sorry it happened, but I couldn't think of any other way to handle Jack. Not after he'd done the fire. I thought she was dead, you see. I wasn't half pissed off when I heard you saved her life.' She laughed affectionately. 'You are a twit. I thought about killing you. You're probably the only one who'd guess. But I like you too much.'

An owl hooted out in the garden. Somehow it added to the unreality of what I was hearing. For a moment, I flexed my muscles, squeezing my fingers together to feel the pain, like pinching myself awake.

'You know you need help, don't you?'

'Oh, sure,' she said carelessly. 'But this is just an episode. Give it time and it will seem like a dream, like everything else. Wyndham will probably commission a script about it.'

I made up my mind.

'Why don't you call the police? Give yourself up. It might be easier that way.'

She turned and looked at me curiously.

'Come off it. I know you're going to do the right thing and denounce me. But there's no evidence. Not without this.' She had the gun in her hand again, and she waggled it at me. 'Face it, Sammy, when you walk in with this crazy story, the first thing they'll do is look at you and suspect you're up to something. I'll say we were lovers. They won't like that at all. And I'll say I gave you the push, which they'll understand, and you started threatening me, which they'll believe. Honestly, even if you can convince them you'll have a terrible time, and without some solid evidence there's a good chance it will never come to court. Wanna bet?'

I shook my head.

'I'm going to dump it,' she said. 'When I get back I'm going to bed. Why don't you wait for me? Tomorrow we can zip across the Channel, take some time off. Play in the garden. Forget it.'

'I can't,' I said.

Her eyes didn't change, but somehow I knew she understood that neither of us would forget. Instead it would become part of the current running between our bodies. Late in the shadowed night she would be beautiful and mysterious, her sex a dark magnet.

A spasm crossed her face, as if my reply had given her a sudden, sharp pain.

'Suit yourself,' she said, 'but think about it.'

She got up and walked out of the sitting room. In a moment I heard the door slam and her car drive away. I knew what I had to do, but for a while I couldn't move. I sat like that for what seemed a very long time, thinking idly, without purpose, about the things she'd done and what she'd just said. After a while I closed my eyes and saw an image of Sarah lying on the floor in front of me, her naked body writhing slowly, her long hair shrouding her face. The impression was so strong that when I opened my eyes I almost expected to see her there. But the illusion seemed to break the spell which had been holding me, and I found the energy to look at my watch. An hour had gone by, so I pushed myself off the sofa, and moving slowly, went to pick up the phone.

Discover Mike Phillips' gripping and authentic Sam Dean mysteries

In the 1980s, London is a melting pot of cultures, but race and class create sharp divisions.

Black British journalist Sam Dean looks for stories, not missing persons. When an old friend asks for help tracking down a White Conservative MP's daughter, he feels he can't say no. Especially as Virginia's disappearance is tangled with the fate of Roy, a young mixed-race boy who reminds Sam of his own son.

A trail of secrets leads Sam into the backstreets of Black British culture, to the crossroads of race and class where you'll find seedy walk-up flats, betting parlours, and smoky nightclubs.

In 1980s London, Black political leaders who can straddle the racial divide are a rarity.

So when a rising Black politician, Aston Edwards, is murdered, the effects quickly ripple through London's Afro-Caribbean community.

Then a young Black boy is arrested for his murder, surrounded by rumours of an affair with Aston's wife.

Sammy Dean, journalist-turned-investigator, is determined to find the truth. He believes the death of a Black activist, written off as a suicide, might be linked to Aston's killing. With tensions running high, can Sam find the truth before the city erupts?

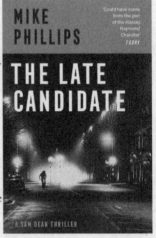